"A TALE FULL OF FIERCE LONGING AND BRIGHT COURAGE . . . RICHLY INTOXICATING."°

THE TOWER AT STONY WOOD

She saw the knight in the mirror at

During the wedding festivities
of Gloinmere, is sought out by
terrifying tale: that the king ha
cloaked in ancient and powerf
steadfast honor and loyalty, C
quest to rescue the real quee~~n from her tower prison,~~
prevent war, and to awaken magic in a land that has lost its
way. . . .

"McKillip's iridescent prose cloaks a simple quest with effervescing images and tantalizing, shifting arpeggios of shapes, as a Celtic triple goddess spins and weaves Cyan Dag's fate. By showing that out of her hero's forgotten gesture of mercy in battle long ago came hope, compassion, peace, McKillip concurs with the poet Rilke that perhaps everything terrible is in its deepest being something that needs our love."

— °*Publishers Weekly* (starred review)

"The real strengths of the book are the splendor of its imagery, the elegance of its prose, and the character of Cyan, whose own nobility, rather than anything external, holds the key to the success of his quest."

—*Booklist*

"Mesmerizing and unforgettable—a true flowering of a major talent."

—*Kirkus Reviews*

"A new book from the pen of Patricia McKillip is always a thing of beauty, and . . . *The Tower at Stony Wood* is no exception. . . . Ms. McKillip is in fine form indeed, creating one of her most appealing heroes and an ambiance of pure enchantment for lucky readers."

—*Romantic Times*

"An elegant, eloquent fantasy . . . *The Tower at Stony Wood*, a beautiful fantasy about the power of story in our lives and how sometimes the purpose of a life is simply to live it, is McKillip at her best, and will only enhance her already impressive reputation."

—*Locus*

WITH*continued . . .*DRAWN

continued . . .

The Tower at
Stony Wood

Patricia A. McKillip

ACE BOOKS, NEW YORK

THE TOWER AT STONY WOOD

An Ace Book / published by arrangement with
the author

PRINTING HISTORY
Ace hardcover edition / May 2000
Ace trade paperback edition / May 2001

The Penguin Putnam Inc. World Wide Web site address is
http://www.penguinputnam.com

Check out the ACE Science Fiction & Fantasy
newsletter and much more at Club PPI!

ISBN: 0-441-00829-1

ACE®
Ace Books are published by
The Berkley Publishing Group, a division of Penguin Putnam Inc.,
375 Hudson Street, New York, New York 10014.
ACE and the "A" design are trademarks
belonging to Penguin Putnam Inc.

PRINTED IN THE UNITED STATES OF AMERICA

10 9 8 7 6 5 4 3 2 1

For Dave,
mi corazón,
who gave me Loreena McKennitt's "The Visit"

The Tower at Stony Wood

ONE

S he saw the knight in the mirror at sunset.
He rode alone down a road along a river. Where
the black cloak he wore parted over his surcoat, she
glimpsed towers of gold; the cloak fanned behind his back
down the horse's golden flanks. The knight's head was
bowed, his face in shadow. The jewel in the pommel of the
sword hanging from his saddle flashed a bloody crimson in
the last ray of light. His hair, swept back and gathered into
a silver ring at his neck, was black as jet.

She mused over him, scratching absently at a fleabite.
Her own long, woody hair, tangled and bunched as if small
animals lived in it, fell over kelp-dark eyes that glittered
now and then with uncertain color. She brushed at the hair
in her face, then touched the mirror in its plain round frame
lightly, as if to hold the image in place. The horse's steady

pace might have found its unchanging rhythm across miles, across countries. The knight followed the water's slow path toward night. That much she could see from the way the light faded, faster than the water flowed, all down the river, leaving it mysterious with color. Beyond the tall trees growing along the river, she could see little; she had no idea where in the world he might be.

Melanthos, someone called far below. She shifted on her straw pallet, slapping the air as at a mosquito's whine. At that moment, entranced by the mirror's dreaming, she did not recognize her name. But the knight raised his head abruptly, as if he had heard.

A strong, sun-browned face looked out of the mirror at her. His eyes were unexpectedly light, the color of water, of the blade at his knee. She studied him, wondering curiously at the grim set of his mouth, the mingling of apprehension and resolve that honed the taut, clean lines of his face. Without taking her eyes from him, she reached beyond the mirror on the stone window ledge for an untidy pile of thread. The knight rode out of the mirror. The images in it faded until only her own face remained, her intent, curious eyes. But she remembered his colors. They remained reflected in her mind's eye: gold, blood, silver, night.

She sorted through her threads with slender, bitten fingers, chose a needle and a square of linen. She threaded the needle and began with his face.

The story would come later.

TWO

When the Lady from Skye rode through the gates of
Gloinmere to marry Regis Aurum, King of Yves, an
old woman in her retinue caught the eye of Cyan Dag as
he stood in welcome with the knights of Gloinmere. Eager,
as they all were, for a glimpse of the stranger who would
be queen, he found his attention snared by the crone who
turned her head to look at him as she passed. Her dark,
softly crumpled eyes held his gaze as if, he thought, she
recognized him. But he knew Skye only as a nebulous, unpredictable land along the western sea. It had been overrun,
a century before, by the restless armies of Yves, who had
not realized, until they conquered it, what a strange country
they had made their own. Poets came out of Skye, and
rumors of magic, and the odd warrior seeking a place in
Gloinmere, with a cloak smelling of sheepskin and a name

older than Yves. High on a wall, trumpeters blew a fanfare to the king's bride. The old woman loosed Cyan's eyes and disappeared into the patchwork swirl of dismounting guests. Cyan searched through the confusion; the Lady from Skye had apparently added herself to it.

The knights around Cyan had not been so distracted.

"Is she beautiful?" one demanded. "Or isn't she?"

"She has a face like a fish."

"She is the most beautiful woman I have ever seen in my life."

"She's too tall, and colorless as cloud."

"I would lay my body in the mud for her to walk across. Anyway, the king looks like a bear."

"Which is she?" Cyan asked, wondering what he had missed, and how.

"You didn't see her, Cyan? How could you not?" A gauntlet pointed. "Look there. The gawky one with the king. It's a marriage made of money."

"There is no money in Skye," he argued absently, finding nothing gawky with or without the king.

"Then it is a matter of peace."

"Skye is always peaceful," Cyan said, for Skye had paid tribute without comment for a century to the Kings of Yves, in return for being left unnoticed.

"Then it's a matter of sorcery," a dark knight beside him muttered sourly. "She bewitched him, and will bring her monstrous ways into Yves."

Cyan felt a sudden tension at his back, a breath sharply drawn, the shift of metal in a scabbard. The raw, impoverished knights from Skye, drawn to Gloinmere's wealth and power, took suggestions of sorcery personally. Cyan turned. His eyes, clear and light as rain, fell on them and they shifted.

He turned his gaze on the knight beside him and said mildly, "In a hundred years, nothing without honor has come out of Skye, not a knight, not a promise. Why would the king find anything less to bring back to Gloinmere?"

The dour knight blinked, yielded.

"Then it must have been," he amended dubiously, "a matter of love."

The shadow lifted over Skye; there was a soft laugh behind them. Cyan brought his attention back to the yard.

"I still haven't seen her."

"There—on the steps."

Cyan looked, but missed her again. The company of knights moved then to follow the king to the hall. Their silken surcoats were bright with the symbols of family and rank: birds and animals, suns and shooting stars, pyramids and lightning bolts and the phases of the moon. Cyan wore three gold towers on a field of midnight blue. Through centuries, the towers had lost their doors and windows, had become only the idea of towers. It was an ancient emblem, but beyond honor and a name older than the king's, his family possessed little. He had been brought to court by his father when he was twelve to be raised and trained with the young prince. Cyan grew up in the sprawling shadow his father had cast, and then out of it, abruptly, when he saved the newly crowned Regis's life during a border brawl with the North Islands. Younger than most of the knights of Gloinmere, he wore his formidable reputation lightly. A tall, sinewy man, he carried his strength lightly as well; most recognized it too late. His hair, long and black, he kept neatly tied at his neck. His eyes rarely lost their calm, even when he fought.

He walked with the knights across the yard. A pale-haired figure going up the steps caught his attention, but it seemed laden with baggage. The guests had gone inside. They were nowhere to be seen in the hall, where brilliantly dressed lords and ladies waited to welcome the king's bride more formally. The king's bard, in a tabard of cloth-of-gold, softly played a ballad from Skye on his harp. The trumpeters had joined the ranks of other musicians and singers, their purple tabards mingling with blue, silver, scarlet, green. Cyan set his shoulders against a carved column of oak near the musicians and absently watched for the ambiguous beauty of Skye.

Cria came to him, as he hoped.

"You look pensive," she said. "My lord Dag."

He looked down into her smile. She had skin as white as peeled almonds, hair as dark as winter solstice, eyes the color of wild violets. She wore the green, gold-scalloped tabard of a singer. Her voice was deep, sweet. Late at night it grew smoky; embers flared in it. He lifted a hand to touch her and did not, remembering where they were.

"I was looking for the king's bride," he answered. "My lady Greenwood. Tell me: is she beautiful?"

"Gwynne of Skye? You haven't seen her?"

"I was distracted."

Her smile widened, amused. "By what? Another woman?"

"Yes."

"Was she beautiful?"

"I have no idea. She had cobweb hair and eyes like new moons. She rode past me, her eyes caught mine, and in that moment that's all I knew."

"And in that moment she bewitched you, and you missed the Lady from Skye entirely. Beware the sorcery out of Skye, my lord. Who was she?"

"Someone's grandmother, most likely. Still." He hesitated; Cria watched him curiously. "She looked at me as if she knew me."

"Perhaps she only wanted to." Her eyes fell away from him then; her smile began to fade. She glanced at the musicians; the clusters of color were growing, but as yet no one had called them to order.

Familiar with her expressions, he asked, "What's wrong?"

Her shoulders moved, fidgeting as against a hold. "My father is here for the wedding. I will not dare come to you."

Again his hand resisted its desire to fill itself with her soft, cloudy hair, to measure her eyelashes against his thumb. "I'm sorry," he breathed.

"So am I." She folded her arms tightly across her tabard, looked at him again, but without seeing him. "I don't like what I think he is thinking, these days. He complains about the time I spend here among the king's musicians; he complains about what I wear, about my hair —"

"Your hair?"

"As if he sees me suddenly as someone else. Someone who dresses more respectably and does not sing, who might bring him gold and meadows and more cows than anyone could milk." He felt the blood leave his face; he linked his fingers behind his back, leaned against the oak, so that he would not reach out to her with both hands. She was seeing him now, a line as fine as thread across her brow. "I think he has someone in mind."

"Who?"

"I don't know yet. I do know that he will not ask me, he will tell me, after he has pledged me to whoever has enough of those things to buy me — "

"I will talk to him," Cyan promised, wondering where, in a day, he could acquire meadows, hawks and hounds, gold to drink, if that would persuade her father. "I don't," he realized bleakly, "even have a roof of my own to offer you. I'll talk to the king."

She nodded. Her face was very calm, as if they had been discussing ancient ballads, and so pale it might have been carved of ice. "Soon," she pleaded. There was a flurry of notes from flute and drum, then; the musicians began to sort themselves out. His hands clenched behind his back; he said softly as she turned, "I love you, my lady Greenwood. And I would let you sing."

He saw the Lady from Skye then, entering the room amid a chattering entourage. She was quite tall, as tall as Regis, who moved to meet her. The braided coils of her hair were as white as gold could be and still be gold. Her eyes seemed to reflect a midsummer sky, an endless, timeless blue filled with light. The long, graceful slope of her profile might be considered fishlike, Cyan saw, but it seemed only to adjust the boundaries of beauty, so that what had been called beauty until then became too small a realm without her. Regis, with his brown, shaggy head, his massive shoulders, and all his teeth bared in a grin, looked more bearlike than ever. She laughed as he reached her, and lifted her left hand to his arm, shedding charm like sorcery throughout the hall.

The trumpeters blew a flourish. She smiled over the court, looking pleased by the noisy welcome, the music, the shouting, the applause. Regis's voice, booming over the hall, fought the noise and took the field. Three days of feasting, he declared. Dancing, falconry, hunting, contests of strength and skill with weapons, and cups of gold awarded by the new queen as prizes. For three days, no words of anger or unkindness would be permitted, no quarrels addressed, all feuds must be held in abeyance. The king loved this pale woman from Skye, Cyan saw. His hands unclenched, fell to his sides. In that mood, Regis would be generous to other lovers; he would refuse to admit the possibility that love might be worth less than cows.

Gwynne of Skye spoke then. "My lords and ladies," she said. "I am grateful for your welcome." Her words had a crispness to them, like the bite of air in the west, that enchanted the court; it fell almost silent, listening for more. "I hope to know you and love you as Regis does. In Skye we are at the mercy of the weather, and we name the winds according to their fierceness. But, fierce or gentle, all the winds blow tales to us of the great court at Gloinmere, and I have been hearing them all my life. I never thought I would be standing here beside Regis Aurum on the day before our wedding, wondering what you all must think of this woman from the unpredictable west about to be called queen."

She was interrupted then, with cheers and drums and an untidy chorus of horns. Someone pounded on Cyan's shoulder, pushed a cup into his hand. He raised it with the king's knights in salute to the Lady from Skye. Regis, his voice sending pigeons in the high windows flying, proclaimed the marriage of Lady Gwynne of Skye to the House of Aurum and the land of Yves in that hall, at that hour the next day, and let no one be a moment later.

And now let the feast of welcome begin.

"Watch her dance," said a woman next to Cyan. He almost did not hear her, for the music had begun, and as always he listened for Cria among the singers. Then the strange urgency in the words struck him and he turned.

The old woman who had caught his eyes in the yard and stolen his attention from the beauty of Skye, captured it again. She was taller and straighter than he would have guessed; she looked as old as the world. Her white, rippling hair swept away from her seamed face down her back, almost to her knees. She wore a long, scarlet robe of fine linen, and a peculiar mantle, a crisscross of faded colors, draped over one shoulder and pinned with gold. One hand flashed gold at every knuckle, the other only a single, silver ring. She carried a harp so pale and plain it might have been made of bone.

Again her eyes held him, black as new moons and as secret.

"Watch —" he repeated, mystified.

"Watch her when she dances. She forgets herself in music and lets her true self show. You have ancient eyes. You will see it."

The music and the chatter grew distant. Something glided over him: the chilly intimation of trouble. "See what?"

"What she is. You'll see it in the sixth fingers on her hands, in the scales on her feet, in her distorted shadow, in her terrible eyes. That is not Gwynne of Skye. There is a woman trapped in a tower in Skye, who cannot free herself, who dares not even look at the world for fear of death. Will you find her, Cyan Dag? Will you free her, for the sake of those who love and need her?"

He swallowed the sudden dryness in his throat. "The king's true bride is imprisoned somewhere in a tower in Skye?"

"You saved your king's life once before. Will you help him now?"

"But how do I—how do you know these things?"

"Watch the lady the king will marry. She will show you herself what she is."

"Who are you?" His voice had gone.

"I am the Bard of Skye." Her ancient eyes looked still as well water and as measureless. "I was trained, long ago, to see what exists and to say the word for it. The woman who calls herself Gwynne of Skye can hide nothing from me. But I can do nothing; your king would never believe me. In this land, a bard speaks only through music; words may be as fickle for them as for anyone. In Skye, it is said that the bard can change the world with a word. You see with your heart, Cyan Dag. You recognized me, in the yard."

"I don't know you," he whispered.

"You saw me instead of that false queen. You recognized what is true. We need you." The dark in her eyes trembled slightly, well water disturbed by the first drop of rain. "All of us in Skye. And all in Yves. Your seeing eyes, your steadfast heart. Help us."

It was the second longest night of Cyan's life.

Perversely, the lady did not dance. She moved among Regis's court after the feast, learning names and faces. Her eyes, always smiling, quickened when she met Cyan.

"The king has spoken of you, my lord," she said as he bent stiffly over her hand, counting fingers. "Of your courage, and great skill, and of your very long friendship. So I must conclude that your three towers had their origins in Skye, since I think that everything extraordinary must have come somehow from my country. Even the king."

He murmured something, and cast a glance at her shadow as she withdrew her hand. Five fingers, her shadow said. Her shod feet told him nothing at all. The only magic he could see lay in her charms.

Later, he sat in the king's chamber with Regis and a dozen of his most trusted lords and knights. Regis, flushed with wine and happiness, assured them that he had found the perfect, the most beautiful, the wisest—for all that her father was an eccentric, absentminded old nodder, peering through lenses in search of dragons and trying to walk on water. Cyan, with three women on his mind, drank little and said less. She did not dance, his perturbed thoughts ran again and again. I saw nothing. I cannot accuse her of nothing. They will marry. The bard is mistaken. Or else the lady is a lie. But if that is true, and I am forced to tell Regis that all he loves is a lie, then all love will become a lie to him, and even my love for Cria will be worth less to him than cows . . .

Late at night, out of a mist of wine and goodwill, Regis fixed him with a disconcertingly probing eye. "Cyan. You aren't smiling. Everyone else is smiling but you. You don't like her."

Cyan opened his mouth; nothing came out. Smiles grew thin around him, curious. He rubbed his eyes, evading the king's, and found words finally. "I'm as bewitched as everyone else. Too bewitched to speak."

The king threw an arm around his shoulders. "Maybe you have fallen a little in love with her yourself. You should marry. Everyone should marry." He poured more wine into Cyan's cup. "Drink with me. To Skye and all the magic that has come out of it."

Cyan coughed on his wine. The king's eye rolled toward him again. But someone else raised his cup to the king's happiness, and that Cyan could swallow. The knights reeled to their beds as the stars began to fade. Cyan, walking along a battlement wall, saw the softly lit tower window framed with roses behind which the lady slept. Did she dream? he wondered. Or did she watch the flickering shadows and wait for dawn, having no need for human sleep?

A shadow melted over the candlelight in the window. He froze on the wall. Jeweled colors flashed in the casement as it opened. He saw her hair, rippling loose and limned with fire. He could not see her face. But he felt her eyes on him, the man on the wall, alone and sleepless, gazing at her across the well of night between them.

She closed the casement; the room grew dark. He went inside, woke a page dozing beside a door, and sent him to find the Bard of Skye. He waited in the great hall while servants moved around him, laden with garlands to hide doorposts, transform the throne, spiral up the oak columns to make a wedding bower. The page came back to him finally. The Bard of Skye was not in her chambers, nor with the lady, nor with the lady's retinue, nor with the king's bard, nor with the musicians, nor, it seemed, anywhere at all.

And that, Cyan thought, baffled, seemed to be that.

He took his place the next day among the men escorting the king through the hall to the flower-strewn dais. Caged doves, released at the entrance of the new queen, flew upward into shafts of light. Her escort of women held her to earth with ribbons of pearl they let fall when she reached Regis. She seemed to be wearing every pearl in the western sea. Like everyone's, her eyes burned with sleeplessness, but with nothing more sinister that Cyan could see. The Bard of Skye had reappeared to play gentle ballads from Skye and Yves with the king's bard, as Regis Aurum and the Lady from Skye pledged their lives to one another. The bard's eyes caught at Cyan once, above the bone harp. *Why,* they demanded, *are you still here?* He heard Cria's voice then, raised alone, sweet and pure, singing verses to the harping. Her gaze had drawn inward; she saw no one, not even Cyan. Chilled, he wondered if her father had already promised her to one of the smiling courtiers watching her. Her voice soared toward the circling doves. The king and queen kissed. Trumpets sounded; bells pealed in answer, passing the message from bell mouth to mouth across the realm. Still, he picked out Cria's voice, like a thread of gold in a tapestry, fine and true, yet fading into the growing tumult until he lost the thread and heard only the memory in his heart.

He had little chance, that day or the next, to speak to her. She seemed always hurrying somewhere with her father, or in her green tabard about to sing. The Bard of Skye was always elsewhere, when he found a scant moment free to question her. Constantly at Regis's side, among an escort of knights, he watched the queen as she rode with falcons, or judged the offerings of a dozen ardent poets, or awarded prizes at the knights' contests. On the field, he found himself battering with his sword at the web of uncertainties that entangled him. Someone pleaded breathlessly, again and again, "Cyan." He blinked sweat out of his eyes and found a knight kneeling on the grass, trying desperately to yield to him. He stood before the queen to take that cup of gold. His head bent; he watched her shadow burning stark black lines across the pavilion carpet. Again, it told him nothing.

Cria, passing him unexpectedly on the field afterward, said bewilderedly, "You are always looking at her. Are you in love with her, now?"

"No," he answered, horrified. "I love you."

She said nothing; her eyes remained perplexed. She seemed weighed down in the hot spring afternoon, by satin and brocade; her hair was drawn tightly away from her face and captured in a gold net. It would take no longer than a breath, he thought, no longer than the thought of it, to slide a finger into the net and pull it down and let her dark, rippling hair fly free again across her shoulders.

"Cria," her father said behind him, and Cyan turned to meet a hard, suspicious stare like a slap, before her father inclined his head the inch or so he accorded landless knights. "My lord Cyan Dag," he added with perfunctory courtesy. "The king is fortunate in your prowess, and in your friendship. No wonder he keeps you close to him. I would not like to make an enemy of you. But prowess passes, prowess passes, in the end, and when you're aging and balding, as I am, it's important to have more tangible possessions. Come, Cria."

"My lord," Cyan said desperately, understanding, very clearly, the final word on the unspoken subject.

"My lord," a page interrupted. "The king asks for your presence in the queen's escort."

"Come, Cria."

Cria closed her eyes briefly. She pulled the net loose abruptly as she turned to follow her father, and flung it onto the grass. Cyan watched her shake her hair loose. He heard her father's rumbling question; she answered shortly, "It fell off."

Cyan looked down, to retrieve the little net of gold, but it had vanished. The page, moving quickly across the grass, was struggling with a button on his tunic above his heart. Cyan was left staring in exasperation at his own shadow. It told him nothing, either.

Finally, the Lady from Skye danced.

She could not resist the enchantments of harp and drum and flute after supper the second night. She danced with everyone, while the king watched from the dais table, entranced and smiling. Cyan, beside him, watched unsmiling, but equally entranced. Her shadow whirled everywhere, candles casting a ghostly second shadow after it. The shadows blurred together at odd angles of light, formed a third that, to Cyan's riveted eyes, seemed not quite human. As she lifted her hands, new fingers formed, then disappeared. Her feet left their shoes behind, in one moment, danced naked and flashing oddly. In another shift of light, her eyes darkened, grew small, and retreated into hollows of bone and shadow. Cyan's breath stopped. Then she moved into torchlight and he saw her smiling, midsummer eyes. He breathed again, reached for his wine. A hand came down over his wrist, brawny and newly ringed with gold.

He looked at Regis, startled. The king asked bluntly, "What is it? You've barely spoken in two days. This is my wedding! In the fifteen years you and I have known each other, I have never seen you like this. What is it you are not telling me?"

Cyan gazed at him mutely. His brain, misty with wine and worry, refused to show him either an answer or a clear path around the question. It was late; the dais was all but empty; the last guests left awake were dancing. A bell tolled some brief hour. The Bard from Skye had vanished again. Cyan's hair hung loosely around his face; the tie had vanished hours or days before. His eyes felt charred. He had worn the same clothes for a month. They had been celebrating the king's wedding for a year . . . I see, he answered silently, helplessly. But I do not know exactly what I see, and I cannot say without accusing your wife or the Bard of Skye, and at this moment I know which of us you would toss out of Gloinmere if I spoke.

The king was still waiting. His eyes, oddly light for a bear, had begun to narrow; his grip on Cyan's arm tightened.

"You have not danced with me, my lord," said the woman from Skye. She stood behind Regis, still panting slightly from her last dance. Her shadow cut across the cloth between king and knight. Regis's eyes flickered at her voice, but refused to loose Cyan. He raised his face to her finally, still unable to answer. But he could smile, and he felt Regis's hand ease at that.

"My lady."

That was all he could think to say to her. She spoke to him as they danced; he heard himself make brief, polite sounds. He tried to keep his hands from speaking suspicions to hers; he tried to keep their shadows from crossing. When he returned her to the king, she had also fallen silent. The king gestured to the musicians; they began putting their instruments away. The king's bard began a harp song that sounded as old as night.

Regis took his wife's hand. "You must be tired," he said. "One more day."

She smiled sweetly at him, while Cyan refrained wearily from counting the fingers the king held. She laid her other hand on Cyan's shoulder, and he started. "One more day," she said to Regis.

But not, the Lady from Skye decided, for Cyan Dag.

She sent for Cyan in the morning, while those who had found their way out of bed were breakfasting with the king. A hunt had been called. The new queen, dressed in raspberry and gold, her hair bound in a net of pearl and gold, seemed to Cyan something out of fable. He found her gazing out the open window as he entered.

She touched one of the tiny roses on the vine, and said at his step, "Close the door."

He did so, and heard the silence throughout her chambers. She turned, then. He caught a glimpse of her eyes, small, deep, without pupils, like something dangerous staring out of a cleft of stone. He backed against the door, his heart pounding, knowing then that she had watched him in the night, and every hour since then: the dark, unsmiling figure at her wedding.

"My lord Cyan Dag," she said briskly, while her shadow crawled like a living thing across the stone toward him, "you are disturbing your friend the king. You are disturbing me. I am Regis's wife and the Queen of Yves; you are his faithful knight who has never failed in any test of strength or honor. Until now. You cannot fight me and win. You cannot tell Regis what you see. What would he say?" She held out her six-fingered hands; their shadows splayed across the wall on either side of him. "When you tell him this? Or this?" She lifted her gown to reveal her naked feet; they glittered silver, scaled like a fish or a snake. "Or this?"

She looked at him again out of the ancient, inhuman eyes of creatures that crept close to earth and had no language. He felt the shadows of her hands grip his arms, and he closed his eyes, trembling, his face drained in the warm morning light.

"What are you?" he whispered.

"Look at me. Brave knight. Open your eyes. This is what I am." He looked, and found the king's wife, with her tall, bewitching grace, her enchanting smile. She laughed a little, a sound as light as water flowing over pebbles. "I am Gwynne of Skye, Regis Aurum's wife. I will be the mother of his heirs."

He had to find breath before he could find words. "I will fight you," he promised, feeling the icy touch of her shadow seeping like death along his bones.

"You cannot. What will you tell Regis? That I have eyes like a snake and feet made of fish scales? He will think you have gone mad. I mean no harm; there is no reason why we all should not be friends."

"You are a lie—some kind of monster. Where is the true Lady of Skye?"

"Her." She smiled again. "In a tower somewhere in Skye. If she leaves it, she will die. If she even looks at the world, she will die. I gave her a mirror in which to watch the world go by, and some threads to busy herself with. Or, if she prefers, she can watch herself stay young forever in the mirror. So you see, you cannot rescue her. You will only kill her."

"I will find her," he said, and saw her eyes grow shriveled, bleak. There is a way, he realized then. She fears it. Her gaze bored into him; he closed his eyes again and saw them, small and dark and merciless, behind his eyelids, and then within his thoughts.

He swallowed a cry of terror at the sorcery, pushing hard against the door to keep himself upright. She only laughed, and turned away from him to smell the roses on the vines. "Please, Cyan Dag, stay with us. The king loves you, your place is here, and I mean only to give Regis what he most wants. So should you. Forget Gwynne of Skye. She has her mirror, and — as long as she does nothing — her life."

He turned without answering, his hands rattling at the door latch until they remembered how to open it. He left her, went to his own chamber, where he threw he knew not what into a leather pack, and carried that and his sword into the yard. As he waited at the stables for his horse, he heard a horn sound the gathering of the hunt.

He rode out of Gloinmere alone, only dragging once at the golden gelding's reins, as a thorn snagged the breath in his throat.

He whispered, "Cria."

He swallowed the thorn, felt it lodge in his heart, and found a road that led beyond the land he knew.

THREE

Melanthos saw the tower in the mirror at sunrise.

Sun struck it, rising over the ring of hills enclosing the plain on which the tower stood. Nothing grew on the plain, possibly because of the monster that had wound itself around the tower. It appeared to be sleeping. But as the hills released the sun, it turned them red, and flooded the wasteland with light. The beast's visible eye opened then, round and golden as the sun.

It yawned, showing sharp crystal teeth through which light blazed and separated into colors. For a moment rainbows trembled over the parched ground. Then fire rolled out of the beast's maw, licking at the dust. Its teeth snapped shut; its flat, triangular head lowered again, both eyes visible now, and watching.

Dragon, she thought, chilled and fascinated.

Its scales seemed luminous, sparkling green, gold,
bronze, copper, outlining paler diamonds of pearl, ash,
bone. It lay with its tail beneath its head, its body circling
the round tower. She watched a wing shift, open slightly
to the air. The other wing was pressed against the tower.
In the new light, the tower, as red as the barren hills,
burned brightly as a flame within the dragon's ring.

She could see no door. The tower showed its back to
her, she thought; it must show its face to the rising sun.
Yet its blindness teased at her, presented an image to her
mind's eye: the tower with no way in, no way out.

What lay inside? she wondered as the image faded.
What did the dragon guard? Who did it watch for, in the
dead, fiery waste?

She chose her threads with difficulty, wanting more colors than she had, wondering that such a deadly place could
be kindled to such astonishing beauty.

She began with the tiny, moving reflection in the
dragon's eye.

FOUR

In a broken tower on the crescent island of Ysse, Thayne Ysse splayed his hands on the crumbling stone along the narrow sides of a lancet window and stared south across the sea. Behind him, his father played with fire and water, mumbling words to himself out of some rotting, mouse-chewed book. Sometimes he spoke to Thayne, though that was rare; more often he spoke to his own brother, who had died thirty years before. Thayne answered to either or not, depending on his patience.

He was a fair, muscular man with a face like a yellow-eyed hawk. The hawk's stare was trained toward Yves. He had been to Gloinmere once, years earlier, to see Regis Aurum crowned King of Yves and the North Islands and the peculiar land of Skye. Thayne had gone with several of the islanders, very young men, watching out of still, unsmiling

25

eyes as Regis paraded through the streets of Gloinmere flanked by his proud knights in their fine leather and silk and glittering mail. The islanders had not traveled so far to swear fealty, but to take a measure of Regis's strength. They had no need to disguise themselves; they stood in the sweaty, screaming crush in their drab mantles and worn boots and looked like what they mostly were: farmers and fishers with the smell of brine blown into their skin and one coin among them to flip for their fortunes.

They tossed what they had and lost, when Regis came with his knights some months later to find out why no one of the North Islands had knelt before him and sworn faith and peace and a portion of their livelihood to him. The war was brief and bloody. Regis himself had nearly lost his life. Thayne had lost cousins barely old enough to fight, and his remaining uncle; his father had been badly wounded. He recovered his strength, but his wits had wandered away into some misty past when Ferle Ysse ruled the North Islands and there was magic in the world.

With the thin blades of wind scoring his palms through the ancient, unmortared stone, and his father muttering and blowing on water behind him, Thayne thought dispassionately: I am descended from kings.

He dropped his hands and turned. His father, gnarled and boled like an old tree with swollen joints, his hair the silvery white of ash bark, blinked as if Thayne had, in the act of turning, changed into someone else entirely.

"Bowan," he said, waving Thayne to his side. "Look at this."

"I am not Bowan," Thayne said in his leashed, even voice. "Bowan is dead. I am Thayne."

But he joined his father anyway, just as his father ignored Thayne's words. He gripped Thayne's sleeve, pulled him to the book on the table. The table was a magpie's nest of odd objects: papers, stones, bowls, candles, bones, jars, lenses, mirrors, dried herbs, feathers, a small, mummified bat. His father turned pages of the book awkwardly, shakily, with his bulging, painful hands. He had grown old long before his time, Thayne knew. He should have been still pepper-bearded and powerful, trimming Thayne's hair with a broadsword in the training yard, and dreaming up ways to annoy Regis Aurum. He tapped at a drawing of someone blowing sails with his breath, and said to Thayne, "You could do this, Ferle. You summoned a fog on a cloudless day over the sea and hid the North Islands from an army from the south."

"I am not Ferle. I am Thayne."

"You understood the language of seals."

"I am Thayne, Father."

"I know that," his father said querulously. "Why do you think I called you here? You are my heir and you will be King of the North Islands."

Thayne started to answer, then didn't bother. He glanced at the open book, brushed a mouse dropping off a page. "What did you want to show me?"

"This."

"This" was a tower without a door or a window, ringed by a monstrous dragon breathing flame at a rider whose face had been blurred away by centuries of fingers turning pages. "Yes," Thayne said patiently.

"I want you to go there, Thayne."

Thayne looked at his father, oddly moved by the unexpected recognition. But who knew, he reminded himself, what "Thayne" meant anymore to his father, who might as easily consider him as real or unreal as Bowan and Ferle, just another ghost. "You want me to get charred into cinders by this dragon. Then who would remember that you are up here, to send you meals and firewood, and take you down to bed at night?"

"You don't always remember that," his father complained lucidly.

Thayne touched a glass jar of what looked like old moldering oysters without their shells. "I try," he answered mildly. "What is this?"

"Pearls."

"Ah."

"You will find a way."

"A way to do what?"

"To fight the dragon. I taught you myself to fight. You were better than anyone but me."

"I still am."

His father blinked at him silently, confused, it seemed, by Thayne's assumption that he was still alive. "You are," he said politely, and Thayne leaned wearily over the book, his elbows on the table, fingers rubbing his eyes.

"And so," he said, quelling impulses to laugh, or weep, or crack the jar of pearls against the wall to reveal the true nature of the world to his father's frayed mind. He gazed down at the dragon, which was drawn with surprising detail in faint red ink. It wound a double loop of its body around the tower; its open lizard's maw revealed a great many even triangles of teeth. "And so what do I gain by disturbing this dragon?"

"Gold."

Thayne grunted. Dragons grew gold, apparently, as oysters grew pearls; one meant the other interchangeably, without the threat of fire or death or the reek of decayed sea life.

"I kill the dragon—"

"Slay. It says here to slay."

"Slay the dragon and take its gold. And then—"

"You free the North Islands from Regis Aurum." His father's voice was suddenly so level and cold that Thayne stared at him in wonder. His eyes were rimmed with yellow like a hunting cat's. "Thayne Ysse. My son. You rule."

Thayne felt the small hairs prick on his neck. He watched his father, hungry for the strong, familiar, unyielding expression that even now faded, became uncertain, fretful. His father laid a hand on his shoulder, patted it awkwardly, trying to remember, Thayne saw, the name he had just spoken.

There is no door, Thayne thought, gazing numbly down at the drawing. There is no door in the tower. No way in. No way out.

He straightened. The thin archer's windows framed slits of twilight purple and gray, the faint memory of gold. He said, "I'll send Hael up with your supper. I'll come back later and take you down. Don't go by yourself; the steps are dangerous."

"Thank you, Bowan."

He walked down in the dark himself, feeling his way from step to crumbled, broken step in the spiraling staircase. At the bottom, he found his younger brother sitting on a step, reading by torchlight. At twelve, Craiche had fought their father to convince him that his rightful place was in a fishing coracle sailing to the mainland to stop Regis Aurum's knights before they crossed the water. The battle had raged down the yard into the cow barn, where their father had left Craiche sprawling in a stall. But Craiche had followed anyway, which was why now, at nineteen, he dragged one withered leg behind him. He still had their father's dauntless, reckless courage, all his love of the wind and the sea, the precarious life on the islands.

He closed his book over a finger and looked up at Thayne. He was dark, like their father, with the same challenging, teasing smile in the face of the raw night wind. He asked, "How is he?"

"Maundering," Thayne said. "He keeps calling me Bowan."

"Which Bowan?"

"His brother, I think. He died years before I was born. Did the sheep get penned?"

"Sheep are penned, cows milked, boats are in, everyone accounted for and at supper, including the stranger who climbed into Dirdre's boat while she was digging for mussels across the channel."

"What stranger?"

"A woman with a harp."

Thayne grunted. "Good. I'll send her up to play for our father." He saw Craiche shiver. "Get inside and eat. You're far too thin."

Craiche rose, balancing against the stones a moment, then pulling himself forward on his own. Sometimes, when his leg ached, he used a sword for a crutch; waving it at straying cows, with his sweet, rakish smile, he could make even Thayne laugh.

They crossed the yard together. It was small, with thick stone walls and outhouses to slow the wind. The tower and the old castle loomed over it, both dark, sagging, ancient. Parts of the castle had been rebuilt with mortared stone, but not in Thayne's lifetime. Possibly in Bowan's, he thought sardonically, keeping an eye on Craiche as they went up the steps. At the top, Thayne set the torch in a sconce, then wheeled abruptly, not wanting more stone, more walls, wanting to clear his head in the night and wind, not listen to his household chew.

"Go in," he said shortly to Craiche. "Send the harper to our father after supper. I'll bring them both down later."

Craiche lingered, looking at him curiously. "You're eaten," he said.

"What?"

"Something's eating you inside."

"You would think," Thayne said harshly, "that after all these years I would have learned not to want my father to remember my name."

Craiche was silent a moment; his smile flashed, edged but without bitterness. "I'd give my other leg for that," he said simply. "I'd give my life to have Regis Aurum dodder-ing in a tower instead of our father."

Thayne dropped a hand on his shoulder, jarring him off balance. He caught himself on Thayne's arm, laughing a little. Thayne touched his hair. "Don't say such things out loud. I'm the will and the sword of Ysse. You are our heart."

He was halfway across the yard when Craiche's voice caught up with him. "Bowan was also Ferle Ysse's grand-father. He spoke magic. He taught it to Ferle."

Thayne turned. In the dark, he could barely see Craiche's face, a pale profile beneath the fire. "What?"

"Something I read. You're right about words. Bowan said they are full of wonder and danger, and they can change into themselves."

Thayne shook his head, trying to untangle that. "Po-etry," he decided, but Craiche did not laugh. He adjusted his stance on the steps, ratcheting himself around to face Thayne, his face entirely dark now, his hair become flame.

"So that when you say cloud, the word itself becomes cloud. That's how Ferle Ysse raised the fog that blinded an army on the sea." He paused, letting Thayne contemplate that; Thayne, contemplating his windblown brother, wished he would go inside. Craiche added, "Or when you say, 'I am the sword of Ysse,' that's what you become. Not just a dream. Not just something rusting in the scabbard."

Thayne drew a breath and loosed it. He said tersely, "You only have me to lose. I have you. And there's our father and this house and this island—"

"And sheep and boats—"

"All," Thayne said with sudden intensity. "Our lives. We need far more than rusty, pocked metal to wave at Regis Aurum. We have no arms, no money, and no power."

He could not see it, but he felt his brother's smile flash across the night between them. "We have words."

Thayne watched him turn again, lift himself jerkily, limb by limb, puppet fashion, up the steps. He got himself inside, and Thayne went out the gates, which had not been closed since the North Islands swore fealty to Yves seven years before.

He went down a short path to the sea, which he found by starlight and memory, and sat down on a stone to watch the waves. Behind him, the tower on the cliff threw its weak, narrow oblongs of candlelight onto the incoming tide. He thought of his father, shut away from the world, nattering over his books, walking a labyrinth of past and present without a center, veering from one blocked path into another. He thought of Craiche, who went to battle smelling of cow dung and whom Thayne carried home in his arms. *Where is the magic word*, he thought, *that will make him walk again?* The tide, dark and silver, coaxed at his attention; he heard it from a distance, ebbing and circling, the birds crying above the deep over something that had died.

He heard the harping woven into the sounds of the sea, inseparable as moonlight is inseparable from water. He listened thoughtlessly to the light, tender rills and phrases, until it seemed he breathed them out of the air, drew them deep into his bones, until his thoughts no longer coiled in endless tight circles around themselves, but flowed everywhere, as shapeless as water, touching everything. He could see the stars then, not just the night. He smelled the peculiar mix of sheep pasture and brine, Ysse and sea, and then, overwhelming them all on a wind from the mainland, the scent of Yves: its harrowed fields and rich forests, its mountains, its bloody earth.

The harping drifted through his thoughts again, luring, coaxing, charming his attention. He rose finally, wanting to meet the harper, for he had not heard anything so lovely in a long time. She might look like her music, some part of him hoped foolishly, as if she were something conjured out of the old tales Craiche was always reading. Her song stopped before he got halfway up the steps. He quickened his pace a little, before she vanished back into the tale. But the harper stood talking quietly to his father. As Thayne entered, she looked across the room at him and smiled thinly, as if she had read his thoughts.

Her face was seamed like a dried pool. Her eyes looked as though they had seen what existed before the world began, and taken their blackness from that. Her loose, white hair swept down past her knees. She was surprisingly tall and straight, for a woman so old; her arms, under the rolled sleeves of the long, gray tunic she wore, looked muscular from wielding the harp. Even that seemed ancient, unadorned, and the color of bone, as if she made her music out of something that had died.

"Bowan," his father said eagerly. "She knows the dragon."

"What?" Thayne, distracted, pulled his eyes from the secret black gaze and saw the tower in the open book his father still pored over.

"It's a tale out of Skye," the harper said. Her voice had grown a trifle hollow, reedy with age, but it was still pleasing, tuned from all the songs she sang. Thayne sighed noiselessly. His father's hand lay on the page as if his touch claimed dragon and tower and all that lay within.

"So it's a tale," Thayne said, summoning patience.

"No." His father tapped the drawing with his forefinger. "The tower is in Skye, she said. And it is full of gold. You must be careful of the dragon, she said."

Thayne looked at her. "There are no dragons."

"There are dragons in Skye," she answered.

"And there is gold." His father tapped the page again, where the faceless, armed figure rode toward the fire. "And there you are. My son."

Thayne gazed at the dragon, wondering which son his father saw: the one who stood before him, or the paper knight endlessly riding toward the tower. He turned to the harper again,

"How do you know—"

"I know," she said, and he saw the memory of dragon in her eyes. "I am the Bard of Skye." She raised her harp again, released a handful of sweet and haunting notes. "It's a tale," she said, "and it is true. Real and dream."

"Which?" he asked harshly, and knew her answer before she spoke.

"Both."

"It's gold I need for the North Islands. To eat, to wear, to build our boats—we're already rich in dreams." He did not say the word for war; it hovered in the air between them like an unplayed note.

"I know some tales of the North Islands," she said thoughtfully, and plucked a single string, as if to begin one. It ended there, on a dying note. "There was magic here, in Ferle Ysse's time."

"A tale."

"Or true?" She raised her eyes; they held the expression she must have carried in her since she had watched the world begin. Behind her, his father was smiling, too, the familiar, wolfish, invincible smile that Thayne had not seen in seven years.

"Thayne," he said. "Go and bring that dragon's gold to Ysse."

Thayne started to speak, stopped. Wonder swept like a wave through his heart at the name his father had given him. It seemed no longer the man he was, but the Lord of Ysse he might become. He turned, before he had to watch the smile fray apart into bewilderment, and went back down the tower steps, feeling his way in the dark. Crossing the yard, he smelled the mainland again, saw it crouched in the night across the narrow channel like some vast beast, its eye turned sleeplessly to the scattering of islands beyond its shore, its breath waiting to flame, its upraised claw to strike at any movement from the North Islands.

He heard himself whisper, "A dragon to fight a dragon."

He felt something fierce, dangerous, as magical as hope rouse within him at the word, and he walked out of the gates to the sea.

FIVE

Melanthos saw the woman in the tower.

She sat in light on an ornate chair covered with carved lions' heads and roses. Melanthos could not see her face, only the white-gold hair that rippled down her back. She worked at a picture in thread on a broad round frame on a stand in front of her. From one side of the frame hung folds and swathes of unworked linen; from the other, transformed on its journey across the frame, bright images painted in thread poured down and piled on the stones.

Melanthos, kneeling in her own tower among her swirls of threads, stared, transfixed, at the vision.

The room seemed large; the window, its casement of colored glass open, was broad enough to sit in and look out. But the woman did not look at the world. She looked instead at the great round mirror angled across the window ledge to catch the scenes below. As she watched, her needle flashed ceaselessly, quickly. She paused only to replace one needle with another from a long row of them pinned to one side of the frame, trailing different colors down the un-worked linen.

Melanthos's eyes slid warily to the mirror. But she did not find herself there, watching the woman in another mirror within another tower. She saw lilies massed against the tower wall, a shallow river flowing past them, a road beyond the trees along the riverbank, and on the other side of the trees, furrowed fields beginning to flush green. A man rode through the mirror, too vague, translated between mirrors, for Melanthos to see clearly. Silver flared like the glance of light off armor. The woman's hand rested briefly on the linen; her head turned very slightly toward the open casement.

She bent over her work again, her long hair trailing over her shoulder, shielding her eyes from the world.

Melanthos, her breath stopped as if the woman in the mirror might hear her, reached soundlessly for threads.

SIX

Cyan Dag lost count of days and nights as he traveled west. He rode through sun and moon, wind and rain, and snow-white flurries of apple blossom without noticing them, as if, intent on Skye, he had already left the world he knew. Skye could be found as far west as one could ride without falling into the sea. How far that was, no one seemed certain. Seven days, he was told. Weeks. It depended, he was told, but on what it depended varied: the direction of the wind, perhaps, or the phase of the moon. He set his face to the path of the falling sun and continued his journey as methodically and relentlessly as he fought. If the sun set before he found a bed, then he slept where he stopped. If a road west took him across a mountain pass as narrow as a blade and so high he felt the cold starlight in his hair, he crossed it. Having left Gloinmere so quickly, he had taken little of anything with him, clothes, money, or arms. Sometimes innkeepers recognized the towers on his surcoat and gave him a bed for the sake of his name. Other times they bound him with a deed: a demand for justice, a rescue, a plea for mercy, or, when that failed, a battle. He did all that he was asked in the king's name, and directed all gratitude and tributes back to Gloinmere. Sometimes, late at night, the lady's eyes cut through his dreams, small and pupilless and ancient as stone. He would wake to find himself on his feet, sword in hand, searching for her shadow in the dark, while disturbed animals or other travelers edged nervously away from him. She haunted his dreams as if she searched for him, the knight who had seen her secret face, to snare him before he dragged her into light.

He thought she had found him one day. He stopped to seek a bed at a crazed inn beside the road he followed. The road ran west into a deep forest not far from the inn, and disappeared from view. The inn was a hunched, soot-blackened place with sagging floors and crooked lintels. He barely noticed such details; his journey west left him sleeping under a tree as often as not. But he did notice the silence. Only one man sat at the hearth, making his way stolidly through what smelled like a bowl of scorched stew. At the sight of the armed knight walking in the door, he rose hastily, and Cyan saw the greasy, beer-stained apron he wore.

"My lord knight," he exclaimed.

"My name is Cyan Dag."

"My lord Cyan Dag—" He wiped his hands on the apron, then clutched Cyan's arm as if the knight might change his mind and flee. "Have you come through that forest?"

Cyan shook his head, recognizing fear in the bloodshot eyes. "I'm riding west from Gloinmere. Are you the inn-keeper?"

The innkeeper, a burly man as bald as an egg, loosed Cyan long enough to wipe the sweat off his head. "I am," he said grimly. "You are the first traveler I have seen in three days. My lord, there is an evil in that forest. It will not let anyone pass without injury, and it's frightening everyone away. You'll be in peril if you continue on this road."

Cyan was silent, trying to see the forest out of the thick, smoke-charred ovals of glass in a casement. He gave up. "I'm on my way to Skye," he answered slowly, wondering if what troubled the forest had been waiting all these weeks, for him. "Skye lies west, so I ride west. If the road west goes through that forest, then so do I."

The innkeeper sighed in relief. "You are a brave man, sir knight. If you choose to fight the evil in the forest, I will give you my softest bed, and whatever I have to eat and drink. Which is not much," he admitted. "But the best I have, you will have."

Cyan detached himself from the innkeeper's hold and went to the door. The great, dark trees, blurred with dusk, might have been painted, they stood so silently. The road ran across a meadow to the edge of the forest, and then shadow swallowed it; he could see nothing beyond the night within.

He asked, thinking of a pale, enchanting face with eyes

turning black as that shadow, "What does this evil look like?"

"Monstrous, they say. Merciless."

"Human? Or animal?"

"Human, after its fashion."

"Does it use magic? I can't fight sorcery."

"Its strength is its power, so they say." The innkeeper watched the forest nervously over Cyan's shoulder. "It attacks travelers, steals their horses and possessions, sends them running for their lives. Four armed men together could not bring it down. But you are a knight of Gloinmere."

"And it is between me and Skye . . . If it stops me, I will fight it," he promised simply, "in the name of Regis Aurum."

He stepped into the yard to get his pack, since even the innkeeper's menials had abandoned him. The innkeeper followed to take the gelding to the ramshackle stable.

"Thank you, Cyan Dag," he said somberly. "You may fight evil in the king's name, but it's your name the plain folk around here will remember."

Dawn was scarcely more than a flush of gray above the forest when Cyan continued his journey west. As he rode into the trees, a damp, webbed lacework of green from the heavy boughs brushed his face. No birds sang at his passage. He kept the gelding at an even pace as he watched for movement within the forest. He kept his thoughts as steady, not trying to guess what might come at him, or when, or how much warning it might give before it struck.

It was not subtle. That he noticed immediately, as it rode toward him down the road. A pack of hounds after a stag might have made less noise. He reined abruptly; his horse started to rear, then checked itself and stood still, trembling. The rider was huge, bulky, twice as tall as any man Cyan had ever seen, and, it seemed, with twice as many heads. One, a mass of white hair, faced backward. The other faced forward, its bell-shaped head flowing into its shoulders without bothering with a neck. Only its mouth and the glint of its eyes were visible beneath a black helm. Its mouth was opened wide, and emitted a strange, continuous noise that sounded midway between the groan of some great bellows and the high, harsh screech of a rusty wheel. It was dressed entirely in black, and rode a black horse, which, for all its broad frame and massive hooves, seemed dwarfed by the giant on its back. Two arms swung a great broadsword through the air in front of it, back and forth, like some demented thresher. Two others guided the horse in a headlong gallop toward Cyan.

He stopped grappling with the strangeness, and let all his attention focus on what he recognized, rather than what he did not. The rider was top-heavy; it would not stop easily; on foot it would be clumsy, slow to turn, possibly confused by its double vision. He gathered his reins, waited until the grim, noisy monstrosity was upon him. Then he dodged the fanning sweep of the blade as he wheeled the gelding out of its path, and aimed a passing blow at the black helm. The helm tolled a deep, sonorous note, as if he had struck cast iron. One of the four hands loosed a rein and rose to still the clang. The backward face, bare, red-eyed, and glaring wildly, startled Cyan as it passed. He urged the gelding after it; its expression changed, in the moment, from fierceness to surprise, and then to apprehension as Cyan neared. Then it gave a yelp as the horse under it wrenched to a halt and spilled its unwieldy burden out of an extraordinarily high saddle onto the ground.

Heads and arms separated into two bodies that turned fully human as they rose. The white-haired one, with oddly pale skin and red eyes like a rat, leaped lithely to his feet, still holding the sword. The other stumbled up and turned in a circle as it struggled to lift the cumbersome helm. The face under it, older and heavier, was bloodied. Cyan swung at the younger man, who was attempting to mount again. His blade snagged the new sun flaring through the trees; the man, wincing at the light, slashed at nothing and slipped on a tree root. The great horse, stung by the flat of Cyan's blade on his haunch, leaped away. Cyan rode at the armed man, and had backed him against an outcrop of rock at the side of the road, when something struck him from above.

The world disappeared in a sudden wash of red. Fire licked jaggedly across his wrist. He flailed desperately at his blindness and lost his balance. A hand gripped the cloth at his chest and heaved; the ground spun up to slam against him. He heard a horse's hooves growing fainter and fainter, and then nothing.

He woke a moment or two later, with the hissing moan and shrill clamoring in his ear, as if the giant's foremost head were trying to warn him of some dire portent. His sword lay beneath him, the angry red glint of its pommel near his eye. Someone, he realized with groggy astonishment, was sitting on his legs and pulling his boots off.

"Put these on," a woman said briefly. "Leave yours for him. They could talk, the way they flap."

"He won't be doing much walking," a young man commented. "That slash in his wrist is bad. He's losing blood."

"So am I," the older man grumbled. "He's got a fighting arm solid as a tree trunk. You wouldn't think so to look at him."

"He's a knight of Gloinmere."

"He's a menace."

"He would have routed the pair of you," the woman said tartly, "if I hadn't dropped a rock on his head. As it is, he's seen both your faces and broken your noise box."

"He'll die soon enough," the older man said dispassionately. "The animals will help him along. But where one knight comes, others may follow, especially if they search for him. We don't want to linger in this forest. Where's his horse?"

"I caught it," the younger said. "There, with ours. He doesn't have much else, for a knight."

"Riding alone away from Gloinmere," the woman mused, "on the road to Skye . . . Where was he going, I wonder, and why?" The weight lifted abruptly off Cyan; her voice grew distant, tangling with the odd, incessant din. "Take his sword. Leave that."

"But I can fix it —"

"It would drive me mad. Leave it with him for company."

Cyan gripped his sword and rolled to his feet. His first thrust, down at the ground to catch his balance, struck a round wooden box to the heart; metal cogs and gears groaned to silence around the blade. The woman shouted; the men groped hastily on the ground for their swords. Cyan shook the box away, and spun a dizzying circle of light around him, keeping the men at bay, trying to keep the woman in sight, while he edged toward the horses. Beyond the flickering, slashing web of silver he wove, someone shifted from view. He turned desperately, searching. A horse galloped up to him; a blade flashed overhead. Cyan ducked, then reached up, caught a wrist, and wrenched a stranger down into the fray. He paused a heartbeat, startled. But the stranger only gave a battle yell that Cyan had not heard for seven years, and hoisted himself up behind the white-haired man mounting Cyan's gelding. A blade swiped at him. He fell over the other side of the horse, taking the rider down with him. The woman had already pulled herself up into the high, unwieldy saddle on the black, and was shouting again. The older man, blood fanning down his face, caught the reins of a snorting piebald mare and fumbled for a stirrup. Cyan started to pursue, then stopped as the trees bent low over him, leaves fluttering and sparking in his eyes. He leaned on his sword, groping suddenly for air. The stranger, one hand gripping the young man's hair, the other hauling at his trousers, brought him to his feet. The woman rode up against them both, knocking them apart.

"Get mounted, you rat-eyed goose," she snapped, and thumped the stranger's head with a dagger's hilt. He staggered. The cob-haired young man leaped up behind the hillock of saddle and clung to it as she plunged after the mare down the road toward Gloinmere.

"Thank you," Cyan gasped through the close and oddly shimmering air. For a moment the stranger, with his gold hair and eyes, his blurred, flickering face, seemed something not quite human, another mystery along the road to Skye. Then the mystery rubbed his head violently and spat.

"Vultures."

"I'm sorry I dragged you into it."

"I was looking for a way in."

"How did you know —" He stopped, until the leaves had floated back to the trees and he saw the man's face clearly, spare and proud, scoured by wind and weather, young yet, but harrowed, it seemed to Cyan, beyond his years. "Which of us to help?"

The stranger smiled tightly. "You were the one with no boots." He blinked then, at something not quite clear in his own vision. His smile vanished; all expression flowed out of him, as if he saw a ghost standing between them on their battlefield. He said very softly, "Three gold towers on a dark field of blue . . ."

"My name is Cyan Dag. I am a knight of Gloinmere, on my way to Skye. Do you know Skye?" he asked, for the stranger might as well have come from there as anywhere. "I need to find a certain tower."

The stranger reached him in two steps. One hand closed with a hawk's grip around Cyan's torn wrist; the other caught the sword he dropped as he fell to his knees. He groaned, the trees rustling close again. The blade seared his throat. He shook leaves out of his eyes, bewildered, and saw the strange fury in the fierce, yellow eyes.

"I am Thayne Ysse. If you make it back to Gloinmere alive, remind Regis Aurum that Ysse once ruled the North Islands, and we will, with that tower and the dragon who guards it, rule again. If I see you in Skye, I will kill you."

"There is no dragon," Cyan told him, amazed. "There is a woman."

But he only thought he spoke. The bloody jewel on his sword flared above him and the wind that roared among the leaves blew out the sun.

When he woke, the world was dark and the Lady from Skye watched him across her fire.

He caught breath painfully, choked on hot, charred air. She loomed over him suddenly, impossibly tall and angular, her face in shadow, the full moon rising out of her hair. Then she knelt, and he saw that what he had thought were the pale coils of her braids had been the aura of moonlight behind her. Her hair was long, straight, and black as night, falling around her like a mantle. She could fold herself into it, he thought feverishly, disappear into herself like a forest animal.

Fire shimmered over her eyes as over water; he could not see their color, or the thoughts in them. Her face, in the shifting light, seemed weathered smooth and dark as polished wood. A long, slender hand rose from within her hair, shifting gleaming strands and opening as it moved toward him. A silver ring flashed as it slid loosely between the knuckles of her middle finger. Then the hand disappeared; he felt it ease beneath his head, raise him a little. Something rough and dank, like wet bark, touched his lips.

He pulled away from it, though his throat was raw with

thirst. "Who are you?" he whispered, trying to see beyond the fire in her eyes.

"Don't be afraid." The voice he heard seemed oddly familiar, and inside his head, rather than in his ears. Cria's voice, he realized suddenly, deep and haunting, like a horn heard from far away in a wood.

"Drink. You must be thirsty. So thirsty you taste ashes when you swallow, you taste dry, bitter leaves. There is a little stream not far from here; the water is so cold and sweet . . ."

He drained the cup. She smiled and he glimpsed, in the graceful bones of her face, the tender, luminous expression, what he had feared across her fire. Then the night whirled around her and poured into his eyes.

He asked again, clinging desperately to his question, as if it was the one thing that might keep him alive, "Who are you?"

If she answered, he did not hear.

He woke on a lumpy bed he recognized: the innkeeper's best. His sword and pack lay on top of a scarred clothes chest. The wounded noise box sat on a chair, the cracked boots he had inherited stood beside the bed, one sole gaping speechlessly. Through the window, he could see the gold gelding in the yard, feeding from a bucket. From beyond the walls came murmuring, sudden calls and laughter, the gabbling of returning guests.

He questioned the innkeeper before he left, the next morning. "No one brought you here," the innkeeper said. "I found you across your horse's back, coming into my yard.

But someone cared for you. Someone tended your wounds and sent you here. You don't remember?"

He remembered. He searched the forest for her as he rode through it. But he found her only in his thoughts, where her secret, luminous eyes, her smile, stayed with him all down the long road out of Yves into Skye.

SEVEN

Melanthos saw the third tower at night.

It stood in a ring of trees, a squat dark flattened
beehive of stone. Three great worn lichen-covered slabs
formed the doorposts and the lintel. There was no door,
only that yawn into blackness. The waning moon hung
above it, low and cold. In the milky light, the shadows of
trees melted into the elongated, impenetrable shadow of the
tower. Only the doorposts, sagging heavily into the ground,
and the crooked lintel they bore, all made of paler stone,
caught the light in tiny flecks of silver.

Dark, its colors said. Light and dark, and darker still,
with a faint grayish glimmer of green for the trees, and a
blur of muddy white for the hare frozen in the moonlight,
its ears cocked toward a sound.

A moving shadow spilled over the hare. The hunter?

Melanthos guessed, transfixed. But it moved past, and the hare, freed, scuttled away.

The shadow stopped at the edge of the tower's shadow; whoever cast it stood beyond the eye of the mirror.

Man or woman? Melanthos wondered. Hunter or hunted?

The shadow moved again toward the tower, disappearing into the black, until at the very edge of the tower's shadow, the figure stepped into the mirror. It was cloaked, hooded, its face turned away from Melanthos toward the night within the stones.

"I don't have thread that black," Melanthos whispered. "It would not be visible."

She watched the figure move closer to the threshold. It paused there, its back to Melanthos, one hand raised, touching the moonlit stone of a post, its body angled forward, as if it tried to see into the dark.

The image faded. Melanthos stared at the mirror, chilled as if she herself had felt the cold stone beneath her fingers, heard the silence within the tower.

She reached for black.

Melanthos saw the knight ride into Skye.

She had finished the tower at sunrise. She left it on the window ledge as always, and then curled up on the musty pallet to sleep. As always, when she woke, the embroidery was gone. Taken, she thought, but by what or whom she could not guess. Maybe it simply unraveled itself and melted back into the mirror. Desperate, by then, for light, she stepped out of the tower into the brilliant afternoon. She began to walk.

Later, she rested in the middle of a broad, rocky plain, watching sheep drift like sea mist across the grass. She sat in the shadow of one of the abrupt upthrusts of stone that rose starkly out of the ground. She watched the knight appear out of a smudge of forest on the steep, bony ridge of mountain that bordered the plain. He was very far away, picking his way carefully down the slope. But she recognized his colors: black for his long windblown hair and his cloak, gold for his horse, red for the jewel in his sword catching the sun in minute explosions of light, and gray, she remembered, for his eyes.

She watched him motionlessly, intensely, as she watched the images moving through the mirror. Then, her whole body prickling with astonishment, she realized that he was neither reflection nor thread, but as real as she, riding alone into Skye. The beginning of his journey, his tale, lay in the unknown land behind him; the ending was hidden somewhere in Skye. At the foot of the slope he turned north, toward three hills that faced one another, so alike in their wide, smooth lines that they seemed reflections of one another. Three Sisters, they were called, by those who saw them from the south; farther north, they were known by other names.

It was late in the day for such lonely traveling, but the knight would not have seen the village lying between the sudden edge of the world and the sea. The only thing visible of Stony Wood from that distance would be the cluster of oddly shaped stones that might have been wood once, long before there was a village, or even the word for it. Now they resembled trunks and stumps still rooted in the earth and standing. Some were white as bone. Others were variegated and luminous with color, as if they might be turning, more slowly than the stars turned, into shell instead of stone.

"If he is real," she whispered suddenly, her lean fingers digging into the grass roots, "then so might be everything in the mirror."

She rose impulsively, wanting to catch up with the knight and ask him. She was barefoot, but he was riding slowly. He must stop eventually to sleep; if she could keep him in sight, she would find his fire beside a stream, or his horse in an inn yard. One of the wild horses roaming the plain might be in the mood to let her ride it. She bounded a step after the knight and then a voice wound around her ankle and pulled her motionless.

"Melanthos!"

She turned, knowing that of all the many things she could not explain to Anyon, running barefoot after a knight of Gloinmere would be foremost among them. He was already upset with her. Anyon, she thought, was a horse turned human: wild and beautiful, black as night, prone to flaring its nostrils and rolling a wide, nervous eye at anything unpredictable. His father owned half the sheep around them. Anyon sheared the sheep, spun wool into yarn, and wove it into blankets. His intricate and beautiful designs had traveled beyond Stony Wood, up and down the coast. He would spend a night making dyes to match the colors in his head without feeling the need to tell Melanthos. Yet he stood in front of her now, tossing his black hair off his brow, his fingers dyed blue, his dark, liquid eyes wide with exasperation. The sight of his restless beauty against the sky and the wind-scrolled sea took her breath away. She wondered, amazed, what he saw in her tall, scant body, her unkempt hair, her fey, murky eyes full of marsh lights. Whatever it was struck him as mute as she a moment. He went to her, slid one strong blue hand beneath her hair, and kissed her as if he had not seen her for months. She caught her balance, blinking as he surfaced for air. So did he, staring at her as if she had cropped up out of the harsh, beautiful land he loved, like a tor or a twisted tree. Then he remembered that he was angry.

"You vanished last night. All night. Without telling anyone—"

She pushed against his hold, impatient and mystified now, by whatever it was he wanted from her. "You must have guessed where I was. You couldn't have thought I was under a bush with the sail maker's son."

"With him, no. Under a bush, maybe. Or in a wave, or on top of a mountain—I never know where to find you. You go where I can't follow."

"I was in the tower. You can walk up a stairway."

"The tower won't let me," he said stonily. "It only wants you. What does it make you do up there?"

"I embroider. I've told you. You make blankets; I make pictures. You work all night sometimes without explaining. Why can't you give me the same freedom?"

"You can come and go in my house when I work. I can't. The tower keeps everyone away from you. And I can show you what I've done. You never show me anything."

"I can't," she answered tautly. "I've explained that, too. The wind takes my pictures."

"It does." His arms were folded, as hers were; they glowered at one another, in squabblers' stance, still close enough to kiss. "What picture did the wind take this time?"

She opened her mouth, hesitated, then said baldly, "Another tower."

He tossed his hands, whuffing like a horse at a suspicious smell. "The wind. It's magic that takes your pictures, magic that lured you to that tower and keeps you vanishing back into it."

She shrugged, bewildered, smelling magic on the wind, even there, in the ancient scent of stone, the tease of brine. "So it's magic. That's an art, too, like weaving. What—"

"You never ask yourself who put the magic in the tower so that no one else can get up the steps. You don't ask where the images in the mirror come from. Or if the magic is good or evil. You just do what you think it wants, and you want it more than you want me. Why?"

She was silent, thinking of the knight riding out of the mirror onto the plain behind her. "The mirror isn't evil," she said slowly. "It's more like an eye, watching something happening in Skye. Sometimes it lets me see what it watches. And I embroider a picture of that. And then I leave the picture on the window ledge beside the mirror and I never see it again. Wind takes it somewhere, I suppose."

"But what possesses you?" he demanded. "What compels you?"

"They're beautiful," she answered helplessly. "Like fragments of stories that I have to piece together to learn where they begin, and how they will end. Why do you spend days and weeks on your weaving?"

"To get it out of my head and into my hands, where I can see it and feel it. But the image in my head is mine, not in some mirror putting thoughts into my head—"

"It's not—it doesn't—" She held her breath and loosed it, then unfolded her arms and touched him. "Come with me and see."

"Now?"

"Now."

His eyes widened; she saw a muscle jump along his jaw. She knew what he feared. She felt it herself when she entered the old tower in the stone wood. There was something disturbing in the density of shadow, in the age of the stones, that seemed to speak of a time before words, before the trees clustered near it on the cliff had even thought of turning to stone. The broken, spiral steps suggested other things: they led away from life; they led to loss and endings, to the places where time stopped moving and nothing would ever happen again. But she found them unpersuasive. The tower had simply woven spells as harmless as cobweb to guard itself from intruders. What it protected in its secret heart was the strange, mysterious images in its mirror.

"If I come with you, you'll see there's nothing at all to fear."

He snorted at that, and shied uneasily, as if the tower walls had fallen suddenly around him out of the sky. But he met her gaze, held it, drawing from her fearlessness. He said tersely, "Let's go."

As they crossed the plain, the sun began to sink behind a long line of billowing mist beginning to blow inland. At the broken edge of the plain, the village below revealed itself: a meandering network of cobbled roads and stone houses facing the sea. Its harbor was a deep, restless half-moon of water, its rounded sides enclosed by stone. Boats rolling into the harbor moored along its straight side. It was open to the sea at one end through a narrow channel in the rocks, tricky to navigate in good weather, impossible in bad. Half the villagers fished. The others raised sheep and goats on the wild land, which grew grass or rocks indiscriminately, but little else. Others, like the baker Melanthos saw walking to the seaward end of the harbor, tended to the daily needs of the village.

She stopped, gazing down. The road they stood on began in the harbor, wound up the rocky cliff, and ran along the edge of it, until it frayed away in the stone wood. "There's my mother." She frowned absently, studying the tall, bulky, swaying figure. It was her private belief that her mother had once been a seal, who had swum too close to humans without her sealskin on and had been taken. She was shaped like one, she barked, and she knew some very strange things. "She's on her way to the tavern again for her splash of something. She'll be upset with me, too," she added, remembering. "So will Gentian. I was supposed to be up before dawn to help with the morning baking." Anyon, gazing down, looked as if he would rather be following the baker to the tavern instead of the baker's incomprehensible daughter. Melanthos's frown deepened; her fingers worked a knot into a long strand of hair. "She used to make magic, instead of bread."

"What?"

"She did. When Gentian and I were young. She's fey. Now she just turns flour into bread and sells it. I used to think she was as old as the stones on the cliff."

"She's your mother," Anyon said bewilderedly. "She was as young as you are, once."

"So were the stones," Melanthos said pithily. She gave the strand in her hand a sharp tug, and turned down the road toward the tower. "I used to think I understood her."

Mist raced the wind across the sea toward land, swallowing sky and water, and chasing the last of the fishing boats into the harbor. Over the plain, a single star hung beneath the moon's averted face like a tear. Melanthos wondered where the knight was beneath that tear, if he had stopped at some inn, or if he pursued his mysterious, urgent quest into the night. Beside her, Anyon walked silently, apprehensive, she could tell, with what he might meet in the tower. In an odd blurring of their thoughts, she saw the stone wood suddenly out of his eyes: not trees at all, never anything alive, just stones raised for some ancient, obscure, and no longer important reason. The tower changed, too, through his eyes. Black against the twilight mists, sagging with age, its doorway webbed with the coming night, it looked oddly like the tower she had embroidered out of all her darkest threads.

He hesitated at the threshold, then forced himself to take a step. She stopped him.

"I'll go first. Just watch me. Don't look at anything else."

He nodded briefly, without meeting her eyes. She saw him swallow. She stepped through the doorway and began to climb the stairs.

"You see," she said as she reached the top and lit a taper from the little oil lamp she left burning on the floor, "it's simple. You just go up one step and then another, and ignore all the arguments along the way." She turned when he didn't answer. The room was empty but for her.

She heard him call her then, in frustration and fear, from somewhere down the stairs. But the mirror was speaking, too, filling itself with light, colors, movement, another piece of the fragmented tale.

"In a moment," she called to Anyon, and sat down among her threads.

EIGHT

Cyan Dag, following a river across Skye, found the
dead at sunrise. The river had grown shallow, and
spread into thin, silvery fingers across a wide marsh. New
light spilled over him as he dismounted; bright, startled
marsh birds flickered around him, calling to the sun. Clouds
in the distance, bruised purple and tumbled together, told
him of the storm he had missed. He could smell it, rain still
clinging to the leaves of the low, flowering brush he stood
in, rain in the wind from the sea. For a moment the scent
of the tiny, sweet flowers overpowered the stench of death.

He stared at them. Six men, he counted, and two
horses. Even the horses were armed. Two of the warriors
wore rich, embroidered silks over their mail; the others
wore fine black leather trimmed with silver. He did not
recognize the emblems embroidered on the silk: black roses,

or perhaps black suns. They were not of Gloinmere, and looked too rich for Skye. They might have wandered into Skye from some strange land across the sea, though why they had fought there, in that lonely marsh beside the sea, he could not guess. Light sparked in the jeweled chains still hanging around their necks, in the jewels in their ears. Their faces, bloody and smeared with dirt, seemed imperious. They gazed unflinchingly back at the sun, at the flies beginning to swarm, at the weapons scattered on the roiled ground, and explained nothing. But he stood listening to their silence, as if, becoming as motionless, as breathless, he might hear the language they spoke now.

A hawk cried above him, fierce, piercing, and he started. Something moved among the dead that was not windblown cloth or hair. A ring flashed; a hand shifted a spider's step across the ground. He felt the cold, silken glide of horror over his skin. That warrior lay facedown, looking, Cyan had thought, into the black, rain-pocked shadow of his blood. He turned his head slightly, showing hair matted with blood, the bone sheared above his brow.

Cyan swallowed dryly, motionless again, waiting for the man to realize that he was dead. But the searching eye found him, held him until he was recognized: human and alive. Then it closed. The ringed finger beckoned.

Cyan stepped among the dead and knelt beside him. He bent low to catch whatever words the warrior thought he could still speak, and saw then how young he was. His lean jaw was smooth as a child's, his eye golden and fearless, too young to believe in what it saw coming. He wore red and yellow silk; slashed ribbons of it swirled around Cyan as he listened.

"Name," he heard, and said it. The warrior's eye closed, opened when Cyan thought he had finally died. His hand moved; one finger touched Cyan's arm. Words as frail as cobweb catching light among the leaves wove together somehow, made a coherent pattern.

"Who are you?" Cyan asked when he understood. Wind answered; a bird answered. He heard an indrawn breath, and then another. Then he realized that he listened to the sea. The warrior's eye was still open. Cyan closed it gently and straightened, as stiff as if he had knelt there for hours.

His jaw tightened. He turned the young warrior over, knowing then how scavengers felt, prying under mail and cloth for treasure, trying to free it from the weight of flesh and bone growing rigid, unfamiliar. But he found at last what he had been asked to take.

He could make nothing of the plain silver disk. Round and polished to a mirrorlike clarity, it covered his palm. It refused to reflect anything, even his face, as he gazed into it. What it was, or meant, or did, it did not tell him. Magic, he decided finally. Incomprehensible. Still, he slid the heavy chain it hung on over his head, tucked the disk beneath his shirt. It would mean something to someone who knew the young man; perhaps that was why he had been asked to take it. Then he studied the cloth it had been wrapped in.

He felt the blood drain from his face; his skin prickled again with shock. There they all were, the six dead warriors, the armored horses. But they were made of thread now, depicted in bright, precise stitches. He recognized the yellow hair and silk, the golden eye, against a different background. They lay on a brown plain instead of a flowering marsh. A tower stood in the distance. The dragon wrapped around it opened one slitted eye wide, as if it had watched the battle on the plain.

Dragon, Thayne Ysse had said. Gold. Troubled, Cyan searched the picture for some hint of explanation. Neither dead nor dragon offered it. The dragon had killed them, he guessed. But nothing had been burned, and the dragon looked more curious than aroused. More likely, meeting by chance, they had killed one another, fighting over the gold they did not yet possess. But what were their bodies doing in the marsh?

He lifted his head then, perhaps at the odd silence. The relentless buzzing behind him had ceased. He did not want to turn, but he turned finally, slowly, to find that the dead had all unraveled into the wind behind him. There was nothing left of them, except their images in thread on the cloth he held, and the silver disk beneath his shirt.

He shivered, unsettled by the power that turned death into thread. He lingered, chilled in the bite of sea wind, but nothing else happened; nothing explained. He let the wind take the cloth, but did not watch to see if it, too, vanished. But he kept the disk, for a ghost had come out of nowhere in Skye and given it to him, like a portent. But of what, for what, why? Nothing said. He mounted finally and rode out of the marsh to the sea.

The tower overlooked the sea. It rose seemingly out of solid stone on a dark wedge of cliff; graceful walls dipped and curved away from it to enclose the castle within. Cyan, putting as much of Skye as he could between himself and the eerie marsh, saw the tower near dusk as he rode along the coast. The castle itself looked worn and unthreatening, stones spilling out of the old wall here and there onto the meadow, one side of the massive gate open and sagging on its hinges. It flew the blue banner of Skye, with its three white doves in flight. Its chimneys looked hearteningly busy.

He found an old man in the turret beside the gate, looking through a long, strange tube out over the fields. Cyan called to him. The man, his hair thin and cloudy white, his chin patched with white-and-gray stubble, removed one eye from the tube and leaned out of the turret.

He ran a sky-blue eye over Cyan, from the dust in his hair down the towers on his surcoat and his sword to his cracked boots. "You look lost," he commented. "Though I couldn't say where from."

"From Gloinmere," Cyan said. "My name is Cyan Dag."

Both brows, fat and furry as caterpillars, went up.

"Cyan Dag is a knight in the court of Regis Aurum."

"Yes."

"Well, what are you doing at my gate in Skye? You're a very long way from home."

Cyan nodded wearily, feeling the sands he had ridden across lodged in his hair, behind his eyes. "A very long way," he agreed. "Do you think that, in the king's name, the lord of this castle might give shelter to a knight of Gloinmere? I have slept on the ground as often as in a bed since I left Yves."

"Why—" The old man waved a hand vaguely at the word, and changed it. "Wait." He took the tube from its stand, tucked it under his arm, and disappeared. He reappeared stepping out of an arch at the bottom of the turret. He wore a long black robe; its sleeves and hem and collar were of scalloped cloth-of-gold. Under his chin, Cyan noted, the gold carried a wine stain, a few morsels of old meals. He patted Cyan's horse, then took the bridle gently.

"I am Verlain," he said, "the Lord of Skye." He walked the gelding through the gate while Cyan gazed at him, dumbfounded. "If you came from Gloinmere, you must have seen my Gwynne married. She would not let me come; she said I am too old to cross the mountains. Did you see them marry?"

Cyan closed his eyes, felt the grit in them. "Yes."

"You must have left Gloinmere shortly afterward. No one of my household or family is back yet. Is Gwynne happy? Tell me. Do you think the king will love her?"

"From what I saw he loves her past doubt."

Her father heaved a sigh. "Thank you." He stopped, lifted the tube he carried. "Would you hold this for me?"

Cyan took it. It was broader than he expected, and heavy with circles of glass at both ends. He balanced it awkwardly against the pommel of his saddle, letting the Lord of Skye guide his horse. "What is it?"

"It sees dragons. At least," Verlain amended, "it does when there are any to see. Sometimes there are, but I always miss them . . . But why did you leave Gloinmere to come to Skye? You look as though you left in a hurry, without an escort, without armor except for that sword. And your boots—"

"They aren't mine. Mine were stolen."

Verlain rolled a dubious eye as blue, Cyan realized, as his daughter's. "No one would dare steal the boots off such a formidable knight."

"They didn't know it was me."

"Oh. Why didn't you stop them?"

"They threw rocks at me." Cyan sighed. "It is not a pretty tale."

The old man snorted in amusement. Then he patted the gelding's neck, as if in apology. "In the name of Regis Aurum, who seems to have made himself my son by marriage, let me offer you a few things to help you on your way. Which, by the way, is where?"

Cyan hesitated. The woman in the tower might be anyone, he decided, and so might the woman who sent him on his bewildering path. "I am looking for a woman in a tower," he said, watching Verlain's face. The hoary brows lifted again, in surprise.

"You rode that hard, from Gloinmere to Skye, to look for a woman in a tower?"

"She is in very great danger. I was sent to rescue her. I was told only that she is in Skye, but not where . . . You have a tower," he added suddenly, remembering the dark stones rising above the sea.

"Yes, but I don't keep women in it," Verlain said reasonably. "I go there sometimes to watch for dragons from the roof. Who is this woman?"

"A lady of Yves, who is trapped in Skye. Regis," he

added, inspired, "was so moved by the tale that he sent me without delay. So I went alone. So moved, myself, that I forgot a few things."

"I never travel without a small village," Verlain mused. "Attendants, guards, pots, dogs, spare horses, pavilions in case there are no suitable lodgings . . ." He summoned a stabler for the gelding. A liveried servant came down the steps to take the dragon tube so that Cyan could dismount. He cradled it in his arms as carefully as a baby.

Verlain said to him, "This is Cyan Dag, from the court of Regis Aurum, a knight of great renown. Treat him so."

"Yes, my lord."

"Find him suitable clothes, a proper pair of boots, and—"

"A bath," Cyan pleaded.

"Yes, my lords."

"Bring him to the hall to eat with me. You can tell me about the wedding," he added eagerly to Cyan. "The feasts, the celebrations, the games. And have the tube set on its stand on the roof of the tower for us to view the skies after supper. Tonight there might be dragons."

The servant bowed. Cyan blinked, suddenly remembering Thayne Ysse's dragon. But that was another tale, he decided tiredly, another tower. After he freed Gwynne of Skye from her prison, he would search for Thayne. He might have entered Skye, but Cyan guessed that even the smoldering Lord of Ysse, with all his dangerous intentions, would have trouble riding onto a plain made out of thread.

Washed, dressed in light wool and linen that did not have dirt and sweat ground into their seams, and in fine, supple boots that did not try to walk away without him, the towers on his surcoat golden again instead of dust, he presented himself to Verlain of Skye. Supper in the great hall seemed a haphazard affair, with dogs wandering loose among children eating on the floor, lovers feeding each other in corners, musicians with harp and flute and lute snatching bites between songs, and long gaps of empty, sky-blue cloth between courtiers.

"Everyone left me to go to the wedding," Verlain explained, patting the cloth beside him for Cyan to sit. "And when they all return, my Gwynne will not be with them . . ." He brooded a moment, then added more cheerfully, "But my bard will. I miss her almost as much. Did you see her there?"

Cyan pulled the seamed, secret-eyed face out of memory. "A tall woman with long white hair and a very odd harp? Oh, yes. How could I not have noticed her?"

"The harp is quite old, made of swan and dragon bone, she says. She can pick songs out of the wind that have lingered there forgotten for centuries. She can hear the moon sing. Did you listen to her?"

"Yes."

"She might know something about a tower . . . But she is not here."

Of course not, Cyan thought. Like your dragons, she vanishes every time I look for her. He said cautiously, feeling his way into his questioning so not to appall the innocent Lord of Skye, "Your daughter is very beautiful. She charmed the court at Gloinmere with her grace and courtesy."

Verlain clapped his hands, delighted. "Her mother was like that," he said, signaling servants to heap salmon and lamb to overflowing on Cyan's plate. "She knew everyone's name, down to the boy in the cow barn who forked out the stalls."

"She did everything equally well—she hunted, she judged poetry, she danced—"

"She loves to dance." He picked a fish bone out of a bite, still beaming. "My bard taught her. We are so far from Gloinmere that dances change, she said, between there and here, passing from court to court."

Cyan ate fish he did not taste, watching, in a flicker of candlelight, shadows appearing and vanishing on the cloth. "How did your bard know the court dances of Yves?"

"How do bards know anything? Will the king be kind to my daughter?"

Cyan looked into the sagging, sky-blue eyes, in which the hope of dragons flew. "Will she be kind to him?" he asked softly. "He has given her his heart."

Verlain drew breath, loosed it in a long, surfeited sigh. "Then I can live without her. Thank you. Now. Tell me everything you remember of the wedding. Every tiny detail."

Cyan sighed, too, soundlessly, and did his best to pick a harmless path around the nightmare wedding.

After supper, Verlain took him to the tower on the cliff. Servants followed them to the roof with torches and wine, dried fruit and cakes, and left them there alone at the boundary of two vast plains of darkness. One sang with the voice of water, the other with the voices of trees. Dragons flying at night could best be seen against the moon, Verlain explained, aiming his tube on its stand at a cluster of stars as thick as bees around their waning queen. Cyan searched the night, saw mists sharpen into stars, and stars bloom into impossible fires. He saw the dark and pitted hollows in the moon. But he saw no dragons. Verlain watched one distant, glowing eye shoot past the moon; he swore that night wings had opened, their bones patterned with stars, to catch the wild currents above the sea so effortlessly that they did not seem to move as they flew. Cyan, giving up on dragons, swung the tube toward land and found, among the wind-swept trees, stars that burned and moved but did not fly.

He raised his head after a moment. "You have company." The Lord of Skye applied his eye to the tube while beyond him the slow tide of stars flowed raggedly toward his gate.

Verlain gave a cry. "They're back! My house is back from Gloinmere." He leaned precariously over the edge and shouted down into the yard. Then he snatched a torch from its sconce and spiraled back down the tower steps. Cyan, smiling, watched the torch fire tumble across the yard below to stop beside the gate.

He turned to go down himself, and saw the eye of the dragon tube flash suddenly, a molten, heart-stopping gold. He stepped toward it, his lips parted in wonder. The lens flashed again, this time with darker fires. Breathless, not daring to touch it, he looked into the opposite lens.

He saw the dragon.

The broad plain it lay on was ringed with barren hills. The ground was so parched it seemed to shed flakes of gold.

The tower of flame-red stone the dragon protected had no windows, no visible door. Both the dragon's eyes had opened. One burned gold; the other, in shadow, fumed iridescent blazes of blue, green, black. The arch of one folded wing rose as high as the middle of the tower.

Cyan stared at it, stunned. A single claw looked longer than his body; he might have ducked into the glowing fires of its eyes. That was the deadly, gorgeous monster Thayne Ysse dreamed of unleashing at Regis Aurum. It looked impossible. The dragon could kill Thayne like an insect with a flick of a claw. If he could even find it. There were legends, Cyan remembered, of magic in the North Islands. But they were as threadbare as an islander's cloak. And there had been nothing at all magical in their desperate, ill-fated battle with Regis Aurum. Thayne, eaten by passion and delusion, could do nothing more than add his bones to the dead on the plain. So Yves could hope. But if, in seven years since that battle, he had learned to harness and unleash such power, the dragon would rend Yves like a tattered banner on its flight to Gloinmere.

Someone spoke behind him. He whirled, his muscles locking, his hand trying to shape the air at his side into the sword he had left below. The Bard of Skye waited patiently until he remembered his own name, and wondered, for the first time, about hers.

"Verlain told me you were here. You are a brave man, Cyan Dag, and true to your king." Her face was in shadow, but her hair gleamed white as the moon behind her. "I'm sorry I cannot help you. I must go back soon to Gloinmere.

The queen asked me to return. I think she does not trust me out of her sight."

"Did you—" He stopped to swallow, still shaken by his vision, and the fierce, overwhelming urge to battle. "Have you seen that?"

"What?"

"Thayne Ysse's dragon."

She was silent; he felt her gaze, intense and unyielding as the night. "What dragon?"

"The dragon guarding its tower full of treasure. He wants it to—"

She shook her head quickly, impatiently. "Cyan, that is not the tower you are looking for."

"But—"

"You must keep your mind on the Lady of Skye. You have no time for dragon hunting."

"I'm not. It's Thayne Ysse who wants—"

"Never mind Thayne Ysse. I know you've had a hard journey, and you don't know where to go, that's why I came up here in secret. I must go down again. Verlain will be looking for me."

"Please—"

"Listen to me. You've said nothing about this to frighten Verlain. I can tell: he is still smiling. You must leave soon. At dawn and ride south—"

"I've just ridden north."

"South," she said firmly. "Until you see three hills to the west exactly even with each other, so that they seem reflections of one another. They are called the Three Sisters. Ride west into them. They may be farther than they look.

Skye is sometimes imprecise. But you'll find it."

"What — "

"The tower you need to find. Be very careful there. It will be dangerous for you, and for Gwynne of Skye. I must go. I don't," she added, moving toward the stairs, "exactly know how you can rescue her. Only that there will be a way. Farewell, Cyan Dag."

He felt her cool, strong hand on his cheek. Then she took the torch and left him in the dark.

NINE

Thayne Ysse, following the wind, rode west to the edge of the world and watched the sun burn out like a candle flame in the sea.

The sound of the waves was different in Skye. They boomed down a long, endless boundary of land, broke against high cliffs and broad stretches of white sand longer than some of the North Islands. A village in the crook of a bluff to the south had begun to burn its evening lights; the tiny fires looked frail as insect wings against the vastness of sea and the night flowing toward it with the tide. He would find shelter there. But he lingered on the cliff, watching waves below curl and burst into butterflies, feathers, fingers beckoning from the deep. He wondered where Skye hid its dragons. Crossing it, he had scented for sulfur on the wind, for charred earth and bone, for gold. Words,

Craiche had said. They could change into themselves. If he said the word for dragon, the word would become dragon. He whispered it slowly, let the wind drag it out of him like flame. Nothing happened. His mouth crooked. In what world could he bring words to life? Not even in Skye, apparently, where the wind, insistent, chilly, everywhere, in his ear, up his sleeve, down his throat, seemed to want to knead him out of the shape he knew into something other. He let it blow him off the cliff, finally, toward the distant lights. Words were what people gave even strangers for nothing. If there was a tower full of gold in Skye that no one had managed to plunder, then truth would have turned into many tales, by now, and tales cost nothing either, especially in a tavern.

But the tavern he found had few travelers and they spoke of fish and families and the weather instead of dragons. He turned inland again, for the image in his father's book had been precise: a plain, ringed by what looked like craggy hills blasted treeless by the dragon's breath. Both tale and true, the bard had said; it was up to him, he knew, to recognize the difference. But where to find such barrenness, such danger and magic, in that green, misty, peaceful country, he had no idea.

He caught a glimpse of direction a day or two later, when his drifting path crossed the trail the knight of Gloinmere had left across Skye.

"You're the second man from beyond Skye staying here in three days," the innkeeper told him as she set ale and lamb stew in front of him. She had a slanting smile, a rook's nest of straw-colored hair, and shrewd blue eyes. She lingered as he began to eat. "It's rare for a knight of Yves to come this far west. And I don't remember anyone at all of the North Islands finding his way here before."

Thayne, chewing a tender bite of spring lamb, and watching the innkeeper's charming, quirky smile, blinked. The stew grew suddenly tasteless in his mouth. He swallowed, asked calmly, "Who was he, this knight of Yves?"

She told him. "I didn't believe him at first," she added. "Anyone can wear a sword and call himself a knight. But he spoke to me so courteously, and he wore those towers."

Thayne took a sip of bitter ale. "He is one of the most powerful and honored knights of Gloinmere."

"I always thought knights looked less — well, bedraggled. I cobbled one of his boots back together."

"Where was he going? Did he say?"

"He was trying to find a tower . . ." She held his eyes then, in an open, disconcerting gaze. "Why? Do you know him?"

"We met, in Yves." He stirred up a piece of leek, added briefly, "He was fighting some thieves, when I came across him. They had already stolen his boots."

"Which explains his boots. So you stopped to help him?"

"I did what I could," he answered evenly. "He was wounded. I didn't think he would make it into Skye."

"He did. But I don't know where he went from here, to look for his tower. It sounded like something out of a tale, to me. A dream." She wiped a corner of apron across a spill on the table, slowly enough for him to see the pearl on her finger, and the milky underside of her wrist. She said without looking at him, "My husband is out on his boat; he'll be gone for days. The salmon are running, up north. Travelers are scarce yet, which is why I can remember one from the next." She gave him a sidelong flash of her smile. "You'll let me know if you want anything else." She turned away briskly, left him to consider what else he might need.

He considered the knight. If a man of Yves who knew no more of magic than what he could do with a sword were searching for that tower, then it existed. The thought of the dragon slain according to the ruthless, efficient, unquestioning methods of Gloinmere, its magic destroyed and its treasure snatched away from the desperate North Islands, fed the fury and desperation that had impelled him on his improbable journey. The image of the stranger in the forest, standing his ground barefoot against armed riders, blood running through his hair, his broadsword leaving patterns of light in the air, faded from memory. Only his eyes, the color of cold, tempered metal and the gold towers that linked him to Regis Aurum remained. Thayne, his own eyes on the split, seared logs on the hearth, heard himself whisper, "You should have gone back to Gloinmere."

The dragon possessed his dreams that night: a bright, sinuous, deadly thing that tore out his heart with the flick of one claw and swallowed it. He saw out of the dragon's eyes, then, felt the fire pulsing through him. He coiled himself around the gold in the tower, and watched the knight riding toward him across the wasteland. Fire the color of gold billowed out of him, ate everything living in its path. Only the knight's surcoat remained, lying like a fallen banner on the scorched ground. He spread his wings then, and uncoiled his body in a spiraling flight toward the sun, smelling more gold, more death, in the towers of Gloinmere.

He rose early the next morning, still feeling the dragon fire smoldering behind his eyes, in his heart. He lost himself in Skye, drifting away from roads, for no road he had ever heard of led to dragons. The land turned lonely, unpredictable. A lake might appear out of nowhere, stretching flat, still, and cold as a blade on the horizon. Rivers he followed seemed to change the direction of their flow. A ridge of stones on a high peak slowly turned into an intricate lacework of wall and window, ruins older than Yves, and with no name anyone could remember. He met few people in the woods and marshlands. Those he chanced across seemed to see the dragon he looked for coiled in his eyes, and answered his questions uneasily. No, they had never heard of a plain where nothing grew, and there were old towers of various origin scattered all over Skye. There was one in the birch wood; he couldn't miss it, heading that direction. There was nothing in the tower, though, but bats.

He rode among the pale, slender trees, with their new leaves of green whispering around him, the dead leaves that had turned to gold luminous beneath shafts of light. He missed the tower; it had fallen, or moved itself, or it was hidden within a blur of brightness falling through the trees. Coming out of the wood, he crossed a meadow and followed the shallow, silvery stream flowing through it. As dusk fell, he startled a hare in the grass and shot it. He made a fire beside the stream, skinned the hare, and spitted it above the flames. He ate it with bread the innkeeper had given him. When the makeshift spit and the bones collapsed into the fire, he lay back to watch the moon rise. It dropped its reflection among the stones in the stream. Water tried to drag the moon away; it rippled, wavered, but clung stubbornly to the bottom of the stream. Thayne's eyes closed. The water chattered at him, like some old crone trying to tell him a story he couldn't understand. He saw her finally, wading in the water, trying to rescue the horned moon. Fishlike, it eluded her; she kept catching at it, still talking breathlessly. He could not see her face clearly, but he thought he might recognize her. The ring on her left hand sparked silver white now and then, catching at moonlight. He interrupted her finally.

"Dragon," he said. "Tell me how to say the word for dragon."

It opened a baleful maw that could have swallowed him standing, and howled fire. He felt it engulf him, charring his skin and then his flesh, and then changing the shape and position of his bones, until he realized that he was the hare on the spit, slowly turning to face the flames.

He jerked himself awake, saw an ember in his own fire flare, and pulled away from it, gasping. Still shaken, he rolled toward the stream, drank from it to clear the charred taste out of his mouth. The smoldering embers dragged at his eyes again; the small bones in it, he saw starkly, might well be his own. He wondered what word in any language might get a dragon's attention in the middle of its mindless burning. None he knew. He lay back down finally, staring inward, for the first time, at the bleak, unremitting notion that he might lose his life in a strange country, on a plain in a tale that no one even knew existed.

At sunrise, he saw three hills in the distance, green and silvery with ash, so alike they seemed reflections of one another. He rode toward them. They disappeared for a while as he made his way through a forest of oak so old and massive they might, petrified with centuries, grow into towers. He saw the hills again in the afternoon, across a broad valley. The placid river that flowed through it disappeared between two hills; the third hill was visible between them.

He stopped at the river to let his horse drink. Gazing absently at the placid hills, he saw that their close flanks nearly touched; the three broad, rounded hills made a ring around whatever lay within them. He thought of the picture in his father's book. But that plain was circled by harsh peaks, sharpened into teeth as if by the constant dry pound of light. These, with their linked, green slopes, seemed to surround some secret loveliness.

He followed the river toward them. They were not so far as they had looked; he came swiftly to the place where the river began its curve between the two closest hills. It quickened there, grew narrower, shallower. It took forever, he felt, to make his way between the hills. They seemed to shift closer, flinging their shadows over him. The ash forests growing on them thinned, dwindled into brush, and then into grass. In the late afternoon, the grasses on the slopes began to turn brown, as if he had spent a season or two trying to round the hills. He felt the sweat on his face from the hot afternoon light, and stopped again for water. The banks of the river were hard, cracked mud now; grass grew sparsely along them. He felt his heartbeat then, knowing what secret the hills held in their midst. He had been, without thinking, testing the wind for the smell of dragon for some time now.

He saw Craiche's face, very clearly, lifting out of a book and giving Thayne his sweet, dauntless smile. He saw their father, recognizing Thayne, speaking his name. A longing for home swept through him then. He could simply turn, ride out of the hills and all the way back to the North Islands, defeated but alive. It seemed worth it, simply to see Craiche smile at him again. "I am not Bowan," he whispered. "I am not Ferle, who had a way with words. I can't make magic out of nothing. I don't want to die for gold."

He saw the knight's eyes then, clear and cold, fearless. *Then go home,* they said to him, without judgment, without surprise. *I will do what you cannot.*

He mounted again after a swallow of warm, murky water, and continued his journey.

Near sunset, the river trickled to a stain on the cracked earth. The endless hillsides were barren now, jagged, ground down to stone. His horse's black hide was silvery with a gloss of sweat. The hills pushed closer together, loomed above him, their peaks fiery against a blazing, changeless blue so parched it could not even make a cloud. Thayne urged his weary mount forward, through an opening between the hills so narrow that they nearly formed an arch above his head.

On the other side, he stopped. Dust shimmered across a plain ringed by three hills on which nothing could ever have grown. Light from the lowering sun scorched the earth like dragon's breath. The immensity of stone rising out of the parched ground cast a shadow halfway across the plain.

The dragon coiled around the tower opened its eyes.

TEN

In Stony Wood, the baker lumbered her slow, implacable way down the cobbled street between the bakery and the tavern at the bottom of the half-moon harbor. The fishers tended toward an older, brinier tavern at the end of the pier. There the floorboards were warped from their wet boots, and the only adornment among the scarred tables and benches was a jar in which something scaly green, pale as pearl, with tangled strands of dark moss or hair dimly floated. A mermaid, the tavernkeeper called it. Late at night, her face grew almost visible to those who stayed that long. Then, they would swear, she sometimes turned her head and smiled.

Sel preferred a quieter tavern with no drowned, pickled mermaids in it. She went to a place at the bottom of the harbor, where she could watch the waves scroll across the endless sea before they heaved into the harbor mouth, bringing the boats back with them. In that tavern, the stone sills were littered with odd pebbles and shells. Old fishing nets hung along the windows for curtains. In the distance, on the opposite cliff, she could see the strange stumps of the stone wood, that could take on the dark, silken sheen of mother-of-pearl when the last light touched them.

The baker eased her long, heavy seal's body onto a bench at her favorite window overlooking both the harbor mouth and the open sea. Her eyes, wide set like a fish's, were kelp dark, hiding thoughts and stray flecks of color deep in them. Her hair, which was long and wild when she loosed it, hung in a single braid of black and silver. As she watched the sea and drank there, she let old memories stir up from the bottom of her mind like things in the deep unburying themselves, drawn up to light.

"What can I get you, Sel?" Brenna asked her. She was a massive, cheerful, round-faced woman with butter-colored hair and long, graceful hands. Her children had collected the shells and stones in the tavern; they were out on the rocks now, fishing in the incoming tide.

"My youth," Sel said. "My husband. A spell to get my child out of that tower."

"What about your usual?"

"My usual," Sel agreed. Brenna brought her dark ale as bitter as brine. Then she poured one for herself and sat down with Sel, since the place was empty but for them.

"What keeps her up there?" she asked puzzledly. "It's a dank, solitary thing, standing there in the stone wood."

"Stories," Melanthos's mother said dourly.

"Stories?"

"And magic. She's caught up in it. It's like being in love, only with nothing real. And she refuses to see the danger. She thinks it's all innocent."

"Well, nothing's happened," Brenna said soothingly. "Nothing yet."

Sel looked at her silently, color flashing unexpectedly in one eye, vague and swiftly gone. She took a sip of ale and answered obliquely. "I hoped that Anyon would be enough to keep her out of it. But no. She's willful. She prefers mystery to love."

"Well, sometimes . . ." Brenna murmured, gazing reminiscently out to sea herself, until a movement caught her eye and she leaned forward to push the casement wider. "Hol! The baby's eating your bait!"

"She's up there all night sometimes. She embroiders pictures, she says. Things she sees in a mirror. But she never shows them to us. They're gone, like words are gone on the wind as soon as they're spoken."

"Have you been up to see?"

Sel shook her head. "I've sent Gentian. It won't let her up. And Anyon has tried."

Brenna stirred. "Oh, well, Anyon—"

"I know; he hates walls. But he tried, for her. And even he can't follow her."

Brenna contemplated her ale, honey brown, sweeter than Sel's. She smiled suddenly. "They're a pair."

"They would be," Sel said darkly, "but for that tower."

The door opened. One of Brenna's froth-haired children came in, one hand carrying a shell, the other dragging the baby. "Look at this—"

"What was she eating?" Brenna asked, dipping two fingers into her ale and wiping the baby's dirty, sticky face.

"Herring guts. Look at this shell! It's like the stone wood—so old it turned to stone."

Brenna took the shell without looking at it, laid it down abruptly. "Then you must go," she said to Sel. "Go into the tower yourself and see if she's in danger."

Sel turned the shell; its delicate ribbing fanned across a stony underside. "It must be as old as the world," she murmured. "I don't care for the idea. I don't have a mind for such things anymore. I don't know if I could make it up the steps without getting stuck like a slug in a chambered shell, inching into smaller and smaller spaces until I couldn't go in or out. I don't know if I remember how to do it."

"Remember what?" Brenna asked blankly.

Sel gave the shell back to the child. "Pretty. Well. We'll never get the work done without her. She's taken lodgings there, it seems. And I have to listen to Anyon complain."

Brenna snorted back a laugh. "Then you'd better go," she said.

Sel went back to check her ovens first. She found Gentian wrapping a loaf and a half-dozen currant rolls for old Cray Given, who after sixty years of fishing smelled like a dried haddock and had about as many teeth. He showed Gentian the ones he had left, grinning at her as he edged out of the door. Then he encountered Sel's fishy stare and jumped. She snorted at his back, saw his shoulders hunch. Gentian, dropping his coins into a pot, bit back a smile. She checked the baby, who was sleeping in a breadbasket on the counter, then leaned next to it, chin on her hand, looking curiously at her mother.

"Melanthos?" Sel inquired. Gentian shook her head.

"Either in the tower or anywhere in Skye but here. Do you want me to find her?"

"No," Sel said. "I'll do it." She opened an oven door, checked the nut tarts inside, then the fire beneath them. She closed the door gently and stood without moving, part of her mind on the tower in that strange, ancient wood, the other part hearing seagulls and the following tide, and seals barking on the flat rocks out beyond the breakers. Once her small daughters had swum with the seals. She had watched their curly heads above the water, one dark, one light, their paddling hands and small white feet flashing through the foam.

"Mother?" she heard, and blinked at a tall young woman with long copper hair and eyes as lucent as the summer sea.

My children swam away from me, she thought. They left me watching them across the waves. She sighed and turned to the door. "Don't forget the tarts," she said. "When they come out of the oven, you can close the shop."

Gentian's bright brows twitched together, trying to frown. "Are you sure?" she asked. "If you stand at the tower stairs and call, and she doesn't answer, then come back here, and I'll look for her at Anyon's. I could use a walk."

Sel nodded. "I'll come back here," she said. "But if Melanthos is with Anyon, I'll let them be."

She left Gentian still hunched over the counter, watching Sel with a gentle, bemused expression in her eyes.

On the road that ran above the cliffs, Sel made her ponderous way, but not alone. Halfway to the stone wood, Joed surfaced and came with her, or at least one version of her. He wouldn't know me now, she thought. My grizzled hair, my great, slow body. He had eyes of slate and hair like loam, earth colors, for all he loved the sea. The sea took all of him: his lean, clever hands, the sunburned skin weathered and molded to his bones, his deep, conch-shell voice saying her name. She could hardly blame the sea, the way he looked at it, his other heart, his paramour. She only blamed it, deeply and past reason, for not taking her as well.

She had begun to bake to have her eyes looking at a bowl, a flour bin, an oven, a fire, a face, anything but water. Her hands shaped loaves like scallop shells, like moon shells, like starfish; she ate them as if she ate the sea, to make it part of her, to transform bone to shell and lose herself in it, eyeless, thoughtless, wrapped in memories and anchored on some hoary rock against the currents of the deep.

She walked among the stone trees, the standing stones, that always asked the same riddling questions. Stone or tree? Were we once alive? Or never? The bone-white stumps were stained with pale greens and grays of lichen. The darker stones, touched by light, smoldered with iridescent fires.

She saw the tower at the edge of the cliff. It looked harmless enough, its old stones dreaming under the fading sun, rooted in grasses and ringed with wildflowers. She went to stand beside it on the cliff, watching birds white as foam soar and dive into the waves. On the sand below, children raced after the receding tide, then turned and ran away from it as it foamed toward their heels. She felt something emanate from the weathered stones as she stood feeling as bulky and as weathered beside them. As if, she thought, the tower had looked at her.

"Well," she said after a while as the sun dipped into the scalloped cloud at the edge of the horizon. "It seems I must enter. You have my spellbound child."

Light drew back across the face of the sea, a brilliant tide rolling after the sun, breaking against cloud and vanishing. Cloud turned to silver; the sheen on the tower melted like water into sand. Sel felt the warmth drain out of the stones. She put her hand on one, let the sunlight pour out of it into her palm.

She turned, walked around the tower to the open doorway that faced the wood.

The worn, chipped steps were dark beyond the stone. They fanned out from a central core of stone and circled upward. She could not see where they went. She followed them slowly, panting a little, and expecting the stairs to narrow and leave her there, too bulky with memory and age and life to get into its secret heart. But its spells were more subtle. It turned to her the blank, dark, motionless face of death and she shrugged past it; she had seen it before. It warned her of a place without dreams, without hope; she only laughed once, sharply, and the warnings tore apart like spiderweb under a bitter wind. She wound her

way up into a blankness like the dark of the moon, where
the walls and the stairs seemed to vanish in front of her,
and there was no place to step except into nothing. She
snorted, stepping into nothing. Do you think I care? she
asked the tower. It showed her the steps again, grudgingly,
and was silent until she reached the top.

The chamber was empty. She looked around it, surprised, wondering if the tower had somehow made Melanthos invisible. But nothing stirred the dust on the musty
pallet. A blanket or two that Anyon had made swirled together in the middle of it. An untidy collection of threads
of every color, needles, pieces of linen, lay scattered on the
floor beneath the window facing the sea.

She saw her face in the mirror.

It seemed a stranger's face, for she looked at it as little
as possible, and even then scarcely saw it anymore. Now it
made her laugh again, at the chips and cracks and hairs on
it, the strange, troubled eyes, the silver in the dark brows,
in the hair rippling into its braid.

"Who might you be?" she asked. The face in the mirror
asked her the same question.

She glanced around her at the other windows. One saw
along the cliff road and down to the village. Another looked
out across the stone wood to the plains and tors beyond,
and farther, to the jagged line of mountain where Skye
ended or began, depending.

She poked at the pallet with her foot and sighed. "I
made it this far," she said to herself. "I might as well wait,
let her show me what she does. She'll come eventually . . ."

She settled herself on the pallet, drew one of Anyon's

blankets over her shoulders, for the mist was blowing in from the sea. She stirred the threads absently with her fingers, as though they were the pelt of some pet animal. She watched the cold gray sky reflected from a far window in the mirror. Her thoughts strayed, fashioned pieces of her life that seemed not soft paintings done in thread and finished with a knot, but more like the pieces of a broken mirror, jagged angles full of color, faces, movement, that did not fit together and could hurt. Joed's empty boat. Gentian when she was small and wore a cap of copper curls. The cold ovens of the bakery waiting to be warmed when the moon had set and the sky above the sea was black. The stranger's face she wore, in a life that she barely recognized except in memory.

She was gazing, she realized slowly, at a woman in the mirror.

Above the mirror the stars had been swallowed by the mist. The dark sea crumpled endlessly against the cliffs in distant, dreamy cadences, as if, in that unknown hour of night, the waves traveled beyond time and sang to an older moon. Within the tower in the mirror, a web of light and shadow trembled on the stones from a fire the mirror did not see. The woman sat in the chair, her hands curved motionlessly along the carved wood of its arms. Her fingers, long, slender, pale, were ringed with gold and jewels, as if once they had been considered precious, presented with gifts. Down one side of the circular frame in front of her, unworked linen trailed a line of needles and colored threads. From the other side, bright, finished images flowed onto the floor. On her window ledge, the mirror was a dark moon, disturbed now and then by a fleeting shimmer of firelight, like an indecipherable expression.

The woman sat very still; so did Sel, watching her. Her hands tightened now and then on the chair arms; sapphire, emerald, gold flashed. So abruptly that she startled Sel, she stood up and stepped away from the chair.

Sel still could not see her face. Her head was bowed; her loose, pale, rippling hair hid her profile. She walked; the scene in the mirror shifted. The woman turned her back again, stood facing the fire.

The fireplace was an enormous piece of marble into which a graceful lily opening a bell-shaped mouth had been carved on either side. The woman's gown, blue gray, embroidered with lilies and white birds, showed no sign of having been worn beyond the moment she had risen: not a crease, a strained seam, a stain.

She stood quietly in front of the fire, her head still bowed. Light shifted in a fluid sheen along her tight sleeves, as if her unseen hands moved, Sel thought, tightening and turning around themselves.

Her head lifted suddenly; she turned, as if she felt eyes on her beyond her tower, beyond her night. Sel saw her face.

She heard herself breathe after a long silence; she heard the sea again. "Once," she whispered, as if she were telling the woman's story to herself, "I swam out of the sea and stood on new feet on the shore of the world . . ."

The mirror blinked like an eye, and shone with all the colors of the sea.

ELEVEN

Cyan Dag came to the dark tower at sunset.

It stood, as the bard had told him, in the small valley between three hills. A grove of oak surrounded it; beyond the trees stretched meadows of long sweet grasses and wildflowers. Across one meadow, near another wood, he saw a stag crowned with hoary tiers of antlers raise its head at the unexpected scent and look at him.

The tower was nothing like what he had envisioned. Something loftier, more elegant, more dangerous than this, he thought he would come to, in the end. This one was squat, sagging, its rough stones tossed onto one another and mortared together with nothing but age. Anyone could have walked in and out of its door, which was a crooked lintel balanced on a couple of slabs. Beyond the dusty threshold, black so profound it seemed to have texture and weight like a stone filled the entry. He could see no windows.

He dismounted slowly, perplexed by the darkness, the silence within it. But the bard had told him to find the tower within these hills and so he had. Nothing left but to enter it, he thought. He could see nothing to stop him; whatever danger there was to be faced must lie within.

He left his horse cropping among the wildflowers and walked to the door, unsheathing his sword out of habit, though he doubted that any traps within the tower for unwary knights would be that unsubtle. The utter blackness made him hesitate. But he could not do what he needed to do standing around in the tranquil light of day. He put one hand on a worn doorpost, bowing his head a little, for the lintel was not high. He had taken the first step across the stark line between light and night, when he felt something rouse in the blackness so close to him he thought they shared the same breath of dusty air. Startled, he swung the broadsword awkwardly; the blade sparked against the lintel and froze there, as if it had driven into stone.

Someone pushed past him out of the shadow, gathering form and color as it moved, dark slipping away from it like a cloak. He let go of the sword, which had been rendered useless, and stepped into the tower to make himself invisible while he watched whatever had come out. It did not let him get far; a hand caught his wrist as inexorably as the stone had caught his sword. A woman cried, "Stop!"

He felt an immensity open around him in the blackness. He did not know anymore what there was to fear, since anything within that strange tower seemed possible. He could barely see his own hand, all that was left of him in the light, and the other hand, long and brown, with a silver ring on one finger, locked around his.

"Come back!"

He could not move. More than an absence of light held him still. There were voices just beyond his hearing, words of immense and complex power and meaning. There were visions beyond the black: colors that had never existed before, places reached by endless, intricate paths, so beautiful he could search for them in one lifetime, then linger in them for another. There were promises of unimaginable rewards for impossible dangers overcome, for precious things found, for those in dire distress and mortal need rescued and made safe. They pulled at him with a hundred whispering voices, a hundred gentle touches. Come, Cyan Dag. Go there. Do this. Learn that. Take this path, find, fight, save, kill, kneel, swear, love. If he could only free himself and turn, he would serve the perfect king, do the impossible deed, achieve his heart's desire, transform his world.

"Come back."

The voice sounded very far away. He heard his breath suddenly, quick and sharp, as if he had been running. He had pushed his free hand hard against a post stone, using all his strength as leverage against the hand pulling him back into the light of day. He wrenched at it; it tugged as fiercely at him. Somehow, despite his formidable strength and longing, he was jerked across the threshold into light. He stumbled, caught his balance and his breath, his face slick with sweat or tears. He stared bewilderedly at the woman who had forced him back into the world. Behind him, his sword dropped to earth with a clang.

He cried at her, "Why did you stop me?"

Then he recognized her.

She had lost the eerie, frightening beauty he had glimpsed the night she had rescued him in the forest. She had taken it off like a mask, or hidden it somewhere within what he saw now. She could do such things, he sensed. She was tall, long-boned and lean, brown as earth; her astonishing hair, night black and straight as straw, still seemed something she could vanish into. By daylight, he could see her eyes clearly: amber flecked with gold. She smiled at the recognition; fine lines fanned away from her eyes, framed her smile.

"Sidera," she said, before he could speak. "You asked me my name," she reminded him gently, and he remembered.

"You saved my life. You left me at that inn and I couldn't thank you."

"I told your horse to take you there," she answered. "I don't care for such places. I'm not like my sister. I'm more comfortable with the foxes and deer than king's courts."

"Your sister—" He stopped, confused, as three faces imposed themselves over one another in his mind: the one he had glimpsed across her fire, the face he saw now, the face of the woman who had sent him to that tower.

"The Bard of Skye."

He stared at her. The bard intruded between them, in his thoughts, tall and sinewy, with her black, sunken eyes, her long, rippling hair, her strong veined hands caressing the strings of her harp. He saw her in Sidera, then, in her height, her straight shoulders, her compelling eyes. But Sidera's eyes held light, and they seemed kind.

"Does your sister have a name?" he asked finally. "I only know her as the Bard of Skye."

"Her name is Idra. She didn't tell you?"

"I never asked," he said tautly. "I just seem to do what she tells me to do. She sent me here; she told me to find this tower, and rescue the woman trapped in it —"

Her brows went up; her eyes lost their smile at his distress. "But that's another tower entirely." Her hand emerged from her hair quickly as he felt the blood flare into his face. "What is your name? She didn't tell me."

"My name is Cyan Dag." His voice shook with leashed anger. "I thought that bards in Skye never lie."

"Did she? Did she lie to you?"

"She said—" He stopped, running a hand over his face, trying to remember exactly what she had said, that night on Verlain's dragon tower. "She said that finding the tower would be dangerous. And that this is the tower I needed to find."

"What you need," Sidera said, "is not always what you are looking for."

His mouth tightened. He turned, before he shouted, and picked up his sword. He said tersely, as he sheathed it, "She tells me what to look for. I didn't need this tower." It pulled at his heart then, as he faced it; he saw again the hundred tantalizing paths, the nameless kingdoms. "But I wanted it," he whispered.

"Cyan Dag," she said softly, before he took a step toward the dreaming darkness. He turned away from it to look at her, the woman who had come out of nowhere to thwart him. Then it struck him: she had not come out of nowhere, she had come from within. As if, he thought, she had been waiting for him.

He said a word finally; it did not come easily. "Sorcery."

She nodded. Her brows were crooked; she stood very still, watching him, as if she were luring a wary animal with her stillness and her calm. "Magic," she said. "Witch, I suppose you could call me. I am adept in the ancient ways of Skye. Which is why I am more often found in wild places instead of the civilized world. Some of the things I know are older than the coming of humans into Skye. The language of horses, for instance. The healing powers of plants."

He felt the tension in his body ease; the confusion in his thoughts yielded, like cloud, to a ray of certainty. She had saved his life; she meant him no harm.

"I'm grateful for that magic," he said simply. "But I don't understand why the bard sent me to this place."

"I'm not sure what she is doing, either." She folded her arms within her cloak of hair, paced a step, musing. Light was fading around them, leaving the air silvery with dusk. "Bards do speak truth, but sometimes in riddling ways."

"Nor do I understand," he added steadily, "what you were doing in the tower."

Something in her eyes warned him that he would not like the answer. "She sent me here to stop the knight who would enter."

He drew breath sharply, wanting to blaze at them both, the bard for sending him to the wrong tower, the witch for rescuing him from it. His hands clenched; he said tightly,

"I have never wanted anything more than the worlds I glimpsed in that tower."

"Well, you must be content with this one," she sighed, "with all its ambiguities and magic." She paced another step or two, trying to riddle from the passing breeze what the bard was thinking. Her steps, Cyan noticed, made no more sound in the grass than air. "She wanted me in there, you there, both of us lost to the world for a while. If you had pulled free of me, I would have had to search for you . . ."

He watched her, calmer now, trying to think in unaccustomed ways, as bards or witches thought. "She didn't expect you to stop me?"

"I don't think so. You think with your heart, Cyan Dag. It's an unusual and risky magic. She expected you to enter, me to follow . . . So there we are, lost in the dark, while she—does what?"

"Maybe the path to the lady in the tower is somewhere in there. It seemed the beginning place for many paths."

"It seems."

"What?"

"That tower. It's best at seeming."

He gazed at it, bewildered again, tempted simply to walk into it and let it answer their questions. She turned, as if she felt his impulse, and added, "I know my sister well, and I trust her as I trust the wind when it tells me what I smell, or the rain to go down instead of up. She does not lie. But she does not state the obvious, or take the shortest path, or do anything that might make life simpler if for her own reasons she prefers it complicated."

He shook his head, baffled, murmuring, "There are too

many towers . . . She sent me to Skye to find one, not three — "

"Three?" She turned so quickly that her hair clung to the spare, graceful lines of her body. A small bird flew out of it; he blinked. "What three?"

"This dark tower. Thayne's dragon tower. And the one with the woman trapped in it."

Her eyes glimmered oddly in the dusk. "The dragon tower . . . Someone is searching for it?"

"Thayne Ysse. The man who left me to die in the forest. He wants the dragon and its gold for the North Islands. I saw the dragon," he added, "on a piece of embroidery. I took the embroidery from the dead it watched."

She did not comment on the embroidery; such things, he guessed, happened daily in Skye. Her head was bent; he could not see her face. But he knew from her quick, certain steps that her thoughts were circling just as quickly, homing toward a point. "That is the way Idra thinks," she said. "At a tangent, like a weaver connecting threads beginning so far away that you don't even see them."

"I saw the dragon Thayne Ysse is looking for through Verlain of Skye's dragon lens."

She grunted, surprised. "I didn't know it worked. Nobody has ever seen a dragon in it before."

"Do you know that plain? That dragon?"

"I've heard of it."

"Would it be easy for Thayne to find?"

"If he wants it badly enough . . . Why? Do you want this dragon, too?"

"Only to stop Thayne from destroying Yves with it."

"So you want to kill it first?"

"No," he said starkly. "I've seen it. I'd rather just forget about it. But I am sworn to guard Regis Aurum and protect Yves. I must stop Thayne Ysse any way I can. The bard refused to listen to me when I told her about Thayne. She sent me here to rescue a woman. So here I am. The only woman I found was you. I have no idea where to go now, except back into this tower where I was sent in the first place."

The witch looked as if she were trying to hear a voice beneath the chatter of birds settling for the night. Her hair fell like a hood around her face. Cloaked in such darkness she looked, he thought uneasily, something other than human. She shook her hair back, frowning. "Bards listen to everything. They hear everything. They hear stones age. I can find Thayne Ysse for you, if he is in Skye. It's a very simple kind of magic, done with water. You'll know then if he has found the dragon."

"Yes," he said recklessly, too relieved to fear her sorcery. "Thank you."

"Come with me."

"Where?"

She smiled. "Not far at all. A slight adjustment to the heart." She raised her hand. The gelding, pulling grass idly until then, crossed the clearing to her. She took its reins, held the stirrup for Cyan to mount.

"Now," she said. "We will follow the stream a little, watch what might flow down it. Don't move, don't speak, whatever you see, do not make a sound . . ."

He started to pull himself up. Then he heard harp notes

as delicate as bird bone spiral around him. Sidera said something; she seemed suddenly too far away for him to hear her. The gelding vanished under his hands. The dense night inside the tower filled his eyes again; he wondered, astonished, if he had ever really left it. He heard a thin, bitter wind weave into the harping, pick it apart and scatter it, until nothing was left but wind roaring through the darkness now, revealing the shapes of harried trees, torch fire stretched thin as thread.

"Cyan Dag," someone said from very far away: Sidera, perhaps, or the bard, or someone else entirely.

He tasted rain and recognized that dark.

TWELVE

Thayne Ysse saw himself reflected in the dragon's eye.
The eye itself was enormous, a pool of liquid gold circled by dry, rough ridges of scale and skin. A very thin, pointed oval of dark slit the gold from top to bottom; paler streaks of gold rayed away from it. Thayne was a splinter of something human within the dark.

He did not dare move. His horse had thrown him and bolted, halfway across the plain, when the dragon had opened its maw and a tongue of fire uncoiled out of it, licking the ground into a frozen shimmer of glass. Thayne, desperately picking himself up as the dust and scorched air roiled over him, stood in the full glare of the dragon's eyes when the fire died away. It had not reached him, though he felt scoured and drained in the aftermath. The sun, a second watching eye, wended a leisurely path down a slope and paused, forever it seemed, wedged in the cleft between two hills. Thayne, motionless and sweating, waited for night.

The sun shifted slightly, after what seemed hours, and loosed a scarlet ray across the wasteland. On the plain, long shadows stretched away from odd things littering the ground. Some of them he recognized. A horned skull. A dead horse, its skin dried to parchment and sagging between its ribs. The wheel of a cart. A shield stripped of its emblem. What looked like a wooden rake, which seemed wildly improbable in that wasteland. A complex mingling of bones, human and horse, pieces of armor, swords, shields, shredded silk, and jewels, lying on earth too parched to give them any kind of burial. A human skull, which had somehow rolled itself away from the confusion, gazed, upside down, at Thayne. The sun slid another fraction of an inch. The dragon, with Thayne trapped in its eye, did not move. Neither did Thayne.

Finally, the cracked, barren ground grew less raw. The shadows faded. A little smoke trickled out of the dragon's nostrils, which were as broad and black as cauldrons. A translucent eyelid rolled down over its staring eye. Thayne stayed still. A moment later, the eyelid slid back up; the dark slit of its pupil widened so abruptly that Thayne nearly jumped. He swallowed, his body rigid, his throat so dry that he might have kindled his own flame out of it. The dragon sighed languidly, blowing dust all over Thayne. It swung its head, coiled its neck more securely about itself. Its baleful eye closed. Thayne, gritting his teeth, his hands and face clenched, imploded with a sneeze.

He took a step sometime later, then another. Above him, a beast with a million eyes opened them one by one, stared down at him. He tried to walk on air. The dragon rumbled, and he melted breathlessly into the motionless night. But it only shifted a little, turning its head more tightly into itself. Thayne waited, watching the humps and hillocks of dragon around the tower. The stars and the risen moon, hanging like a scythe blade above the hills, gave the ground a faint, silvery sheen. Thayne, moving silently around the tower, away from the dragon's eyes, could see no door anywhere.

There had been none in the drawing, either, unless it was hidden behind the dragon. It seemed to be sleeping deeply now, its rumbling soft and regular, as if it were snoring. The tower, with its thick red rings of stones glowing faintly in the moonlight, looked formidable, forbidding and impregnable. It seemed to have no opening anywhere; he could not find even a single window. Baffled, he wondered if the dragon dropped its gold down the open top of the tower like rain dropping down a chimney.

He felt a sudden, intense impatience with himself and this mysterious tower. He had journeyed so far, found the plain that seemed to exist only on a page in a book; he had outfaced the dragon. Here in front of him was treasure to save the North Islands. And he could not claw his way into the tower, nor climb its steep walls, nor burrow under it: the foundation stones, visible under an arch of dragon's tail, looked as if they ran down into the center of the earth. Weary, at last, of ringing the tower with footprints for the knight to find, he slipped recklessly under the dragon's tail to reach the tower wall. If the massive loop of tail shifted, he could be crushed between stone and dragon; he was too frayed with tension and exasperation to care. He slumped a moment against the wall, rested. The stones were still warm from the merciless light of day, or maybe from the dragon's seething inner fires. He felt a heartbeat of utter astonishment as the stones closed about him like water and drew him in.

He found himself in the dragon's heart.

So it seemed, to his stunned eyes. The inner stones of the tower glowed a rich, warm gold, as if the heaps and scatterings of coin, the jeweled cups and patterned bowls, the plates, the scabbards of beaten gold, all kindled their own light. Here was the treasure promised in his father's book, that would fall across the North Islanders like rain, feed them and their animals, mend their broken walls and leaky roofs, arm them, bring back the power they once possessed, and set a ruler's throne again in the House of Ysse. There were crowns in that crazed mass of wealth, one or two still attached to skulls; gold-hilted swords in their bright scabbards clung to thighbones. Dazed, he waded ankle-deep through coin stamped with faces he did not recognize. The dragon had carried away even princes from distant places, dressed in cloth-of-gold, crowned and ringed with gold. One tried to grasp at Thayne's foot, it seemed; he tripped in its hold. Fingerbones and rings went flying everywhere. Looking at the severed wrist, the neckbone snapped where it had fallen, Thayne felt his stomach lurch, his skin grow suddenly cold. The place was oddly full of ghosts.

He looked around for something to fill with gold, for he did not want to leave with nothing. Thoughts, confused and unfinished, collided in his head. He had to find his horse. He either had to slay the dragon or figure out how to speak its language of fire and gold. He had to watch for the knight of Gloinmere, who would try to kill the dragon, being ignorant of magic, and believing that gold had more value. He found a golden helm and dragged it like a cup through a pile of coin, filling it to its neckpiece. Perhaps, in Skye, he could find someone to teach him . . . Stumbling a little on the slippery piles, hugging his unwieldy burden, he searched for the place in the wall where he had entered. He found it, exactly opposite a crowned skeleton sitting on top of a gold breastplate. He stopped, before he left, to cast an incredulous glance back at the riches that turned the air itself gold. He stepped into the wall.

Stone stopped him.

Again.

And again.

And again.

And then he felt the horror still trapped in the bones scattered around him on the floor.

The tower was the door leading into itself. The drawing in his father's book had told him plainly: there was no way out.

Sitting on a pile of gold, he waited.

For what, he was not exactly sure. It came stealing mouselike out of a crowned skull; he glimpsed it in the corner of his eye as it slipped into the hollow of a gold cup and turned to shadow. Something small, ignominious, and silent kept intruding into his thoughts, teasing his vision, as maybe time passed, and maybe it didn't in that changeless, soundless place. If he listened, he heard his heartbeat; if he moved, he heard coins shift. Beyond that nothing, not even a spider moved. In that silence he could have heard the sound of one thread dropping onto another as it built its web.

He had spent some time trying to shift every stone he could reach, more time moving mountains of gold across the floor to find some hidden passageway beneath them. He wore his hands bloody trying to pry through stone. The stones bent gold, snapped blades, even broke a gold-handled mace. Later, he began beating on the walls with swords, flinging shields and plates across the room, shouting until his voice was raw, trying to get the dragon's attention. If he annoyed it, he thought, it might push its head through the stones to silence him. Perhaps he could follow it out, if it didn't eat him first. He felt it shift once. Coins jumped and rang on the floor; shields clanged; bones knocked hollowly against the stones. He reached for a sword and waited. But it went back to sleep, apparently, as if all his raging among the gold made no more noise than the whirl of seed off a dandelion stem.

Finally, spent, he slumped onto the gold as if it were a pile of straw. *Craiche,* he thought numbly. *He will never know what happened to me.* That was his last coherent thought for a long time. He simply watched the little, skulking, ignoble idea of death skitter soundlessly through a row of collapsed ribs, duck beneath the outflung bones of a hand. He slept finally, or at least he dreamed. The tower grew so dark that the air seemed to take on density and weight; he felt the blackness that he breathed.

He heard harping.

He walked up the steps in the tower on Ysse, where his father waited for him. The harping surprised him; he thought the harper had gone. But her playing lingered, lovely and ancient as something spun out of sea and wind. When he opened the door at the top of the stairs, he found a room full of gold and the bones of lost princes. His father was not in this tower, only an old woman sitting on a hillock of coins, playing a harp made of bone.

She smiled at him above her harp, her sunken eyes as black as the shadow beyond the glow of gold.

"Thayne Ysse."

"Yes," he answered, wondering, in his dream, why he was not surprised to find her there.

"You have something I want."

He laughed sharply, to hide his sudden fear. "I have all the gold in the world and nothing."

"You have something I want." She released a final, deliberate note with her thumbnail, and put the harp aside. She looked at him out of eyes as dark as the new moon within the ring of the old. "If you give it to me, I will show you the way out of here."

He found the cloying dark suddenly heavy to breathe. He remembered the old crone he had dreamed about, trying to fish the horned moon out of water. He had spoken the word for dragon and she had turned into fire. He said again, "I have nothing to give you."

She plucked another string with a fingernail, a high nick of sound, watching him. "I will show you how to become the words for dragon and gold."

He whispered, "What do you want?"

"Give me Craiche."

"No!" he shouted with such horror and fury that she seemed to blur in the force of it. Her hair streamed into the dark; a string on the harp hummed an overtone. "I will never give you Craiche!"

"Never is a long time."

"I will die here first."

"Yes. It is getting warm, isn't it?"

"What do you want with Craiche?"

"I have my eye on him." She rose then, a little taller than he had remembered. She smiled, her face like the cracked, dry waste outside. "I could take him anyway, while you are dying in here. You will go mad from boredom before you starve. A mercy, I think. The dragon sees you through those stones. He knows you are here. You brought him nothing but your golden hair; even that will not outlast your bones. If you do not return to Ysse, Craiche will rouse the North Islands against Yves again, and no one will be left on the islands but the birds."

"He couldn't — No one would listen —"

"I listen." She smiled again, a skull's smile, he thought, at everything and nothing. "He has already called my name."

"No," he shouted again, and woke himself.

The air had grown stifling; the noon sun, he guessed, was scorching the plain. He wiped sweat from his face, his mouth as dry as the hot metal mouths of the cups on the stones. He contemplated his dream, and thought dispassionately: she was wrong. I will go mad from thirst before boredom. He lay back on the coins. From that angle he could see, very far away, an oblong of blue where the tower opened to the sky. In the dream, he realized, there was a way out. What had the old crone said? I will show you the way out of here . . . "If," he whispered. "If." What would she do with Craiche, anyway? he wondered. It didn't matter; he would never bargain with Craiche's life, for anyone or anything. He would drink this molten fiery air and die first.

It took an exhaustingly long time. He counted coins, picking them out of the pile he lay on and tossing them against the wall, while he watched the oblong of blue narrow into a slit. Later, watching a sapphire mine itself out of the matrix of the night, he thought about the harper. She led him here, he remembered. She had told his father that the dragon existed somewhere in Skye. "Well," he murmured, feverish with thirst, "all I have left to do is pick a crown and call myself King of the North Islands. She is ridding Regis Aurum of the gadfly family that challenged his rule . . . I didn't bend my head low enough for his taste when we surrendered in that dreary rain . . ." His mind seized on the rain, the endless water falling as freely as words for anyone to drink. Rain changed to gold in the merciless crucible of the tower . . . He tasted a coin, searching it for the memory of water, and choked on dry metal. He closed his eyes, felt tears run down the side of his face, and tasted them. They were as bitter as the gold.

Craiche stood in his thoughts, smiled his wild, sweet smile that was afraid of nothing. Thayne, soothed by it, told him: *I tried. That's all. I tried.* Then Craiche was crawling on his belly out of the dark rain into firelight, one leg pushing him, the other useless, bleeding from a sword slash that severed the tendon behind his knee. He wept silently when Thayne picked him up, his body shaking as he stifled the noise, so that his enemy would not hear him cry. "I carried you," Thayne whispered to him, "nearly the whole way back to Ysse."

He fell silent, dreamed a little, of cups of gold that turned to gold dust as he swallowed them. He dragged his eyes open after a while, thinking: *There is a way out. She said there is a way.* His thoughts slid to Craiche again, sitting on the tower steps with a book, trying to persuade Thayne that there was magic in what lay between his hands.

"Maybe," Thayne whispered, "there is a way with words . . ."

He pulled himself upright, off the pile of coins, stood shaking, dizzy, wondering which portion of the dragon he might be addressing through the wall. He said finally, his voice worn so ragged he scarcely recognized it, "I don't know how to talk to dragons. I came here to steal your gold and take you away with me to the North Islands, where it's cold and wet and noisy with the sea. I wanted you to burn a path for the army of Ysse and the North Islands to march south down Yves to Gloinmere, to strike at Regis Aurum where he rules. I wanted your gold to buy bread and arms for the North Islands. I wanted you to fight with us for our freedom. I don't know what you are, or what you want besides gold. I don't have gold to give you. I don't have much of anything. Maybe there is something I can do for you."

He waited. The night beyond the tower seemed so still it might have been stone itself. The stars had vanished from the top of the tower; he could barely see the faintest line where dark separated itself from the deeper black of stone. Then a handful of coins slid down the pile where he had been lying. A cup overturned with a sudden clink. Thayne felt the vibration under his feet, the massive movement of dragon as it shifted a boulder's weight of bone and let it settle.

He swallowed, or tried to. He said, "Is there anything? I'm an ignorant northerner in a land full of magic. All I know is war and work. And a little of love. No magic words. I don't know what language dragons speak. I can say the words I see here in this tower. Wealth. Beauty. Power. Death. They're what I want to take back with me to Ysse. I don't know what the price for them might be."

The dragon stirred again. A sword angled against the wall slid and struck the stones; a jewel spun out of its hilt. A crown shivered away from a skull and rolled across the floor. Beyond the thick tower walls, Thayne heard the faint sigh of dragon breath blowing up dust storms, sending whirlwinds spinning across the waste. For an instant his head filled with gold, as if the sun had poured itself into his eyes and turned his thoughts to light. He found himself on the floor, arms pushed against his eyes. When he opened them finally, the world was drenched with gold; he wondered if he had been blinded by light.

Then he saw the vast eye staring at him through the tower wall. He got to his feet unsteadily. The words he had spoken seemed to echo through him. He had not spoken fear; he had no place left for it under that gold, unwinking scrutiny. In the stillness, he heard the dragon's heartbeat.

"Thayne Ysse." Its voice was a hollow hiss, like wind in a cavern.

He heard his own heartbeat then, slowing to match the dragon's; his blood seemed to run in small rivers, secret chasms, burning like fire and the color of gold. He could fly, he felt suddenly; he could suck stars out of the sky with the powerful drag of his wings; he could spit fire at the sun.

He answered, aware of himself only as a reflection of the dragon's eye, a thought in the dragon's fiery brain. "Yes."

"I will give you everything in this tower. Wealth. Beauty. Power. Death."

"Yes."

"I will burn the towers of Gloinmere for you."

"Yes," he whispered.

"Give me one thing."

He said one letter, then stopped, letting the word fade into breath. He heard his own heart again, faster now, a small, secret thing outracing the dragon's heart. He answered finally, "What one thing?"

"Give me Craiche."

He moved finally, after time had shaped his heart again, his trembling, parched body, his mortal thoughts. He turned his back to the dragon's eye, slumped down on the floor against a pile of gold, and waited.

THIRTEEN

On a hillside in the northernmost parts of Yves, Cyan knelt within a thick line of vine and bramble and brush growing along a ditch between fields. The brush dripped endlessly with rain. The fields, thick with pasture grass, were sodden underfoot; they glittered, under torch fire, as if the stars had rained out of the sky, leaving the thick, blank black overhead. In the deepest part of the brush, Regis Aurum lay shivering beneath Cyan's sodden cloak. The fields were quiet around them for the moment; the nearest torch had passed them, hissing and smoking in the rain. It was cresting the hill now, snaking out from side to side, searching for the dead.

Regis muttered something. Cyan felt for his shoulder. He could see nothing of the king's face, but he knew that he was on a hillside in north Yves with a memory: a newly crowned king warring to keep his kingdom together, and, having won this battle, fighting under a bush in the endless rain for his life.

"Where is everyone?" the king demanded suddenly, furiously. "Tell them to bring fire! And why is it raining in my bed?" His voice broke with a hiss of pain; his flailing hand found Cyan's arm. "Who are you?"

Who indeed? Cyan wondered, feeling the cold rain drip down his neck, smelling the sweet, sticky leaves of the underbrush, as he had years before. Why he had been plunged into this particular memory, he could not imagine. The king was bleeding badly from a stray arrow shot as the ragged army from the North Islands retreated. It had been almost the last bolt fired, as Regis's knights chased them uphill into a wood, leaving a wake of dead and wounded in the grass. Cyan, leaping off his horse, had pulled Regis under the brush out of the deadly path of the warhorses. The knights and the North Islanders disappeared into the wood, leaving him alone with the wounded king, not knowing, as twilight seeped into night, that the North Islanders were scattering for their lives down the other side of the hill. They won a few parting arguments as they retreated. The king's most valued adviser caught an arrow in his throat and was speechless for the rest of his life. The king's youngest cousin threw up a palm to ward away an arrow and fell with his hand pinned to his eye. Fury over their own dead drove the knights to follow the retreating army farther than they had to. When they collected themselves and their fallen, in the bleak twilight, no one remembered when the king, in the midst of his victory, had disappeared.

"Who are you?"

All Cyan knew, in the underbrush with the lost king, was that everyone around them except for the dead and wounded had vanished. He tried to keep the king sheltered and quiet, while he watched for the returning knights. When night fell, he saw the first torches move slowly up from the bottom of the hill. They did not get far before the busy flames found what they sought in the long grass. They took the dead away and returned for more. Cyan heard their voices, hushed and cautious, as they called to one another across the field.

While the North Islanders were gleaning their own off the battlefield, Regis, making his unexpected complaints about the cold and the wet, was one more random voice among the cries and groans and weeping on the field. As the torches grew closer to them, Cyan tried to quiet him, whispering desperately, knowing that if the North Islanders found the king, he would die there, under a bush in the rain, victory or no victory. Cyan, though he might pull a few under the ground with him as he went, would fare no better.

"Who?"

"Regis," he breathed, "you must be quiet. I am hurt, and they will kill me if you are not quiet."

"Cyan," the king whispered back, his fingers tight on Cyan's arm. "Don't be afraid. I will kill them before they harm you."

"I'm very cold."

"I know. It's wet in here. Where are you hurt?"

"In my left side, above my heart. I think they may not

find me if you stay very quiet. Very still. Now."

Torch fire passed over them, searched into the leaves and vines and brambles with their tiny white flowers. The king made a noise and quelled it, his lips caught tight between his teeth. The torchbearers chose that place to gather, a dozen weary, muddy, bitter men searching the unfamiliar field in the dark.

"Who is missing?" they asked each other.

"Ean Muldar."

"He's dead. I took him down."

"My brother," someone said. Torchlight flared, swam across a face, and Cyan bit back a word. Thayne Ysse stood there with his yellow eyes and his gold hair, longer then, lank and streaked with rain.

"You mean your father," a man answered. "They found him earlier in the wood. He's been hurt, but he's safe, now—"

"No," Thayne broke in, the word cutting sharp as an ax into wood. "Craiche."

"Craiche!" someone repeated incredulously. "You left him home to milk the cows, surely—"

"He didn't stay," Thayne said tersely. "I saw him earlier. I told him where to wait, but he didn't stay there, either."

"I saw a boy running with us through the woods," someone said. "I thought he was from these hills."

"Which woods?"

The torch angled, pointed overhead. "Up there. Thayne, he can't have come with us! He's a twelve-year-old boy; someone would have spotted him in one of the boats when we crossed—"

"He knows how to row a boat." Cyan heard the familiar, leashed fury in Thayne's even voice. "He followed us." He turned abruptly, a flame torn away from the circle of fire and heading uphill. Someone breathed a curse onto Regis Aurum's head. The torches separated, lined across the field, still searching as they moved toward the wood.

"Cyan," Regis whispered, when the light was gone. "Are you still alive? Did they find you?"

Cyan did not answer. *No,* he had said in memory. *They did not find me.* In memory, the North Islanders' voices had been indistinguishable, barely comprehensible, as if they spoke another language. In memory, there had been no Thayne Ysse asking about a twelve-year-old brother, but a dozen armed strangers, their faces blurred by fire, saying things that Cyan, listening with all his attention on Regis' silence, barely heard. *Dead,* they said. *Safe. Up there.* And then they followed the fire uphill, and Regis spoke, and Cyan, trembling with cold and relief, answered.

"No," he said to Regis. "They did not find me."

Yes, he said, to whoever was listening in the dark of the tower. *They found me.*

Regis fell asleep then, or what passed for sleep, leaving Cyan alone listening to his ragged, labored breaths. Cyan watched, motionless, one hand on the hilt of his sword, the other hand resting on the king's forehead. After a long time, during which the rain fell with monotonous steadiness, he saw the fires began to come back down the hill, a ragged line of them, the last a roving star just emerging out of the trees as the closest were halfway down the field. The last fire etched a jagged path to the underbrush, began probing into it. Cyan's fingers locked on his sword. The king chose that moment to stir restively, tossing his head back and forth.

"Water," he muttered. Whether it was a demand or a complaint, Cyan was uncertain. Uphill, the torch fire jabbed along the wall of brush, illumining roots, tangles; dry leaves sparked and burned out. Cyan, barely breathing, his attention riveted on the reckless fire, thought coldly: I will kill him when he reaches us. I will catch the torch as he falls, and carry it down the hill, follow until no one notices when I put it out, no one notices that he is missing . . . I will come back and hide his body in the underbrush . . .

"Cyan," the king breathed abruptly, wakened, Cyan guessed, by the murmur of voices, the soft steps.

"You must be quiet again," he whispered, "or they will find me."

He could hear the brush crackling now, tiny explosions of flame that hissed to embers in the rain. The king, facing downhill, could not see it, but he heard; he moved his head fretfully but did not speak. Cyan looked uphill again, watching the fire come.

I did not know then, he thought, *that the fire had a name.*

"Thayne!" someone called, a sharp hiss across the face of the hill. The torch swung away from the brush. "Help me."

The torch moved after a moment, to meet the still fire in the center of the field. The flames, mingling, revealed someone lying on the grass. The fires conferred; one torch fell to the ground. The twisted body sent a raven's cry across the night as it was lifted. A man's voice, Cyan thought, not a boy's. But the other torches had reached the bottom of the hill. The searcher abandoned his search to carry the wounded, leaving his torch to gutter out in the grass.

Cyan unlocked his fingers from the sword hilt, felt his hand tremble. He leaned his brow against a crook of branches, breathing again, unsteadily. Regis's voice, coming out of the dark with unexpected clarity, made him start.

"Will you die?" the king asked.

"No," he whispered fiercely to the endless night. "No. I will not die."

The field was silent for a while. He moved his hand to the king's chest, kept it there lightly to feel him breathe. Cyan's eyes closed. The branches supported his head; he breathed in small leaves, flowers. He dreamed of rain. He woke abruptly, listened for Regis's breathing, to the changeless dark; his eyes closed again. He dreamed of someone crying in the rain.

He woke again, blinking water out of his eyes. He felt the king's breathing under his hand, shallow and fitful; he muttered something, dreaming or feverish, then quieted. Cyan raised his head, scanned the night. He saw nothing but dark, heard nothing but rain. The night, he thought, was frozen in some terrible, enchanted hour; it would never change, dawn would never come, the rain would rain forever . . .

He heard someone crying in the rain.

It was a small, distant sound, a single, sharp sob. He had listened to such noises half the night. But this voice was high, light: a woman's voice, a child's. A boy's. The sound came again, brief, taut. His muscles locked; he felt the sudden bone chill of horror, colder than any rain, as if the faint voice came from the dead already haunting the field.

"Thayne," it pleaded. Then it was still for a long time while Cyan listened, his lips parted, his eyes straining against the dark.

I don't remember this, he thought. *I don't remember. I heard the boy's voice in my sleep, perhaps; I dreamed that I dreamed it . . .*

"Thayne," the voice said again, still faint in the constant rain. As if he heard it, Regis murmured, then stifled a groan. Cyan shifted his hand to Regis's brow. The king drew a shuddering breath and quieted again. Cyan felt him trembling with cold.

"Thayne," the boy said again. He seemed closer now, if only by a matter of raindrops, a few grass blades. Cyan swallowed drily, wondering if he were crawling down the hill.

I did nothing, he thought, *in memory. There is nothing I can do. I cannot change memory.*

"Thayne."

I did not leave the king.

He heard nothing then but the rain, slipping among the leaves, drumming gently, persistently against the ground. He lifted his face to it, opened his mouth, swallowed what the leaves let fall. Then he listened again, as if he could hear the boy breathing across the field.

He fell asleep again. A whimper woke him. The king, he thought. But Regis lay still, so still that Cyan felt for his heartbeat, alarmed. He was clumsy; the king's voice came in a sudden, anguished knot of pain. But he was still alive, and the voice in the dark, no longer alone, had been startled silent.

After a long time Cyan heard the breathing in the grass beside the brush. It shook with effort, dragging for air, keening, but so softly the boy probably did not even realize he made a sound. Cyan closed his eyes.

When he moved, it was as if he moved in a dream, because he would have died before he left the king alone and wounded under a hedge for this. He refused to listen to the brush crackling softly around him, or to the boy's sudden, frightened gasp. He refused to hear Regis's voice; maybe it was raised in a troubled, confused question, maybe not. He groped across the grass, found a slender, shivering body, and rolled it lightly into his arms. The boy hissed as Cyan straightened; one hand, surprisingly strong, dug into his forearm. The boy asked, his teeth chattering, "Who are you?"

Cyan did not answer.

He carried the boy down the hill, striding quickly, wanting to get back to the king before the dream of leaving the king ended. The boy, after a futile question or two, did not speak again; Cyan never spoke. At the bottom of the hill, he saw the fires through a small grove of trees; a few dark figures still moved restlessly among them. The sentry he could see wore the Leviathan of the North Islands.

He set the boy down soundlessly among the trees, hoping the sentries he didn't see would not notice him. Then he turned, as soundlessly, and went back uphill, feeling the dream wearing away at every step, until he was Cyan Dag, listening in the rain for the painful breathing, and terrified that he had misplaced the King of Yves to rescue an islander's brat whimpering on his first battlefield.

So he told himself as he finally heard the broken, chattering breaths under the brush: *It never happened. It was a dream.* He crawled back in beside the king and waited, tense and sleepless, for dawn.

I never left him, he told the knights of Gloinmere when they resumed their search for the king, and Cyan emerged from the underbrush to greet them. That was how Regis, somehow still alive, remembered it as well. *He stayed at my side all night,* the king told his knights. *He never left me.*

So he became then and there, on the sodden field, and more formally later: Cyan Dag, Knight of Gloinmere.

It never happened, he thought as the dark around him grew thick, soundless, and the rain faded into memory. He smelled stone, dust, things that changed so slowly that they would be recognizable when the words for them were forgotten: bone, still water, ash.

He rose as the early light fell through the sagging doorposts of the tower. He stepped, blinking, into the dawn and remembered.

FOURTEEN

S el climbed the spiral steps to the top of the tower.
She paused at the last step, one hand to her heart,
and panted awhile. Melanthos was not there, which suited
Sel. So far, Melanthos did not know she had come there.
Gentian knew, but thought only that Sel came to look for
Melanthos. Time she had whiled away in the harbor tavern
she spent now in the tower, without any noticeable change
in her habits. Both daughters thought she was drinking bitter ale at Brenna's; she had left them to sell the last of the
cakes and pastries. Melanthos tended to come down near
suppertime, which was when Sel went up. She liked looking
into the mirror; she never knew what it was going to show
her next.

This time, as she waited for her heart to quiet, it showed
a roil of slick, dark brown that slid and twisted against

itself, and finally revealed a deep-set eye above a row of long whiskers. She smiled, recognizing one of the seals in the harbor. She knew all their shades of brown, their dapples of black and gray, their scars, their ages, their children. She had watched them for years from Brenna's windows, while she drank her ale. Sometimes one died and washed ashore on the rocks before it got eaten in the water. She would watch the fishers gut it and skin it, holding the skin wide, with the blank sky showing through its empty eye sockets, before they draped it across the high rocks to dry. That drew the children, and the screaming gulls thick as a snow squall above the butchering. The fishers tossed coins to see who would get a coat out of the skin, or a watertight pair of boots. The meat and fat they gave to the oldest villagers, to smoke for winter, to render into soap and lamp oil. The sea got back its bones.

Once, when she was much younger, Sel had left Joed's side at night and gone to the rocks to take a sealskin. She could not remember why she wanted it, only that it drew her, beyond reason, to hold the stinking skin up to the stars and waves and let it see again through her eyes. But the skin was gone. Someone else had gotten there first. Or something. Or maybe the splashed shadows of blood on the rocks around her were old, dry, and that seal had died only in her dreams.

The seal in the mirror dove out of sight; the heaving water slowed, froze, faded. Sel stepped into the room, sat down on the pallet. Behind the mirror the sun was setting. Mist fanned toward land, trying to engulf the boats before they reached the harbor. The still air within the stones felt warm yet with afternoon light. She slipped her shoes off and settled comfortably into the pallet. She tried not to shift things, though she suspected that Melanthos was too untidy to notice a needle moved from floor to ledge, or pieces of linen separated from the jumble of bedclothes. She did refrain from tossing out old tea upon which floated a furry island of mold. Even Melanthos might notice a clean cup.

The mirror showed her scraps of images, as Melanthos had said: broken pieces of stories. One of the oddest, Sel thought, was the woman in the tower who embroidered, as Melanthos did, everything in her mirror. She had a strange, pale, underwater beauty, as if, in a different story, she might have been part fish. She could not seem to find a way out of her tower. Perhaps she did not want to leave. She never leaned out of the window and called for help, though armed and comely knights rode beneath her. Sometimes Sel saw her standing in front of her fire. Sometimes she ate a solitary meal. The building of the fire, the bringing of food, seemed beyond the mirror's notice. Sel never saw anyone else in the room. The beginning and the ending of the woman's tale seemed equally obscure. Sel wondered if the old mirror had forgotten them.

The mirror dreamed privately a little; so did Sel. Images and memories swirled to light, lingered, faded: Joed mending a sail, Gentian running across sand with her hands full of butterfly shells, herself raging and weeping a storm over some small broken thing just before Joed died. Or had it been just after? The mirror went suddenly black as if it had closed its eye. Sel blinked, waited. It gave her nothing. Her attention caught, she watched it. For a long time it remained

mindless and dark as a fish's eye; she wondered what tale
it was trying to begin or end. Then she saw a frost of moonlight on black stone. Peering closer, she separated dark
from dark: stone from night from shadow within the oblong
of stone. The shadow widened, filled the mirror. Within the
utter dark something moved.

An eye opened.

Sel stared into it, astonished. The light in the tower
seemed to fade around her, so intense was the blackness in
the eye. Like the new moon, Sel thought, in the thin, silvery
ring of the old. Thoughts seemed to move across the eye
like clouds over the sea. Sel shifted closer to the mirror, as
if she might see the thoughts reflected in the eye. It gazed
implacably at something. Death? Sel thought, chilled. But
the old eye blinked at the word. Sel leaned closer.

Her hands moved, remembering something. Braiding
hair, she thought. Or maybe it was waves, their silvery foam
she caught just before the waves broke, peeling it away like
lace from cloth, twining froth together so that the waves
slowed, washed in before they crested, with a sigh rather
than a shout. The fishers waiting out the rampaging sea in
their boats far from the harbor, drifted in finally on a docile
tide. *Never saw that happen before,* she heard them say as she
went down the cliff to meet Joed: *High tide rising to meet the
full moon, and the moon letting go of the tide.* And the strange
tide became a tale added to the human faces seen watching
in the water on a misty afternoon, and the fish with the
unicorn's horn.

Once, she thought. *Once I did such things.*

But that young woman seemed no more a part of her

now than what swam so freely in the waves with their curious eyes. She shifted back a little, away from the memory, and the eye in the mirror turned silver.

Sel blinked. The lines around the eye flattened, and became an elaborate frame around the silver. The eye became a mirror, she saw, amazed again, and recognized the mirror.

"But where," she wondered, "is the lady?"

She walked into view a moment later. She was no longer sitting quietly in her chair beside the window, looking at life passing through her mirror. She was doing what Sel, observing anyone in the context of her own life, would call pacing. The force and power of her magical stillness, her spellbound silence and habitual movements, had dissolved for the moment. She moved as restlessly as a fish in a bucket, back and forth across the circular chamber. She avoided the window, Sel noted. She walked with her head bent, her heavy skirts swaying, her hands opening and closing against her thighs. She did not lift her eyes from the strip of carpet on the floor, in which white lilies bloomed against a gold background. She seemed intent on wearing a path through the lilies.

She was very beautiful. Now and then, one hand lifted, uncurled long enough to pull a strand of white-gold hair behind her ear. Sel could see her graceful fish's profile then, her set mouth, an eyebrow of the palest gold slanting over a flash of sky-blue eye. Her lowered eyelids seemed as delicate and translucent as shells. Beyond her, the images in her ornate mirror changed constantly: a hawk plunging out of the sky straight down into water to drag a fish out of the current, the pepper-scatter of blackbirds against the bright sky, the rider just coming into view down the road.

What would happen, Sel wondered, if the woman did not see the rider in the mirror? If she let him pass without a comment among her threads?

What would happen if she leaned past the mirror and looked out the window to watch the rider come to her down the sun-dappled road?

What would happen if she called?

For a moment past and present and the timelessness of tales drew together in Sel's mind. The woman walked out of story and paced, trapped, helpless, under terrible enchantment somewhere in time, somewhere, perhaps, in Skye.

She leaned forward, her lips parting. "I know," she whispered to the woman. "I know."

The woman saw the rider in the mirror. She stopped midstep, gazing at it, her eyes wide now, with despair and hope.

She sat down quickly, reached for threads. So did Sel, not knowing what she might make, but wanting suddenly to feel the magic of making in the movement of her hands.

A cry interrupted her sometime later. Melanthos, she thought, hiding her threads and linen in a cluttered pile on the floor. She went to a far window, looked out at a perplexing sight.

Anyon was moving back and forth below, near the tower door. She leaned farther out. He did not see her, or Melanthos, who was running toward him. He was busy at something nameless, bewildering, something involving a wagon full of huge old tangled vines as spiny as puffer fish

with thorns. He wore heavy gauntlets up to his elbows, and
had stuffed the tower doorway halfway to the top with
thorns.

Melanthos shouted again, too furious to notice her
mother watching in the high window. Anyon, turning to
pick another clump of thorn off the wagon, did not notice
Melanthos until the wave of her fury smacked against him.

"What are you doing?" She careened into him, slapping
and kicking, knocking him off balance with surprise. He
was already bleeding here and there on his face and his
sleeves; she left a new rill of blood beside his mouth with
her open palm. "What do you think you are doing?"

She kicked him in the knee as he stared at her, and he
went down. Her knuckles caught him across the head; her
flailing knee smacked into his jaw. Sel, wincing, heard his
teeth meet with a click. He caught Melanthos's leg as he
reeled over backward, pulling her down on top of him.

He lay panting, holding her tightly while she struggled
against him. "Stop—" he pleaded when he could speak.
"Please."

"I might have been up there!"

"I saw you earlier." He paused, dragging breath wearily. "Working in the bakery. I wanted. I just wanted to talk
to you. Hold you. But you're always up there. And I can't
follow—"

She fought out of his hold, her hair flying wildly; Sel
could not see her face. "So you put up a wall of thorns
between me and what I make."

He pulled her back down. "Between you and what has
you captured—"

"Why," she demanded, her fist thumping down on his heart, "don't you just learn to come up? There's nothing at all to be afraid of in that tower."

"Not for you, there isn't."

"Not for you, either, if you would just listen to me."

He let go of her cautiously with one hand, wiped the blood from his mouth. "I'm sorry." He sighed. "I'll move the thorns. Just let me catch my breath."

"I would have just burned them, anyway. That wouldn't have stopped me."

"Don't you miss me at all?" he asked wistfully. Melanthos straightened, drawing back to study him, not knowing, evidently, the answer to that. Their voices were quieter now. Sel, her chin in her hands, strained to hear them.

"Do you miss me," Melanthos asked steadily, "when you're alone for days working on your blankets?"

"No," he said, surprising Sel. "But it's because I know you will be there when I'm finished. If I didn't know that, I would be out looking for you instead of working. Or looking for whatever would fill the hole you left in my heart when you left me. You don't feel that for me?"

"I don't know." He shifted, his face turning away from her answer; she held him still. "I never thought of it like that. I never thought of how it might be if you weren't there when I wanted you. I always think that of course you will be there."

His face turned to her again, his cracked mouth taut. He moved a little, or Melanthos did. Her head dropped. Their lips touched. Sel's mouth crooked. She turned, moved through memories of Joed down the tower steps. The sound of crackling, rending thorn startled her as she emerged through it; she had forgotten it. The two stared at her, mouths gaping, she thought, like herring.

"What are you doing?" she asked, as near to a sea-lion bellow as she had gotten for some time. "Trying to bury me in thorns?"

"No." Anyon sat up quickly. "I was only trying to—"

"What were you doing up there?" Melanthos asked. Her eyes narrowed, glinting, at her mother, who had just walked through thorns without a scratch. "How did you get up there?"

"I walked," Sel said shortly. "I was looking for you. You're always up there, and I never see you anymore."

"Exactly," Anyon sighed, "what I was telling her. And why I put those thorns there. I'm sorry. I had no idea anyone was in the tower."

"Just get them out of here."

"Mother," Melanthos said.

"I will," Anyon promised.

"That's no way to find your way up, blocking your own path." She straightened a sleeve, set her face to the stone wood like a figurehead on a prow, trying to sail her way out of Melanthos's questions.

"Mother. How did you get through those thorns?"

For a moment she was not going to answer. Then she shrugged, not looking at her daughter. "I thought it was just another trick of the tower's." She moved away among the old stumps. "I've got to get back to the bakery. You stay and help Anyon."

"Mother!" Melanthos cried. Sel ignored her, walking

quickly through the stone wood. It glittered around her with stray pearls of light. She heard running steps behind her, and then Anyon's pleading shout.

"Melanthos!"

The footsteps stopped. Sel walked alone out of the wood.

FIFTEEN

Melanthos watched the woman in the tower.

The woman in the tower was watching the mirror intently, though nothing much was happening in it except a flood of light over the tors from the setting sun. Melanthos wondered if Sel saw private, secret things in the mirror that it would not show Melanthos. Sel had been in the tower all day; she had left the baking to Gentian and Melanthos, who, for once, was up before dawn to do the morning loaves.

Melanthos leaned against the wall at the top of the stairs, her arms folded, yawning noiselessly. Sel had not heard her come up; she had no idea that Melanthos paid any attention at all to her comings and goings. She was doing whatever she did in the privacy of the tower, which involved needle and thread, but no particular image. What she embroidered seemed to have no shape, only vague clouds of pale browns and grays, colors she must have thought Melanthos needed least. Her hands were accustomed to work, stirring, kneading, shaping; empty, they fidgeted. Unlike Melanthos, she did not toss her own needlework out the window. A small pile of it grew, in various shapes and mushroom colors, like a fungus in a corner.

The mirror swam with sudden fire, as if the dragon had looked at them. They both started. Melanthos sucked in a yawn sharply. Sel, pricking herself, loosed a grunt. Fire flowed like windblown swathes of silk across parched ground. The ground glittered oddly in the aftermath, as if sand had melted into glass.

Sel, shaking her hand, turned abruptly. Melanthos, meeting her eyes, thought that for an instant Sel did not recognize her. Sel's eyes, silty, murky, shimmering like kelp with color, seemed flat, expressionless, something inhuman looking at something human. Then she blinked, and recognized her daughter.

She spoke first, gruffly. "There you are."

"Here I am," Melanthos said dryly. "And so are you. What are you doing up here?"

"Looking for you."

"How did you get up the stairs?"

"I walked." She amended that, as Melanthos regarded her dourly. "The tower let me up. I refused to listen to it on the stairs."

"You've been here before. You're making something."

Sel shrugged. "To keep busy." She watched her daughter, who was still hovering at the steps. "Do you mind?"

Melanthos shook her head, moving finally. "No." She crossed the room, dropped down on the pallet beside her mother. "I know you come up here. I just don't know why."

"It's peaceful up here. I didn't know it would be peaceful." She gestured at the mirror. "Except for that. What was that?"

"I don't know. Unless someone annoyed the dragon."

"What dragon?"

"It guards a tower in a wasteland."

"In Skye?" Sel asked incredulously.

"In a story," Melanthos answered absently, watching the mirror for more. "Or in Skye. What else have you seen?"

"An eye."

Melanthos stared at her. "An eye?"

"It opened in the dark and looked at me."

"Was it human?"

"Human," Sel said after a moment, and added, "Old."

"You woke something, I think."

"What?"

"I don't know. It doesn't want to look at me." She grew still then, remembering the knight. "Something real, I think," she said softly. "I've been wondering about that . . . Some of this might be stories. But some of it . . . I don't know. May not be."

"The lady in the tower," Sel suggested.

"Have you seen her?"

"She can't get out of the tower because the mirror doesn't remember how her story ends."

Melanthos smiled suddenly. "Maybe. Of course she

would call for help, if she were real. I haven't seen anyone forcing her to stay there."

"She's what you'll become," Sel said, but without force, "if you stay up here with these threads."

Melanthos ignored that. "What else has the mirror shown you?"

"One of the harbor seals." She hesitated, suddenly shy in front of her own daughter. "Rogue, I call him. He has the longest whiskers and pelt like brown silk."

"You name the harbor seals?" Melanthos said, astonished. "So do I. That small pearly one — brown and ivory —"

"Selkie."

"Hero." She paused, looking at her mother curiously. "Why did you give it a name so close to your name?"

"I liked watching it," Sel said obliquely. "I wasn't thinking of the name, just marking it for memory."

Melanthos grunted, prodding a needle in and out of the straw pallet. Sel studied the empty mirror, evading her eyes. *My eyes*, Melanthos thought. *My eyes*. "Have you made any pictures?" she asked.

"No. My fingers are too big and clumsy for such work. And I wasn't asked."

"Nobody asked me. I just did it."

"I didn't. So there you are."

"But where?" Melanthos muttered perplexedly as darkness gathered in the mirror. It shifted, took shape, became a black moon with strange, rippling dunes around it. Then it blinked. Melanthos caught her breath. Sel only shifted to see it more closely, as if she might catch the reflection in it of what it watched. The darkness thinned like a mist, let them see.

A woman walked alone through a forest. The road she traveled was matted with green needles and gold flakes of dried leaves. Oak sent vast tangled mazes of branch toward the light still lingering in the ancient wood. Their boughs were still. The road, dipping and curving around roots, held a steady pace toward the setting sun. Shafts of late light ran thin and straight as needles through the stitchery of branch and leaf. They faded in a breath, leaving dusk to gather among the trees, lie in wait within the underbrush.

Melanthos mused over her, wondering where the woman walked from and to. She was tall, with long hair falling freely down her back. It was unadorned and white as milk. She wore a long plain tunic that covered her arms and nearly all of her leggings and boots. She carried a weathered staff, a straight branch peeled of its bark and twigs, with a bole on the top, worn smooth as from her touch. A leather strap held something that Melanthos could not see slung across her back. As she came closer, walking toward Melanthos in the mirror, Melanthos saw a silver ring on the middle finger of her left hand, a plain band tarnished nearly black.

The woman's face was a spiderweb of lines. The skin still fitted neatly over bones that once, Melanthos thought, must have made her beautiful. Her eyes, heavy-lidded and sunken now, watched the road beneath her feet, darkening fast with twilight and running on toward night.

Bone, Melanthos thought. *Dust. Silver. But,* she added silently, *I cannot see your eyes.*

As if the woman heard her, the old eyes lifted suddenly, widened to reveal a darkness like the inside of caves. The dark seemed ancient but potent, full of secrets. Melanthos, on her knees now, angling the mirror between both hands, strained to see what had stopped the old woman midstep in the wood.

Her breath blurred the mirror and melted; she saw only herself.

She put the mirror down, crawled back to her pile of threads, her brain busy now with colors. Sel, still staring at the mirror, loosed a sigh like an ebbing wave. "It was her eye," she said obscurely.

"What?"

"Her eye watching us."

Melanthos grunted, sorting thread. "Mother," she complained, "you're using all my browns."

"Here's a few strands left," Sel said unremorsefully, passing them over.

"I'll have to ask Anyon for more, and he is as cross as a crab in a trap, these days."

"I'll get more."

"You could," Melanthos suggested, "use my pinks instead . . . What are you making?"

But her mother did not answer. Melanthos, choosing shades and musing over the mysterious power in the aged eyes, forgot her question.

She remembered it much later as she stumbled down the stairs. It was early; the stone wood was dark, damp with sea mist. In the bakery, Gentian, half-asleep, kneaded and thumped and pulled dough into loaves, lining them up on oiled baking stones. She blinked painfully at Melanthos as she came in.

"Where's our mother?"

"I left her sleeping," Melanthos answered, yawning. She rolled up her sleeves, shook flour into a bowl for sweet almond cakes. "I'll wake her when I go back up."

"Did you get any sleep?"

"A little." She yawned again, then froze as the baby wailed a sudden complaint. Gentian, dough stretched between her hands, stood as motionlessly. The baby searched for a finger. The dough began to droop. The baby settled again, her eyes closing. Gentian sighed. She looked a little off, Melanthos thought, like old cream. Her skin was patchy pale; her reddened eyes seemed to glitter and wince at the sight of the world.

Melanthos said with sympathy, "Was the baby up all night?"

"Only now and then." She caressed the dough into a mounded circle and nicked a crossroads into its top with a sharp knife: north-south, east-west. "And I kept waking myself because I had a feeling no one would be here but me, this morning."

"I'm here."

"But our mother isn't. She spends more time in that tower than you do, these days. What is she doing up there?"

Melanthos shook her head, cracking eggs into the flour. "I don't know. She's brooding, I suppose."

"Over what?"

"Memories. Life. She likes it up there. She's gotten herself drawn into it."

Gentian sighed again. She opened an oven door, checked the fire, then brushed water and coarse flour over half a dozen loaves and slid the stone above the flames. "I wish she'd come back. I miss her."

Melanthos patted her shoulder comfortingly, leaving a floury ghost of fingers. "She's making something," she said. Her brows were drawn hard.

"What?"

"I don't know. Something patchwork." She hesitated, stirring dough violently a moment, then stopped. "She's watching a story in the mirror."

"What kind of story?"

"A woman, trapped in a tower. She can't leave it, she can't even look out of it, except through a mirror. Our mother seems to like watching for her." Gentian stared at her, horrified. "I think she's waiting to see how that story ends."

"Is it a story?" Gentian demanded. "Just one more picture to put into threads? Or is it real?"

"I don't know." She gazed into the bowl, her eyes narrowed, seeing the woman again: her frantic pacing, her unchanging tapestry of days. "I hope it is real," she said softly. "As terrible as that is. Then it might have an ending."

"But how—? But who—?"

"Or maybe she's just there, caught forever in that part of her tale like a warning, a mystery. We'll never know who she is, how she got there, what becomes of her. Our mother needs to see her, and when she stops needing she'll come down."

The baby opened her eyes, gazed at them peacefully a

moment. Then she opened her mouth like a guppy and howled. Gentian picked her up and sat down on a stool. "Melanthos," she said tautly, loosening her bodice, "don't leave me alone here."

"She'll come back," Melanthos said passionately. "She can't forget the world entirely. She's just—"

"Just what?"

Enchanted, Melanthos wanted to say. *Spellbound*. But such words seemed too elaborate for their mother, like putting her into finery worn to a king's ball. "Sad," she heard herself say, the word coming out of nowhere, and she and Gentian gazed at one another silently, above the baby's contented head.

The fishers began coming in an hour later to buy their loaves to take on the boats; the rest of the village wandered in and out for a while after that, for oat biscuits and almond cakes and warm rolls flavored with pepper and anchovies. In the calm aftermath of the morning feeding, Melanthos took off her apron and went back to the tower. It was empty; her mother had wakened and walked down to the sea, perhaps, to watch the boats go out.

Light flooded across the mirror a moment after Melanthos entered. Her gaze was caught in such a flood of gold that her eyes teared in pain. The brightness faded a little; she could pick out shapes here and there: hillocks of coin, cups and crowns and shields of gold, even bones wearing armor and rotting cloth-of-gold. Slowly, within the glimmering mist, a man took shape. He was sitting on one of the piles of coin, staring at nothing, as if he did not notice the immense golden eye with the dark slit down it gazing at him through a wall of flame-red stone.

Melanthos, swallowing dryly, as if she could taste the fiery air, reached for thread.

SIXTEEN

C yan Dag, stumbling into dawn, found his path crossed by an oblong of windblown embroidery fluttering in the grass.

He picked it up absently, part of him still shivering in the rain on a hill in north Yves, and wondering why his clothes were dry. The woman waiting for him, sitting on the grass as silently as dew, said his name. He turned, pulled back into time: Cyan Dag walking out of the wrong tower into the mysterious, light-flooded hills in Skye.

He said, his eyes gritty with sleeplessness, "I had the strangest dream. I thought it was a dream. Out here, in the light of day, I know it wasn't. It was memory. Something I had forgotten."

"What was it?" Sidera asked. She was invisible within the black fall of her hair; he could see only a triangle of her face, one hand resting on her knee, her amber eyes, so bright in the sunlight they seemed to reflect it.

He frowned, perplexed. The incident did not seem significant: he had carried a wounded boy down a hill after a battle. It had happened years ago. That the event had appalled him enough to block it from his mind seemed the result of sitting in the rain and worrying for dark, endless hours. He shook his head.

"Nothing important," he answered; so it seemed now. "Why would I go into a tower in Skye to remember a minor detail from a battle in Yves?"

"For a reason." She did not suggest what. She rose; he watched her hair slide around her, then shift like silk as she parted it with her hands, shook it over her shoulders. He swallowed suddenly, caught in a memory of such soft darkness he had lost himself in. She took a step; the light in her eyes faded a little, making them human again. "What is it?"

He whispered, "Cria."

"Who is Cria?"

"Cria Greenwood. She has such dark hair . . ." He closed his eyes briefly, tightly. "I left her to come here. I did not even tell her why I left her. She might be pledged by now to a loveless marriage. And I am so far away from her in Skye, and as far as ever from doing what I came to do." He glanced around, saw his horse. "I must find that tower."

"The one with the lady in it."

"Yes. I thought she might be in this one after all. But all I found there was Regis Aurum, whom I already rescued."

He looked bewilderedly at the shrunken, silent tower, then turned abruptly, strode toward the gelding.

Sidera said suddenly, "Wait."

He stopped, and felt the cloth in his fingers, the silken threads. He opened it, turned it so that the seated man was upright. For a moment it made no sense. A man sat on a mound of gold within the bright, massive walls of a tower; behind him an enormous golden slitted eye gazed at him through the stones. Then the image solved its riddle: he recognized the man with the golden hair. He said, stunned, "Thayne Ysse found his dragon."

"And my sister," Sidera said softly, "has found Thayne Ysse."

"How do you know?"

She touched the cloth. "Someone embroidered that, and a wayward wind blew it to you."

He caught a breath. "The woman I'm searching for."

"Maybe."

"Weaving and weeping in a tower in Skye."

"This is embroidery."

He brushed the finer point away. "Thread is thread—"

"It is indeed. And it's my sister who is weaving. I think Thayne is in trouble, by the look of this."

He said, tucking the embroidery in his belt, "I'll come back later to help him. I must find the lady first."

"Maybe so, but it's Thayne Ysse who crossed your path this morning."

"You could rescue him," he suggested, pulling himself up onto the gelding's back. "Far better than I could, with your magic. You talk to wild things."

"I do. But this didn't blow a spell across my steps. I told you: Idra weaves."

"It's embroidery," he answered absently. "Not hers." He reached down impulsively to take the witch's hand. "Thank you for helping me again."

"I think I only confused you more."

"You were there waiting for me when I came back." He bent low and kissed her hand, catching a cold kiss back from the worn silver on her finger.

"But you don't know where you're going," she reminded him inarguably, "looking for that tower."

"I never have," he answered, and rode out of the clearing.

He reached the second tower at sunset.

It happened as subtly as in a dream: the landscape changing imperceptibly through the afternoon as he rode upstream along the river to find his way out of the three hills. On the other side of the hill a red sun blazed with terrible fury across a parched wasteland. The river melted away into mud there, and then into dry, cracked earth. The hills around the plain were barren, brown, runneled with crevices and caves. The huge, blind tower rising out of the center of the plain was dwarfed by the dragon coiled around it. The dragon's head, resting on its tail, was angled toward the tower so that one huge, golden eye stared at the stones as if it looked through them. Its other eye rolled lizardlike toward the rider at the edge of the plain.

Cyan reined the gelding, which was snorting at the sudden dust and the charred, sulfurous smell. Cyan wiped sweat from his face, and studied the dragon wearily. Sidera had warned him fairly, he thought, that this was where his path would lead. He could turn and leave. But the dragon was no longer an innocent piece of embroidery. Thayne Ysse would die in that tower. At worst, left to his own devices, he might find a way to free the dragon from the plain and set it raging against Yves. It would be cruel to leave Thayne there to die, and very dangerous to leave him there alive. Cyan, contemplating his choices, realized that he had none. He gave himself one glimpse of Cria's midnight smile, and urged the gelding onto the plain.

The gelding balked. A second later, the dragon swung its head toward them and hissed a shimmering roil of flame across the plain. The fire did not reach them, but Cyan felt a wave of heat slam into him and roll past. It burned metal on the gelding's harness, and the disk beneath Cyan's shirt. The gelding tried to rear; he calmed it, and rode it back to where the river still flowed, shallow and brown, and where a few sparse blades of grass grew on the muddy banks. He left it there.

He drew his sword and walked across the waste. The sun flung a crimson ray between two hills, kindled an answering flare of silver down his blade. The dragon watched him, both eyes on him now, wide and unblinking. Unaccountably, it did not scorch him to a cinder in midstep. Perhaps it did not want to miss again. Cyan stopped, when he came to the edge of the shadow the dying sun, sinking into one wing, flung across half the plain. The dragon's head reared then, its long, sinuous neck arching upward nearly the height of the tower. It did not bother again with fire. It simply flicked one claw through the air and ripped

Cyan's surcoat and shirt open with scythelike precision from throat to hem. Cyan stumbled backward, startled; as he fell out of the dragon's shadow, the sun found him again, burned a moon of fire in the disk at his breast.

The dragon lowered its head and snorted, enveloping Cyan in a sudden dust storm. It asked, as Cyan wiped grit out of his eyes and coughed, "What is your name?"

Another storm rattled around Cyan at the rush of its hollow voice. The dragon waited as Cyan got to his feet. He stared incredulously up at the great, looming wedge of its head, a crystal tooth or two turning bloody from the sun's last rays. He said dazedly, "My name is Cyan Dag. I have come to kill you and rescue the man in your tower."

The slits in the dragon's eyes opened wider. It shifted a foreleg and the earth shook beneath Cyan, throwing him down again. Then it dropped its head with a bone-jarring thud and blew Cyan like a feather across the harsh ground. Cyan, trying to cling with his fingers as he slid, clenched his teeth and bore through the storm. It ended finally; he gathered himself, feeling as if a few of his bones were farther away and heavier than he remembered. He stood up again, his skin flecked with blood and dirt, the disk flashing a colder light now from the wake of the faded sun.

He said, catching his breath, "I have come to rescue the man in your tower. I doubt that I can kill you. I doubt that I could do anything more than annoy you, perhaps only with my bad manners, before you kill me. If you let the man go free, I can promise you gold."

A nostril flared, loosed a smell of ash. "How much gold?"

"As much as I have."

"That would be not much."

"No," Cyan conceded. "I will speak to the King of Yves; he has more than I do, and he would pay for possession of that man."

"I have more gold than a dozen kings; if I want it I will take it. That is truly why you came here: not for the man but for the treasure."

"I truly came to find a tower with a woman in it, not Thayne Ysse sitting on a pile of gold."

"That woman."

He blinked. Then he drew breath soundlessly, realizing what had saved his life. He drew the disk up and looked into it. Now, recognized by the dragon, it revealed the face of the woman within it. She was more beautiful than Cyan remembered, with her rippling white-gold hair falling loosely around her face, and her sky-blue eyes troubled, helpless. He said softly, "Yes. This woman." He let the disk fall, gazed blindly up at the dragon, still seeing her. "Do you know her?"

"Yes." The word was more wind than sound, a reverberation Cyan felt in his bones.

"Where is she?" he pleaded. "I must find her."

"You want this man, that woman, your life . . . You do not offer me as much as a token in return."

Cyan thought. "All I have," he said finally, and drew the needlework out of his belt: the picture of Thayne within the tower watched by the dragon's eye. "The token of the man. You can put this one in your tower instead."

The dragon's head came down so quickly that Cyan

thought he would be crushed or eaten. It took all his will and experience not to thrust his sword up into one descending golden eye and pierce the dragon's brain. He stood still, his mouth tight, one hand gripping the sword, forcing its point against the earth as if it might move of its own accord. One eye and its closed jaws settled at the level of the embroidery. Cyan loosed his fingers, let the sword fall. He held the picture open with both hands.

The dragon rumbled like a small hillside sliding. Then it snorted sharply, turning its nostrils away, and spent a moment hissing noisily. A skull grinning upside down on the plain rolled upright. Cyan wondered if they were both laughing.

"Leave it in the tower," the dragon said. "Tell the man to take nothing but his life with him out of the tower, or he will not even have that."

"And the woman?" Cyan asked desperately. "How do I find her?"

The dragon regarded him silently, its eyes flooded suddenly with pools of dark as its slitted irises opened wide. "You could have killed me, Cyan Dag."

"I know."

"You see with your heart. You will find a way to her." Its head swung away from Cyan, settled, with a small earthquake, near its tail. Cyan heard its voice again as he walked toward the tower. "The way into the tower looks difficult but is far easier."

"Easier?"

"Than the way out. Death is one way out. There are

other words. The man knows them. Tell him that if he takes my gold I will eat him."

"Truly?"

"I eat hearts. On this plain, they all taste of gold."

Cyan reached the tower. He touched the solid wall tentatively; it gave like water beneath his hand. Holding his sword loosely in one hand, the picture of Thayne Ysse in the other, and not knowing which he might need first, he walked blindly through the stones into the dragon's heart.

SEVENTEEN

In the tower at Stony Wood, Sel drew brown threads back and forth across a patch of linen. She barely thought about what she was making. Her hands made it, she told herself, and anyway, it was nothing at all but a pile of bits and pieces of muted colors, all jumbled together, nothing fitting anything. Melanthos had brought up pockets stuffed full of thread Anyon had given her, the grays and creams and browns of his father's sheep. She had asked more than once what Sel was making. *Nothing*, Sel said, *in particular*, or: *I don't know yet.* Her hands seemed to know; Sel did not question them.

Melanthos brought her food, too, when Sel forgot to come down from the tower. She had become engrossed, watching the woman in the tower, waiting for her tale to end, to see how the woman would finally become free. Melanthos warned her now and then that the old mirror might not remember, that the tale might not have an end. But Sel, watching the woman become little by little more restless, more desperate, thought that even if the mirror forgot, the woman herself might give some hint of how the tale began and ended.

So she sewed and waited for the brief, random moments when the mirror turned its memory toward the tower beside the river. The mirror showed her the harbor seals as often as not, which was as close as it ever got to looking at the village. She loved seeing them peering curiously above the waves, diving sleekly after fish without leaving a ripple behind. She wished, occasionally, that the mirror would find the bakery and open an eye into that. But it never did. So Sel, remembering Gentian and the baby, would heave herself stiffly off the pallet and circle down the stairs into the light of day. Gentian, her placid Gentian, had burst into tears in the middle of the bakery the last time Sel appeared.

The baby, starting out of sleep, wailed in sympathy. Sel picked her up and patted Gentian's shoulder awkwardly, amazed.

"What is it?" she asked anxiously. "Don't tell me it's Rawl. I'll put holes in his boat."

"It's you!" Gentian cried. She even wept tidily, Sel saw: one tear out of each eye, traveling to mid-cheekbone and hanging on the fine, flushed skin like pearls. "Rawl goes out in the mornings to fish and comes back to me at night and never complains when I leave him before it's light to bake. But you—you don't even know where your home is now.

You've taken to living in that tower. I see Melanthos in here far more often than I see you!"

Sel was silent, shifting her patting hand to the baby now, while two pearls dissolved on Gentian's cheeks, and two more fell. "I'm sorry," she said vaguely, distressed and mystified at having made Gentian cry. The baby was more easily placated. "I'm just — "

"You're what? Just what?"

"Just — if you'll just be patient."

"Patient!" Gentian stared at her, bewildered. "Patient over what? What are you expecting to happen? Is the tower going to fall down or something?"

"It could be," Sel said, struck, wondering if that was how the tale in the mirror ended. Gentian pulled a clean, hemmed square of an old flour bag out of her pocket and blew her nose once, daintily, as if a flower scent had tickled it.

"Well," she asked, "are you planning to be in it when it does?"

Sel blinked at her. "Oh," she said, illumined. "That old tower in the stone wood. No. That might melt into the earth with age, but it'll never fall." She passed the baby over to Gentian, which soothed her a little. "Just give me some time."

"For what?"

Sel's eyes slid away from her toward the stony streets, the line of houses and shops hiding the sea. "I know it's not fair," she said softly. "And not easy. But I need this time. If you'll just be patient. Get someone to help you in here. One of Lude's older girls could do it. Just for a little."

"But I miss you," Gentian said simply, her eyes filling again with luminous pools that shone but did not spill. "And I'm afraid."

Sel's dark, flickering kelpie eyes came back to Gentian. She patted her daughter's shoulder again, silently a moment. "Don't be," she said at last. "Things will come to an end of themselves."

She sent Gentian home then, and worked, baking and selling and chatting, until she found herself drifting out of the door, through the village, into the stone wood to see if the woman was still in her tower. She was, and so was Melanthos. Sel took a seat beside her on the pallet, and picked up the thread where she had left off.

The mirror showed them the woman in the tower that evening. She sat very still, gazing at what must have been the feverish sky in her mirror: the streaks and washes of rose, purple, gold above the fields where the sun had set. Her hands, invisible in her lap, seemed motionless. The colors in the mirror intensified, grew lustrous; still her hands made no move toward her tidy line of threads. The sun glanced through the cloud as it set, a brilliant, baleful golden eye staring back at the woman through her mirror. Transfixed, it seemed, within her spellbound state, like a bird under a serpent's eye, she might have been a memory of herself; Sel could not even see her breathe. After the sun had set and the colors faded in the sky, she moved, so abruptly that Sel blinked: it was as if a statue had come to life.

She chose odd threads: yellow-green and orange and a bruised red like a black cherry, colors rarely seen in the sky. Maybe there was something coming down the road of such disturbing hues, that Sel could not yet see. The woman bent over her work. Night misted into her mirror, and then spilled out of it across the other mirror, until the woman vanished in a pool of black.

Melanthos grunted. "That was strange." Her fingers hovered over choices: the colors in the woman's mirror, the colors in the woman's hand.

"She's making something of her own," Sel guessed. "She's tired of being told."

"But who tells her, in the first place? And what will happen if she refuses?"

Sel shrugged. *What will happen if you do?* she wanted to ask Melanthos. But she understood too well, now, what lured her daughter: there seemed nothing more compelling in the world than the images spun out of the mind's eye into thread.

Sel worked late, that night, even later than Melanthos. She did not notice when Melanthos left the tower. In her own mind, Sel walked along the harbor cliffs, a tall, slender, barefoot woman with long black windblown hair. Seals swam through the waves pleating and breaking along the stones. The seals had different faces, so long ago, different names. She could not remember those older names now, except that they were odd: a mix of sounds that glided under and twisted back around a human tongue. Wind collided with her, poured around her, gathered and broke like the sea. She did not watch where her feet took her, through tide pools, over barnacles, across narrow shelves of rock slippery with streamers of moss coiling and uncoiling like mermaids' hair. She shouted names, in memory, but Sel, remembering, could no longer hear the sound of them.

She found herself trying to say one, her tongue trying to lick a name into shape. A sound with too many *l*s, maybe, and beginning with a growl in the back of her throat. *What was I thinking?* she wondered, amazed. *What was that young I thinking?*

The young woman in her memory seemed to turn on the cliff to look at her, then. *What are you thinking now?* she asked Sel, who gazed down at the making in her hands.

But she could not even tell herself.

She forced herself to put it down, go into the world to help Gentian again for a bit. She baked and sold and patted the baby and listened to Gentian talk about Rawl and storms, and what the baby had tried to say. Her own mouth made appropriate noises, she thought. But still she caught Gentian looking at her out of those wide, lovely, perplexed eyes, as if Sel herself had wandered into life out of some forgotten tale. Sel, half her mind still waiting in the tower for her body to come back to it, did as much as she could, absently, perfunctorily, to persuade Gentian that she still knew how to cope with life. When she could do no more, she took off her apron with relief and slipped away when Gentian's back was turned.

She found Melanthos in the tower among the broken ends of daylight, sitting on the pallet and staring at the mirror.

"Look what she's doing," Melanthos breathed as Sel knelt down beside her. "Look at it."

The woman sat in her chair as usual, embroidering. But

the side of the cloth that flowed with images down to the floor was oddly broken up with scatterings of thread on the pale background. Sel studied them, astonished. *Tree*, one group of threads said. Another, in an elongated strip of repetition said: *Road road road road . . . Rider*, said a third, at a tangent to *Road*, and in a different color. Above the *Rider*, in black, flew many tiny *Crows*.

"She's making everything into words," Melanthos said, entranced and nibbling on a thumbnail. "I wonder why?"

Sel gazed at the words, felt something stir in her, like some great, dark, amorphous sound on the verge of taking shape. "Magic," she said suddenly, as close as she could get to the sound. "Magic put her in there, magic must get her out."

Melanthos dragged her eyes from the mirror, flicked her mother a glance. "They're just words."

"So far."

"Well, how much farther can they go?"

"I don't know," Sel mused, watching, while her hands reached for an unfinished patch of gray. "We don't know her. But it must be magic trapping her there. Whether or not the story is true, it must be magic. She never changes, she never needs her hair combed, she never sees anyone that we can see, she never—"

"She never speaks," Melanthos said softly.

"Until now."

"She never—so." She stirred, her hands clasping, unclasping. "Magic keeps her there, in a timeless enchantment."

"She needs magic to fight magic."

Melanthos looked at Sel again, out of her sea-fay eyes. "She'd get rescued in the tale. That's how they end."

"Maybe," Sel murmured, drawing her needle out, "she's gotten tired of waiting."

Melanthos studied the woman, until tors grew out of her words, and the reflection of rocky fields. The woman melted away. Melanthos puzzled over threads; Sel wondered if she were contemplating some variations of her own: *Woman*, perhaps, in blues and pale golds, instead of the woman's immaculate image. But it seemed more that her thoughts could not settle yet on what it had been given.

"How can she make magic out of nothing?" Melanthos asked finally. "How can she just sit there and make endless days of changing the world into threads into something powerful?"

"I don't know."

"Well, think about it. If you're caught in a web and can't move—if every line trapping you is a magic not your own—how could you spin magic out of yourself?"

"What's the alternative?

Melanthos opened her mouth, closed it. She studied the mirror as though she could still see the woman in it. "She will die? But she's safe enough in there now. She never seems to go hungry or be tired, she's always tidy—she'll die if she tries to leave," she added, illumined. "As long as she keeps doing what she's doing, not looking at the world, not going into it, only seeing it backward and through her pictures, she'll be safe."

"She'll be lonely," Sel said to her threads. "Never speaking, never touching, never looked at . . . You could die of that."

"So someone put her there to punish her?"

"Maybe." Sel's needle slowed; her own eyes shifted, gazing backward. "Or maybe she's something not quite human, from a place beyond the world, elsewhere. The tower is the only safe place between her and the human world . . . If she looks at the human world, takes it into her mind and her eyes, she will die because she can never belong to it. The tower is the doorway between the worlds."

"She'll die of loneliness."

"Maybe."

"So." Melanthos pulled her knees to her chin, rocked a little, thinking. "She must make herself human."

"It's one way to look at it."

"She can't go back to where she came from?"

"I suppose that's one way the tale could end," Sel said.

"I suppose if it were that easy, there wouldn't be a tale."

Melanthos reached toward thread. Her hand hovered, dropped and drew back, empty. Sel looked a question at her. Melanthos shook her head. "There must be something else . . . I don't want to do her words. I don't feel the urge. There's no magic in it."

"Maybe not yet . . ."

"I mean for the mirror. It doesn't want that." Her eyes slid again to Sel; she wrapped her arms more tightly around her knees and asked tentatively, "Speaking of magic, do you remember the magic you used to do when we were small? When you were young and our father was alive?"

Sel remembered. For an instant all the magic flowed

like tide into her, catching light, dark tumbling within it, nameless creatures and unimaginably beautiful treasures. Then it was gone, like a vision of water on a waste.

"No," she said briefly to the memory and to Melanthos, whose eyes were wide and vulnerable. "I don't." She looked away from her daughter and saw the knight in the mirror.

He was just stepping out of a squat, dark tower. Sel, who had never seen a knight, recognized the details: the towers on his surcoat, the sword, the suggestion of power and skill in his movements. There was a strange look on the knight's face, wonder and bewilderment, as if whatever he had found in the tower was the last thing he had expected. Dawn, touching the sword with a golden fingertip, sparked a glitter of fire within the jewel.

Behind the tower, in the distance, rose the smooth, graceful slopes of hills that seemed to mirror one another against the sky.

Melanthos leaned forward suddenly, reaching out with both hands to the mirror, or to the knight. "Three Sisters," she whispered. "That's where he is."

She loosed the mirror, and sorted through her threads for green.

EIGHTEEN

Thayne, lost in a memory of rain on a dark hillside in north Yves, saw the armed warrior come at him out of nowhere. Yet one more of Regis Aurum's interminable army, he thought grimly. He would make one less of this one . . . Some bony hand left from another battle had gotten hold of his sword; he felt the fingerbones scatter as he pulled it free. The hillside was slippery; he nearly lost his balance, rising, and again when he swung the broadsword slashing through a quarter circle of air before it struck the deadweight of the blade the knight had raised, as fixed in his grip as an old stump in the ground. The fury in his own blow shocked through the metal into Thayne's hands. He hung on obdurately, raising the sword again.

Someone was calling his name. He ignored it, shearing air downward this time, toward the silver disk the knight wore like a small, peculiar piece of armor. He had lost whatever else he had. His shirt and surcoat were ripped apart, his skin scraped and bloodied with battle. He had no shield; the torn emblem on his surcoat was undecipherable; nothing told who he was. But he was not an islander, with hardship and desperation beaten into his eyes. The knight's eyes were clear, cold, and merciless, trained that way to look so at anything beyond the graceful towers of Gloinmere, at anyone who wore thread spun out of wind, whose hands smelled of fish, who dared question a word that came from Regis Aurum's lips. "One more," Thayne whispered between his teeth, aiming for the heart beneath the disk. "One more for Ysse."

But the knight's sword was in the way again, a diagonal flare of silver crossing Thayne's. He felt the strength behind it, pushing at him, not letting him pull free, bearing down at him until he lost his balance again, falling back against a pile of bracken, or a field wall, something he hadn't noticed. The knight's hand closed on Thayne's wrist, his thumb digging into the veins, until Thayne, hissing, dropped the sword. His other hand, scrabbling in the bracken, found small flat pebbles. He flung them into the knight's face. The knight flinched from what looked oddly like a shower of gold. Thayne, sliding down a sudden spill of fieldstone, drew back his feet and kicked.

The knight stumbled backward, slipped on what looked like a skull lying in the field. The skull, chattering, flew into the bracken. Thayne found his sword again, pulled himself up, and drove the blade hard at the knight, who seemed flung back against a wall of night and half-stunned by it.

He lifted his own sword, but without strength. Thayne flicked it aside. The knight, trying to evade the death coming at him, had only time for a breath that made the silver disk slide on its chain and fall to meet Thayne's sword. The point, battering into it, bounced away as if it had struck stone, and then did strike stone, as the knight twisted out from under it. Thayne heard him groping harshly for air. His own arm half-numb, Thayne backed a few steps. He kicked something in his path, and started as an entire skeleton bowed over his feet. A crown, precariously balanced, dropped down the skull to its throat, hung there like a collar.

"Thayne," it said, oddly breathless for something that no longer needed air. "Thayne Ysse."

"What is this place?" he wondered aloud, straining to see through the dark and the rain that streaked the air, but never seemed to touch him. "What is this battlefield?"

The knight attacked again, or so Thayne thought, seeing silver flash out of the corner of his eye. He turned and sheared the arm off another skeleton dropping, armed, out of the bracken. Its fall was accompanied by the ringing of many tiny bells. Thayne swallowed, then choked at the sudden dry pain in his throat; he had been wounded, he guessed, though he did not remember how. The knight, quiet again, was not where Thayne had left him. Thayne whirled, and saw him coming from behind. As if the moon had parted the heavy clouds with a finger of light and reached down to touch the knight's face, it grew suddenly clear. Thayne recognized him.

"You."

He slashed at Cyan Dag, whom he seemed to find everywhere he found himself. Memory tugged bewilderingly against memory: gold illumined the darkness, then faded again. He stood in rain he could not feel, opened his mouth to catch but could not taste. Elsewhere molten gold burned in his throat; thirst gnawed at him with an old wolf's blunt teeth. Elsewhere, he also fought Cyan Dag, but in another battle; in this dreary field of shadows, he would never have recognized the knight. He caught glimpses then, as their swords sparked silver and reflected gold, of a different landscape: burned dry and barren, with air that could kindle itself into flame if it ever moved. Nothing in the land but a tower, nothing in the tower but —

Gold. Ringed by a tower, ringed by a dragon, ringed by a wasteland somewhere in Skye. And the knight of Gloinmere had followed Thayne to this secret place, to take the dragon and the gold for Regis Aurum. The knight had recovered his strength, and was beating back Thayne's attack with a relentless, rhythmical, tireless force, as if, Thayne thought, he were scything wheat. He would kill Thayne, and then turn that cold fire in his eyes toward the dragon, offering it whatever it wanted, since he had all the riches of Gloinmere to back his promises, all of Yves. He would leave Thayne's bones along with the collection in the tower and let the dragon burn the North Islands down to stone, in Regis Aurum's name.

"Craiche," Thayne whispered between set teeth, a private battle cry. The knight's methodical attack faltered a beat. His eyes lost their remoteness; he seemed about to speak. But Thayne's sword drove under his guard toward his heart again. The knight, without seeming to move, was suddenly beyond Thayne's reach, halfway up what Thayne had taken for a pile of bracken in the rain, and which had transformed itself into a pile of gold. He fought there like a man defending his territory, his hillock of treasure, against the traitor from Ysse, who had never learned to bow his head low enough to the King of Yves. Thayne swung a sideways cut at the back of one leg, aiming for the tendon. He caught a boot in the throat that knocked him into a clatter of plate and some astonishing gold armor filched, apparently while occupied, from an ill-fated coronation ceremony. The knight flung himself after Thayne, pinned him down on the floor, knocking the breath out of him. Thayne felt the edge of the knight's blade across his throat.

"Listen to me," Cyan Dag said. "Thayne. Listen."

No, Thayne thought, staring fiercely back into those eyes like cold rain. *You hear me.*

He saw the dragon watching, then, its enormous eye an oval of roiling gold inset in stone, with the dark slit fanning wide across it. He heard his own blood pounding in his ears, and beneath him, beneath the stones he sprawled on, he heard the secret course of dragon's blood. The dry, golden waste stretched like skin over the dragon's veins and bones; he felt its heartbeat deep within the plain, as if the earth itself were dragon, the mountains its backbone, the forests and plains its scales, the wind its breath, the tower full of gold its burning heart. His blood measured itself again to the pulse of dragon's blood; the eye, gazing at him, reflected him like thought.

He saw with sudden, mad clarity, as if he had drunk

its blood or breathed its fire: we are all part of the dragon.
Fire and bone and claw, waste, tower, gold: we are the
dragon.

He felt the fire then, everywhere in the air, there for
the taking. All he had to do was recognize it.

The knight was still talking at Thayne, the sword still
pushing into his throat. *Regis Aurum*, he said, and *north Yves*.
Then he spoke a word like a spell, the last name Thayne
expected to hear out of his mouth: *Craiche*.

Thayne kindled lightning in the hot, dry air and spat
the name back at him. Then he caught fire in his eyes from
everyplace he looked: the fire within the gold, within the
dragon's eye. When he spoke again, the word came out of
his bones in a furious shimmer of fire and light. It hit the
silver disk dangling in the air between them with a sound
like sky shredded by thunder. The knight vanished. He
reappeared briefly, splayed against the wall within the
dragon's eye. Then he slid to the floor and disappeared
again behind the drifts and mounds of gold.

Thayne moved after a moment, slowly. Something had
burned out of him. He was made of paper, moth wings,
ash, so dry and weak he could barely pick himself up. He
stumbled across the floor, dragging a sword behind him, in
case the knight was still not convinced that he should die.

He lay on his back among scattered helmets and shields
of gold. The disk on his breast was smoldering, veined with
black, its perfect circle blurred and ragged, as if the edges
had melted. Thayne sank wearily to his knees, balancing
himself with the blade. Sweat poured down his face, though
he would have sworn that the heavy, burning vise of heat

had wrung all the water out of him long before. He wiped his eyes, blinked at the knight. He breathed, Thayne saw, but barely. His face looked blanched, even under the fey glow of gold. Thayne swayed against the sword that held him up, reluctant to kill the knight before he understood why.

He said slowly, peeling each word out of his dry mouth, "Craiche is my brother. He was twelve when the North Islands fought the king in north Yves. My father was badly wounded, then. He lost his wits and his strength. I paid tribute to the king with that. I paid with Craiche, who was crippled by some great knight taking a slash at a running boy the way you'd slap at a fly. I paid tribute with Ysse, on which we make our living catching fish and raising sheep. Half the working men did not return to that island where once kings were born. The king wants the first bite we put into our mouths. He wants the pearl in every oyster. He wants us to bend our heads so low he never has to look into our eyes. That's why I came here. That's why I'll leave you here, when I take the dragon and its gold to the North Islands. I know now that I can take it. I found its fire and swallowed it. Its gold is my heart. I'll kill you before I go. It's an easier death than dying of thirst."

The knight's head moved a little, as if he finally heard a word he understood. He tried to swallow; his eyes flickered open, oddly dark in his bloodless face. They closed again. He lifted his hand somehow, his brows twisting together with the effort. He touched the disk, shifted it, and Thayne saw the brand seared into his skin, the perfect circle before the dragon's breath warped it out of shape.

He spoke finally, his voice not much more than a whisper. "I remember Craiche."

Thayne blinked. "How could—" His hands tightened suddenly on the sword hilt. "What do you remember?" he asked harshly. "The running boy you crippled?"

The knight's eyes opened again, searched for Thayne, wincing at the flare of gold up the blade, until he found Thayne's face above it. "No." He stopped to swallow. "I heard him crying. On that hillside, after you searched it for your wounded. You didn't find the king under the hedge."

"He was there?" Thayne whispered.

"With me. I guarded him all night in the rain. Except—" He paused again, looking back into memory, into the rain that Thayne had dreamed of in the tower. "When I left him. For only a few moments. To carry a boy who was crawling down the hill back to your camp."

Thayne stared at him. Something bulky and sharp seemed to shift painfully inside of him, as if his heart were changing shape. *A strong, armed, faceless knight,* Craiche had told him for years, until the telling wove itself seamlessly into the lore of the battle. *He came out of nowhere, picked me up, and carried me down the hill.* "What was his name, I asked Craiche," he whispered, "after the sentries found him crawling through the trees into the camp. This faceless knight who came out of nowhere and saved your life? I don't know, Craiche told me. I asked him, but he never spoke . . ."

"Cyan Dag," the knight said, and was silent again, leaving Thayne alone under the dragon's eye.

NINETEEN

Melanthos watched the woman in the tower. She was lying at the edge of the pallet, snoring softly. She had burned candles through the night, making her interminable patches of smoke and dust and ivory. They lay in a heap against the wall, patches for a drab quilt, or an unlikely cloak. Twice Anyon had to bring more thread; she must have gone through several sheep already, and she had not even begun to piece them together. Perhaps she never would; she would just make and make until there was not one cloudy, irregular shape left in her. Then she would leave the tower and return to life, her baking, her children, her cups of bitter ale with Brenna while she watched the sun go down.

She looked thinner, Melanthos thought; she kept forgetting to eat. And she left her hair loose, except when she braided it to go back to the bakery for an afternoon. It fanned across one shoulder and down her back as she slept, a rippling mass of tarnished silver. Her back to Melanthos, her hair flowing into the dark of her skirt, her hands and feet tucked away somewhere out of sight around her long body, she looked scarcely human. Melanthos contemplated her silently, sitting motionlessly in front of the mirror, her eyes narrowed, flecked with tiny flames from the candles.

Maybe, she thought finally, *I should just toss the patches out the window.*

But that seemed cruel, even unnecessary. Maybe she had in mind some brighter thread to join all the patches together, so that it would look like stones under flowing silvery water in the end, or a cobbled street seamed with gold. Maybe there was magic in the making of this odd thing, so that in the end it would bring Sel peace.

The mirror opened its eye then, showed Melanthos another tower, the woman in it busy at her own embroidery. Her elegant mirror reflected the blank face of night; the woman, threading crimson into her linen, was not paying attention to the mirror. As she drew the needle through and lifted her arm to tighten thread, she gave Melanthos glimpses of her night vision: a tower on an island within a deep, slow-moving river thick with water lilies. From the blank windows of the tower crimson petals of flame opened toward the trees across the narrow channel between the island and the bank. Above the tower, a strange bird with a long neck and pale wings of a swan, a predator's fierce hooked beak and talons, flew away from the flames gripping a white, twisting snake with a woman's face. The eyes of the bird and the snake were sky-blue.

As Melanthos watched in wonder, the woman knotted her thread and snapped it. She tore the picture out of the long swath of linen as she might have torn a memory out of her life. Then, without looking away from her threads, she reached out, tossed the burning tower into the night.

She waited a little, still, tense, as if she expected the image to come flying back through the window, or something to emerge out of the dark, crawling up the steep walls on its white belly, a forked tongue flickering out of its human lips. Nothing happened. Her hands moved after a while, pieced the ripped edges of the linen together; she took a needle threaded with the color of flax and began to mend the rent.

How strange, Melanthos thought, her skin prickling. Perhaps you are as real as the knight . . .

Her own hands moved toward thread, compelled not by the woman's burning image but by her face, no longer a beautiful, nameless, thoughtless face out of story, but the face of a desperate woman threading her needle with hope, trying to work magic into her stitches, to transform the world that trapped her. Could she change her shape? Melanthos wondered. Could she fly out of her prison, eluding the eye of the mirror which would no longer recognize her?

Sel was awake, Melanthos realized just before she lost herself, became her threads and her image until it was finished, out of her mind. Sel had stopped snoring, some time ago. Her body held the silent tenseness of one awake in the dark, remembering a dream. She faced the mirror; she might have seen the burning tower, the woman transformed into that shape of grace and danger gripping the deadly sorcery in her talons. As the mirror darkened, Sel sat up. Melanthos, drawing thread the tender blue of the woman's eyes through her needle, disappeared into her picture.

At dawn she threw the haunted, beautiful face out the window. Emptied like an old bucket, and stupid for sleep, she crawled under a blanket on the pallet. She scarcely noticed that Sel was gone. She woke hours later, sweating in a flood of light, thirsty and ravenous. She was alone, she realized groggily. Her mother must have felt an urge for the human world. She put her shoes on and stumbled down the stairs. She found Anyon sitting on the bottom steps.

"I called you earlier," he said. "Nobody heard me." He paused at something in her eyes. She could not, she realized, go one step farther in the world without paying some attention to the wonderful line of Anyon's mouth. She bent thoughtlessly to kiss it. He added breathlessly a moment or an hour later, draped on his back over the steps with Melanthos blinking in his arms, "Gentian wants your mother."

She lifted her head after a moment, looked at him. "She's not in the bakery?"

"No."

"She's not in the tower."

"She's not?"

"No." She pulled herself up, puzzled. "I wonder where she is. Has Gentian got someone to help her?"

"With the baking, yes. With the baby, no. It's snuffling or something." His hands tugged at her lightly, coaxing her back. "Do that again."

"Later . . ." She stood up, frowning, and gave him a hand, peeling him ungently off the steps. "I want to find her."

"She's probably at Brenna's."

"Maybe." She thumped him sharply on the chest for the grin on his face. "Don't laugh at my mother."

"I wasn't! Don't I give her all my earth colors? What is she making with them?"

"I don't know yet. Maybe nothing." She took his arm in both her hands, smelling sharp soap on him, oil from the wool, the tangy scent of bracken. She pushed against him, sniffing like a dog, then pulled him through the stone wood. "Hurry. I want to find her."

They walked along the harbor cliff and talked to Brenna, who gave Melanthos a pickled egg and told her she had not seen Sel for days. But don't worry; Sel was tough as an old piece of driftwood and she was probably out negotiating the price of sugar, anyway she'd never go far from her children. All of which gave Melanthos an odd pang of worry. She swallowed the last of the egg and headed for the bakery.

There she found the baby in a squall and Gentian looking disheveled, a hair out of place, a thumbprint of dough on one cheek. The young girl helping her, one of Lude's, was putting buns in a basket, counting each one loudly and carefully. Anyon hauled the baby over his shoulder, rubbed her back, and she subsided, wiping her nose on his neck. Gentian sighed deeply, dislodging another hair.

"Where's our mother?" she asked Melanthos.

"I don't know." She took one of the warm buns out of

the basket and bit into it, causing Lude's daughter to stare at her in consternation. "She was in that tower all night, making her shapes. Maybe she just went to bed."

"I looked for her in the house." Gentian, brows crooked prettily, like a fretting mermaid, gazed back at Melanthos questioningly.

"Maybe she went for a walk," Anyon suggested. Both their gazes swung to him. He shrugged. "Maybe she went to another tavern, or she's visiting someone. Maybe she's just doing something ordinary."

The two sisters consulted one another wordlessly. Melanthos said, "You go find her. I'll watch the store."

"No." Gentian sighed. "You go. I need to feed the baby. Here." She gave Melanthos a warm meat pie, then tossed Anyon one, too, at the expression on his face. She took the baby from him. Lude's daughter started her counting again, sounding aggrieved. Melanthos crossed her eyes at Lude's daughter, but Gentian, nursing the baby, only smiled peacefully.

They found Sel at twilight on the cliff near the stone wood, when it was almost too dark to see anything but a monolith standing alone on the cliff edge, looking out to sea. They argued over it a little, before they recognized her.

"It has always been there," Anyon insisted.

"No, it hasn't. It's as if a dead tree wandered out of the stony wood . . ."

"You just never noticed."

"I notice all the stones," Melanthos protested. "I have counted all the trees in the stone wood—" Then the monolith moved, turning slowly in the wind, and took her breath away. She saw a graceful, sinuous swirl of long hair, long skirts flowing around a woman's body pulled tight by the wind, only a little drift of cloth, like the foamy ruffle of a wave, fluttering free at her ankles. Beside Melanthos, Anyon had fallen as abruptly still.

Then the wind unwound the skirt, and hands came up, swept the hair back and twisted it into submission. Melanthos, gripping Anyon's arm, made a noise.

"That's her. Your monolith that's always been there . . ."

"Well, it looked . . ." Anyon began, and followed Melanthos along the grassy lip of the cliff.

Sel waited for them, still holding her hair. "Where were you?" Melanthos demanded. "What have you been doing?"

It seemed a long time before her mother spoke, as if she had trouble remembering. But the answer itself was simple enough. "I went swimming," Sel said. "Then I sat here for a while and watched the seals. Why? Did Gentian need me?"

"She wanted you," Melanthos said. "The baby has a cold." It sounded trivial to her ears, suddenly. She could almost hear her mother's thoughts: Two grown young women and you can't take care of a few loaves of bread and a baby? What will you do if? When? But Sel only grunted and followed them, tying her hair with a streamer of kelp as she walked.

Melanthos did not find her in the tower again until the baby abandoned her cold and produced a tooth. By then, Melanthos had studied every bit of needlework in Sel's pile. It all seemed as formless and innocuous as cloud. Nothing caught the eye, nothing suggested . . . Melanthos put them back into the clutter in which Sel kept them, and pondered. Maybe that was all her mother had in her head, those days, she decided. Misty, shapeless thoughts that hid other things she wouldn't say. Maybe when they all came out of her, the other things would be revealed. Or maybe . . . She gave up trying to guess.

"She's changing," Gentian said to Melanthos one morning, when Melanthos had gotten up early to help with the baking and found Sel gone again. Yawning over the breakfast rolls she shaped, Melanthos looked a question at Gentian.

"Well," Gentian answered, putting loaves in the oven, "for one thing she lets her hair down sometimes. And she's getting thinner."

"There's not much to eat in the tower."

"And there's the look in her eyes. As if she's watching something very far away. Or listening for it."

"She's fey," Melanthos said, yawning again.

"You say that. But you never really mean it." She paused, shaking flour onto a board. "Besides, what does it mean, exactly?"

"Magic," Melanthos answered vaguely.

"I mean what does it mean to us if she is?"

Melanthos pummeled some dough, thinking about the question. She pulled it into pieces, shaped the pieces into starfish, scallop shells, as Sel had taught her, thinking about Sel finding her way up the tower, moving through Anyon's thorns as if they—or she—did not exist. She twisted a handful of dough into a spiraling auger shell, wondering what her mother was doing now, thinking, feeling. She rarely told them anything, Melanthos realized, not even when they asked. Did she tell herself what she thought, what she felt? Or did she just make another amorphous shape and let that speak for her?

She pulled starfish legs out of another bit of dough impatiently, set all the shapes on the baking stone, and propelled them into the oven, slamming the door behind them. "I don't know," she said tersely. "I'll ask her. Is someone coming to help you this morning?"

Gentian nodded. "Lude's eldest. She's not so noisy as her sister." She draped her sticky fingers over the board and leaned against it, gazing at nothing. Melanthos saw the worry in her eyes. "I'm afraid," she said softly. "And I don't know why. Ask her about that, too."

In the tower, Melanthos found Sel sitting placidly on the pallet, sorting through her patches. Sel lifted her head, turning as Melanthos walked in, and in that sudden glance, she glimpsed the stranger's face beneath her mother's face: another woman, secret-eyed, graceful in her bones, maybe wild, maybe fey, old or young, but not clearly revealing which.

"What are you doing?" Melanthos asked.

The woman answered in Sel's prosaic voice. "It's time," she said, "to piece them together."

"Why now?" Melanthos asked sharply, and Sel looked at her, surprised.

"Because I've got all the shapes I need."

"For what?"

"A sort of cloak, I think . . . It's not very colorful, but

it suits me, and the wool will keep me warm. And you need all the brightest threads."

She smiled unexpectedly at Melanthos, who felt a sudden, augury turn of pure terror, for her mother had already vanished, left this smiling stranger to lie for her.

She said nothing. When Sel left the tower to go back to the village, Melanthos left also, to cross the plains among the sheep. There she found one of the wild ponies she used to catch when she was young. She rode north out of the plain, toward the Three Sisters.

TWENTY

In the squat, dark tower with the open doorway, Cyan Dag talked to the Bard of Skye. They sat on massive oblongs of stone, like doorposts that had fallen down and been replaced. The floor was dirt; there seemed nothing else in the tower but stone and shadow, and the two of them, illumined by a silvery light shining from a ring on Idra's finger. Beyond the doorway, evening stood at the threshold. The air smelled of damp grass, earth, wildflowers. The palest, most tender shades of green were still visible in the dusk.

"The difference," the bard said, "between weaving and embroidery becomes most obvious if you happen to do one or the other. Most knights don't. The looms are different, the threads are different, the stitches, the instruments that

186 Patricia A. McKillip

carry the thread . . . Are you planning to stay here long? There is still another tower to get to."

"It's pleasant here," Cyan said. "Peaceful. I might stay the night."

"Nights are long here. Nights can be endless."

"You sent me here," he reminded her. "I have been trying to find that tower with Gwynne of Skye in it, but the towers keep changing . . . Is she weaving? Or embroidering?"

"Gwynne?"

"The monster who married the king said she weaves and weeps."

"I doubt that she knows enough about either to tell the difference."

"Gwynne?"

"She was never one for sitting still. That you have with you is embroidery."

He pulled it out of his sleeve, where it had somehow gotten wedged, and spread it on the stones between them. He studied the fine stitches, the bright threads making a picture of the gold-haired man sitting on a pile of gold. He said softly, "I could have done without that tower."

"He needs you," the bard said, her old eyes black and flat as beetles' wings in the silvery light. She wore black now, from throat to heel; her long white hair rippled over her straight shoulders down her back to flow across the stone. "We embroider our days. Life weaves."

"I didn't come to Skye for Thayne Ysse."

"How do you know why you came here? The woven

thread touches many other threads on its journey across the loom."

He did not answer; he had no answer for her yet, though he knew what she wanted. They sat in his silence, she waiting, watching him, while he watched the still evening outside the door. So still it was, nothing stirred, nothing made a sound. Only bright young leaves of ferns and lilies changed, their hues of green turning to darker greens, the shifts of color the only movement in the tranquil dark.

I could stay here, he thought, looking back at his failed journey across Yves and Skye, watching himself leave king and court without a word of explanation. No one knew where he was but Thayne Ysse. And the Bard of Skye, with her eyes like pools so deep nothing stirred the surface from within. But he could feel what she wanted from him. She wanted something; why else was she there?

I am no closer to doing what I came to do than I was when I left Gloinmere, he thought dispassionately. *I am farther away than ever, now, thanks to Thayne Ysse. I am so far away I might never find my way back.*

"I know," she said.

"So," he answered, unsurprised that she had read his thoughts, "maybe I will stay. I remember what I glimpsed in this tower when you sent me here. Dreams, quests, wonderful lands, strange kings with ancient and magnificent courts . . . Was it real? Or did you work some illusion to twist my heart with longings?"

"What you see here," she said, glancing around at the worn stones, the relentless, motionless darkness overhead, black as a toad's eye and as senseless, "is all."

"So you say now."

"So I say," she answered in her riddling way, giving him truth or lie and letting him choose.

"Still," he mused, leaning back against the stone, watching a star form through the doorway, "it's far more appealing than the dragon's tower. That place reeks; it's full of bones; the stones sweat in the heat. And if I go back, Thayne will only kill me. So he said. I'll spare myself the trouble, staying here."

"You told him you saved his brother's life. Thayne would die in that tower himself rather than allow harm to come to Craiche. Perhaps he changed his mind about killing you."

"Perhaps it's not worth going back to find out. My last glimpse of life would be Thayne Ysse's harrowed face blaming me for all the sorrow in the North Islands. I'd rather watch the night fall, here. Its face is calm and lovely, and full of mysteries."

She picked up the harp lying beside her on the stones, flicked a few sweet notes into the air. "You should make up your mind." She did not meet his eyes. "It's a long way back and you'll get lost trying to find your way in the night."

He looked at her thoughtfully, the Bard of Skye sitting with him in the dark tower. "Why do you care?" he asked her. "What do you want from me?"

Her eyes flickered at him, then. "There's still another tower."

"There are many other knights."

"But only one of you, Cyan Dag. I need you."

He was silent again, with wonder; it sounded, for once, like truth. Still, her need was complex, bewildering, and extremely dangerous. He said indifferently, for there seemed nothing left to tempt him, "Make it worth my while."

"Is the Lady from Skye not worth your while?"

"Not at this particular moment. You want me to choose between a tower of night and a tower of fire. You don't offer me the tower with the lady in it. Not yet. Never yet. Always something else first. Do I go or do I stay? Which tower do I choose? You want me to choose fire. Make it worth my while."

He saw the first flicker of expression in her ancient eyes, uncertainty, perhaps even the pain of some memory. He waited, watching the gentle evening darken, smelling the mysteries of bracken, fungus, rotting wood, flowers scattering their faded petals over the grass. The bard asked finally, pulling him back out of the night, "What do you want?"

Nothing, he thought. *Nothing.*

Then the answer washed over him, through him, in a color: the faint, young green still visible just beyond the door. "Cria," he whispered. "Cria Greenwood." And she was there between him and the night, with her violet eyes and smoky hair, her sweet, husky voice full of flaring embers and wine. *Cyan,* she said. *Where are you?* "Tell her," he pleaded to the Bard of Skye, "that I will come back."

The bard bowed her head above the harp. She seemed, as he watched her, to shape herself into it, until her bones formed its bones, her hair strung it; the harper became the harp. He heard her play.

He listened for a long time, it seemed, until the darkness dissolved around him. Gold burned behind his eyes. He struggled to find his way back into the tower of shadows, but he had left it and he could no longer find the door. The sun was rising. It spilled over him, stifling, blinding, merciless. He drew a sudden long, shuddering breath, as if he had been under water and had finally reached the surface. Then he felt the fire all through his bones.

He tried to roll away from himself. Hands closed on his arms, held him still. He cried out against the pain; his voice sounded cracked, frayed. His mouth burned like metal in the heat.

"Cyan," someone kept saying insistently. "Cyan Dag."

He dragged his burning eyes open. Thayne Ysse's face loomed over him, blanched, haggard, his own eyes smoldering with gold, luminous and inhuman. Dragon's eyes, Cyan saw. The fire licked through him again. He twisted in Thayne's hold, his lips so tight between his teeth he swallowed blood.

"Don't die," Thayne begged. "Craiche would never forgive me."

"I thought," he whispered when he could speak, "you wanted me dead."

"I changed my mind."

Cyan closed his eyes again, remembering the dark hillside, the boy crawling through the grass, the rain. The rain. He opened his lips, searching for it blindly; it fell everywhere around him but not on him, not in his mouth, though he turned his head frantically to catch it.

"There is no rain," he said, his throat tight with despair. "Only gold."

Thayne loosed him and stood up. Cyan watched the gold around him blur to his movements, move with him like wings, cling to him like armor, turn his fingers to long shafts of light. He saw the dragon then, in every stone of the tower; the stones rippled to its breathing, bright, scaly shades of green, bronze, copper, flame. The jagged profile of its nostrils and jaw were clear now; its enormous eye, staring at them, opened its slitted iris wide, like a door opening. One of Thayne's burning fingers illuminated the dark within it.

"Freedom," said the gold-shrouded figure that was once Thayne, "lies in the dragon's eye." Or the dragon spoke, giving them a riddle: truth or lie? Cyan tensed, torn between the two words. Fire that was not fire swept through him, hollowing his bones, until he felt he would become like the forgotten dead on the plain, flayed by the sun, pared down to what could outlast the burning day.

Thayne or the dragon spoke again. A great, curved scythelike claw moved from the dragon's side through the circle of its body toward Cyan. He gasped, trying to pull himself away from it. Its shadow harvested his heart before it reached him. The shafts of light that were Thayne's hands gripped him, raised his body to meet the dragon's claw. It touched the blackened, melted disk on his chest, and a sudden flare of silver cracked through the air, so bright it blinded him. He fell back against Thayne, and then into a rattling pile of coin as the floor rumbled and jolted under them. Silver streaked the air again. He dropped his arms over his eyes; his bones seemed to scatter in all directions at the sound the air made as it split in two.

And then he felt the rain.

It was as if a river in the sky had sagged through its bed, torn it open, and emptied its water endlessly onto the plain. For a moment he let it pour into his throat; he tried to fill his bones with it. Then he turned his back to it so he could breathe, and saw the river of mud he lay in. He lifted his head, trying to find Thayne through the flickering sheets of rain.

He saw the dragon rising.

It burned like a sun on the other side of the rain. Its vast wings seemed to span the plain; it could have caught the lightning in its claws. Its back seemed made of gold. As Cyan watched, something spun away from it, flashing as it turned through light and mist, a falling tear of gold within the rain. It hit the mud near Cyan: a coin with Regis Aurum's face on it.

Lightning, or the fire of the dragon's farewell, seared the sky. Thunder bellowed and bounced, echoing from hill to hill. Cyan dropped his face against one arm and closed his eyes, while the rain pounded against him, seeped beneath his skin, searched out the smoldering embers of dragon fire within his bones.

He woke smelling grass and wood smoke, and a breath of chill dark air out of stone as old as the world.

He rolled wearily onto his back, knowing without opening his eyes where he must be. He felt the sun fall on his face, gentle now, dappled with shadow from the trees. The wood smoke, the soft rustlings of fire, were puzzling. He opened his eyes finally. The tower stood where he had left it, in the little glade ringed by trees. Something else caught his eye: a flash of gold in the grass.

He reached for it, turned the small circle until the king's profile rolled upright between his finger and thumb. Thayne Ysse had flown away with the dragon and its magnificent treasure; in Ysse, he would hammer Regis Aurum's profile into the mask of war and give it back to him. Cyan tasted a bitter breath of smoke in the back of his throat, the taste of this failure. He dropped the coin in his boot and began what seemed an arduous challenge to get up.

Someone touched him.

He started. At first, glimpsing the long dark hair, he thought: Sidera. But this young woman with her wild, tangled hair, her eyes flecked with unusual colors, was a stranger. He struggled to rise; she helped him sit. She was lean and long-limbed, with what looked like a dusting of flour in her hair. Her clothes were simple, linen and wool, crumpled from riding. She was barefoot. The wary-eyed horse snorting at Cyan's gelding wore neither reins nor saddle.

It was her fire he smelled, and her fish roasting on it. As if, he realized, she had been waiting for him beside the tower.

"Are you all right?" she asked, her eyes widening at his torn surcoat, the brand the disk had left on his chest. "Did you find the dragon?" Then the tarnished disk caught her eye and she blinked.

"How do you know," he whispered, "the dragon?"

"It was in the mirror. So were you. The mirror told me where to find you." She raised a slender, callused hand, touched the disk very gently, as if she were touching a face.

Cyan raised it, looked into it. Even within the clouds and veins of charred silver, he could see the midsummer blue of the lady's eyes, the long, fine, white-gold hair. She was still there, he thought wearily. Trapped, but still alive. Then, stunned, he saw the recognition in the young woman's eyes.

His breath caught painfully. "You know her?"

"Oh, yes," she said. Her voice sounded plain as stone, eager as flame. "I've seen her many times. Are you hurt anywhere? What did you tangle with?"

"The dragon," he said after a moment, still staring at her. "And a furious lord from the North Islands."

"The man with the golden hair."

"Yes. How do you—how—"

"The mirror," she repeated, and touched the disk again, lightly. "It looks a little like this. Did you kill the dragon?"

"No. Thayne Ysse took it."

She gazed at him, astonished. "Then he must have enormous power. A dragon's power."

"What is your name?" he asked, wondering at the way her strange eyes could so clearly and unflinchingly contemplate such power.

"Melanthos. You are a knight of Yves."

He nodded. "My name is Cyan Dag."

"When I first saw you in the mirror, I thought you were

part of a tale. Then I watched you ride beyond the mirror, into Skye. I came here to ask you for help."

"Help."

"Yes. Knights help people. People in distress. Don't they?"

He closed his eyes, slid his hands over them. The smell of roasting salmon blew his way; he was trembling, he realized, with weariness and hunger. But the pain had gone; the rain had put the dragon fire out. He dropped his hands and nodded, wondering what good he had done anyone in or out of distress since he had left Yves. But he promised her, "I will do what I can for you."

"I can help you find her," Melanthos said, taking his arm. "Can you get up? Come closer to the fire."

"You know where that tower is?" he asked, breathless again, with more than effort. Guiding him, she did not immediately answer. The dark tower called him then, a deepening of shadow beyond the sunlit, drowsing air across its doorway. Something he had left in there, it suggested to him. Or left undone. He left the young woman watching him and walked unsteadily into it.

He found the piece of embroidery spread on one of the fallen stones where he had sat peacefully considering staying forever. There was just enough sun left in the world to show him that the image had changed.

Thayne and the gold and the dragon had gone. There was only the beautiful, troubled face of the Lady from Skye, finely stitched in colors so close to true that truth lay in a change of light. He went to the fire, where Melanthos was taking the bones out of the fish.

She held out a broad leaf full of fish to him as he sat. Then she saw what was in his hands. She gave a small hiccup of astonishment.

"It's one of my pictures. So this is where they go."

Cyan sensed worlds within worlds merge around him; he could almost see the dragon tower within the dark tower. In another shift of perception, he thought dazedly, he might see within the dragon tower to the tower where the Lady of Skye waited, without time, without hope.

He said, his voice shaking, "I kept finding these pictures. So you brought me this far. You know all the towers."

She nodded, her eyes, like dark stones or shells, glinting with unpredictable color, and as unreadable. "I know the tower with the woman in it," she said softly. "Eat your fish, and I'll take you there."

TWENTY-ONE

S el pieced her life together.

To the eye, only the irregular shapes of the embroidered patches, and a preponderance of gray or brown in one or another, made them different. Sel's eyes, as she sorted them at the top of the tower, saw the memories in them. There was the patch with Joed in his boat at the dock lifting an oar to her as he cast off into a dazzle of light at sunrise. Newly wed, she could not stop watching him even when he was a dark fleck on the burning sea, and she could not stop smiling. There was the patch full of harbor seals threading brown and gray stitches in and out of the waves. There was the patch where Gentian was born, and the one where Gentian's child was born, and the one where Melanthos caught the wild pony among the tors and rode it down the cobbled streets of Stony Wood. There was the patch with the stone wood in it, long streaks of brown and gray and ivory; she looked at it and saw the mysterious shapes. *Stone or trees?* they asked as always. *Were we once alive?*

Mostly she saw the sea.

It unwound the long banners of its waves across her days, constantly across her thoughts. It showed her its secrets, the oysters making their pearls, the mermaids among its corals, the luminous, calm-eyed ghosts of those who had once walked on land, and who had their hearts stolen by the sea. Each wave spinning to the shore with its tumbling strands of kelp and mermaid's hair called her name as it broke and foamed and hissed across the sand: *Sel . . .* Dark ancient eyes watched her, harbor seals and others, strangers from the deep. *Sel,* they cried in their rough, tumultuous voices. *Come back.*

She plied her thread, piecing past and future together, so that when she was done, one might become the other: she would be done with memory as well. There would only be the sea.

She put her needle down after hours of sewing. Something had disturbed her, she knew vaguely: something in the world. Besides, her eyes were tired and she needed to rest them on the stone trees or the distant tors. She made her way down and found Gentian sitting at the bottom of the steps in the middle of the morning.

She was alone. She had been crying again, not a sweet spring rain this time, but a full-blown cloudburst. Her nose was red; her eyes were red and green; her apron, already flecked with dough and flour, was patched with tears. Sel gazed at her remotely, puzzled, then sat down. She could fit on a step beside Gentian now; winding up and down the tower steps, living in the tower instead of the bakery, had whittled her smaller.

"What is it?" she asked as Gentian's face disappeared into her apron. "Is it the baby?"

Gentian reappeared, powdery now, and a bit sticky. She shook her head, swallowed once or twice as she looked at Sel. "You've changed," she whispered. "I don't know where you've gone."

"Nowhere," Sel said surprisedly, while the sea spilled all around her, tugged at her, drawing back.

"You've been up there since yesterday!"

"Have I? I'm sorry."

"You say that, and you come back into the world for an hour or a day, and then you vanish again when I turn my back!"

"I'm here now." For some reason that did not comfort Gentian, whose eyes filled again, shiny with brine. Sel patted her hand. "Stop fretting," she said, with a ghost of her old abrupt, booming voice that could halt a whale in its sounding. "You're not a child. You've got one now. Leave me to my life."

"I would," Gentian said, "if I thought that's what you wanted."

"What —"

"If I thought you wanted life."

Sel was silent. *Oh yes,* she thought, feeling the tide tangling in her hair, the seaweed winding its long fingers around her, guiding her into a realm beyond the wind. *Oh, yes, life.*

She heaved herself to her feet after a while, forgetting why Gentian was there. "I must get back to my work. I'm nearly finished."

Gentian stared at her, pale now, her eyes so dry she must have already cried every tear. "With what?" she asked huskily.

"My cloak."

"Will you come down to stay when it's finished?"

Sel nodded. "I won't need the tower after that."

Gentian's face crumpled again. Sel dropped a hand on her head as she turned, having forgotten why she came down, and forgetting, as she settled again to her sewing, that she had ever left it.

The mirror caught her attention after a while, flashing as the mirror within the mirror within the other tower reflected a spark of light from something along the road. The woman in the tower paid no attention to the man riding down the road toward the tower. She was bent over her embroidery, her needle wheeling and diving like a gull. She had turned her loom sideways, Sel saw. The finished images fell to her feet now; she held the unworked linen in her lap. She was making an elongated figure of someone. She must have been working on it day and night, Sel thought, for the face hung invisibly past her knees, and she was busy with the hands now.

They were long and slender, jeweled, in motion against a complex background. A road, it seemed, wound through the fingers; trees were leafing out above the jewels. A small square of unworked linen lay like an empty field beneath one hand. Sel studied the image a moment, curiously. Then her eyes filled with tide; the threads in her hands flowed and tossed restlessly, flinging white stitches of spindrift against the gray.

She saw the riders in the mirror as she was shifting pieces around the floor to figure out the bottom line of her making. She envisioned it swimming, then unfolded, emptied, flattened now, stretched out to dry; this would go here, this maybe here . . . An unexpected color in the mirror caught her eye. She looked at it and saw the knight first, with his graceful, somber face, his long hair as black as mussel shell, his eyes like sea reflecting cloud. He rode a gold horse, with mane and tail of ivory. The dark red jewel on the hilt of his sword glinted at his knee.

After a while she took her eyes off him to study the second rider. She shifted forward, blinking, for a closer look. That lanky body, those bare feet, that wood-bark hair, knotted like vine . . . She whispered, astonished, "Melanthos?" She rode one of the wild, piebald horses from the plain, without a piece of harness on it. As Sel watched, Melanthos leaned forward bonelessly, whispered something in the horse's ear, and it slowed its pace.

Sel felt something rill along her bones, sea or fire, she was not sure. "Where did you learn that?" she asked her daughter abruptly. "To talk to horses, and find your way into mirrors?"

Memory surfaced in answer: herself, when she was a scant half-dozen years older than Melanthos was now, and her children with their sea-anemone hair just walking, and something—a word, a finger, a bite—always in their mouths. Then she did things to amuse them and herself while Joed was away. Things she had learned from her own father, and remembered in bits and pieces, when she left that world for the other. She peeled their shadows off the floor and made them dance. She sent small, sparkling clouds of sand whirling across the floor. She made butterfly shells fly, and slipper limpets shuffle, and plucked the bands of harp shells to sound notes as clear and fragile as glass. She made dead fish swim through the air, blowing schools of silvery bubbles. All to make them laugh, and to charm away the sound of the calling waves. They would not remember, she told herself. When Joed came home, and found her sweeping up the sand, they tried to tell him, pointing delightedly at nothing. But the words they knew then belonged to some other country; they had not yet learned the language of Skye. Joed laughed with them, and understood nothing. Sel, wanting to be as human as Joed, wanting to be loved, kept her secrets. She had not understood then, that Joed might leave her stranded, beached, alone in the world while he himself escaped into the sea.

She had put away her magics when the children learned to talk. Now she knew that she might have made use of her powers in small ways; such things were not uncommon in Skye. But that might have changed Joed's eyes when he looked at her. He knew her as he knew his boat, the fish he caught, the direction of the wind, the changing voices of the tide. For him, she walked on human shores; for him she turned her back on whatever he might fear in her. She walked so far away from what he feared that she thought she had lost even the memory of it.

But there it was, a flame of it, in Melanthos, who walked unafraid up a tower's spellbound steps, and led images in a mirror back into life. That's what she was doing with the knight, Sel guessed. No mirror, no tower, could trap Melanthos. She would find her way out of anything, even grief. So Sel told herself, sewing until the moon set. Then she rose, went down into the raw, chill, starless hour before dawn. The mists were blowing over the cliff. But she could see vague, creamy scallops of waves far below, and hear the restless tide booming hollowly as it hit the rocky sides of the harbor. It was on the verge of turning; she knew the sound of its wildness when it was at its peak. In an hour or so it would be running out, and the fishers would follow it in their boats.

She thought of joining Gentian in the bakery, for she would be up by now, setting loaves to rise. But the village seemed very far away, in another world, too far beyond the stone wood for her to reach now. She turned after a while, went back up the tower steps.

She turned up a lamp and unrolled her cloak.

She positioned the difficult portions, where human hands and head and feet would be, and sewed them into place. When that was done, the sun had risen; the mirror had opened its eye to the distant, glowing tors. She cut the two holes then, and hemmed them neatly. Then she measured it to her body, added a patch here and there so it would cover her hands and feet cleanly. That done, she whipped a hem tidily around the entire shape, with long, quick stitches. She hurried, for the morning was going fast, and she did not know when Melanthos might return.

In the mirror, the woman plied her need as intently. Sel glimpsed her now and then, making the line of birds and lilies at the hem of her dress. She ignored her own mirror, which changed its scenes every time Sel looked up, as if to entice the woman's attention from her work. At one moment Sel saw the sea wash through the woman's mirror, a burst of foam that, draining back, revealed starfish, small white barnacles, sea flowers clinging to a rock. Sel, entranced, stared thoughtlessly. The woman never raised her eyes from her work.

Finally the end of the hem reached the beginning of it. Sel snapped her thread and said softly, "There." She stood up, adjusted the patchwork over her shoulders. She held the hand pieces lightly between her fingers, and let the head fall over her face, shaking her own head until the blank eyeholes met her eyes and she could see. She looked into the mirror, which was reflecting the true world at the moment, and saw her newborn face.

A step behind her made her whirl. She tried to toss the selkie face down her back before Melanthos saw it, but it clung there, its threads snagged in her hair. Then she caught her breath and held it, frozen, while the dark-haired knight, his sword drawn, stared at her from the top of the steps, looking as astonished as she felt.

TWENTY-TWO

C yan sheathed his sword. He did not understand exactly what he faced, but he knew that he could not fight magic, and brandishing a blade at eccentricity in Skye seemed the height of discourtesy. The figure standing in an untidy clutter of blankets and pallet, threads, scissors, pieces of linen, with the strange mask dangling over its face and the smoky threads covering its body, seemed to be spellbound.

He said, while it stared at him through the round eyeholes in the mask, "I'm sorry I startled you. I was looking for a woman in a tower."

The spell broke. The figure moved then, pushing the peculiar patched face back to reveal a woman, inarguably in a tower, but no one he recognized. She had a broad, strong-boned, weathered face, nicked and smudged by time, sun, wind, experience. Her hair spilled in long ripples of gray and black and white down her back. Her eyes were dark, remote with memory or sorrow. Light shifted in them, washing color through the dark, like light on a kelp leaf. He blinked, recognizing them.

"Melanthos brought you here instead," she said abruptly, glancing behind him. "Where is she?"

"I asked her to wait below. I thought—" He sighed, running a hand through his hair. "I thought it would be dangerous."

"Why did she bring you here? To see the lady in the mirror?"

His eyes went past her, to the round mirror in its plain wood frame on the window ledge. It was blandly reflecting the view from the opposite window. He took a step toward it, his voice catching. "You see her in there?"

"Sometimes. Very beautiful, she is—"

"Yes."

"With blue eyes and long—"

"Yes. That's the woman I have been searching for."

The woman nodded, unsurprised. "Something of the sea in her past, it looks to me, with her pale skin and wide-set eyes, and her long butterfly-fish nose."

He saw it then, what had puzzled the knights of Gloinmere when they first saw her. "Yes," he breathed, amazed again.

"You've seen her, then."

"Yes. No. I mean, I've seen the woman pretending to be her."

She let her patches fall and gathered them in her hands,

folding and rolling until they were nothing but a shapeless bundle. She tucked it unobtrusively beside a pile of linen. Then she faced Cyan, opened her mouth and closed it, looking a little fishlike herself. He saw the sudden hunger in her eyes. "Tell me about her," she demanded in her deep, husky voice. "What put her in the tower, what will free her—"

He hesitated. Beyond her, colors in the mirror shifted, gave him a glimpse of sky-blue cloth, hands, delicate and slender, rings glinting as long, fine fingers drew a needle into the air. His lips parted; she faded. A distant mist of sheep grazed in the shadow of a tor.

The woman in the tower gazed at him intently, as if the force of her wanting could draw the story out of him. He drew his attention from the sheep finally, and asked, "Who are you?"

"Sel. I'm the baker, in Stony Wood. Melanthos is my daughter."

"I thought so," he said. "She looks like you."

"What is your name?"

"Cyan Dag. I have come from Gloinmere."

"I knew it. I knew you were a knight when I saw you in the mirror."

"You saw me in that?"

"You and Melanthos, riding together. I thought she was taking you to—" She stopped, stepped to the far window, and looked down, cautiously, he thought, as if she did not want to be noticed. "I don't see her. But then she's always appearing and disappearing." She looked at him suddenly, curiously. "Did you come up alone?"

"Yes."

"Most can't get past the magic. But you weren't afraid of it?"

"I didn't notice any," he answered, puzzled.

"Well," she said slowly, studying him, "if you don't notice the small illusions anymore, you're fey yourself, or you've seen behind them."

"I know nothing about magic," he said ruefully, "except that it exists. I could have used a touch of it on my way through Skye."

"You're here. There's magic in that."

"I'm in the wrong tower. Again."

"Well," she said after a moment, "maybe magic is all in the way you look at things." She paused, studying him again. "And in that disk you're wearing. It's like this mirror . . ."

He touched it gently, as if he might disturb the woman within. "It holds more power than I can understand or imagine. It saved my life twice—three times—"

"Who gave it to you?"

He shook his head, remembering. "Someone dying. Someone long dead, more likely, and made of Melanthos's threads. Who gave it to him to give to me, I can only guess."

"Who?"

But he only shook his head again, his mouth taut. "That's part of a different tale, I think."

Color caught his eyes, flicking across the mirror. Birds, he saw, as yellow as buttercups above the sheep. The woman, Sel, stooped to straighten the pallet, pull the rumpled blankets across it.

"You look a little worse for wear. Take your towers off and sit down," she suggested. "I'll mend them for you. Maybe the mirror will show you where to go next."

It seemed as reasonable as anything else he could think of doing. He shrugged the rent surcoat off and handed it to her. He stopped short of sitting, though, reminded then of what he had seen when he first came in, of what she had bundled away into a corner for him to forget.

"What was that you were wearing when I first saw you?"

Her eyes flickered away from him, then back, and were caught in his steady gaze. He glimpsed trouble in them, mystery, sorrow, secret shifts of darkness stirring like shapes beneath tide. *Magic,* he thought, recognizing it in memory: the inhuman mask over the human face, threads that he had seen, in other places, come to life.

"I'll tell you a story," she said finally, "if you tell me one."

He hesitated, then nodded. They were so far from Gloinmere and its dangerous secret in this small, ancient, windswept tower, that Gloinmere itself seemed like a place out of a tale. "But I don't know," he warned her, "how it will end."

"Neither do I," she said.

She left him for a little, to get him something to eat and drink. He watched the mirror intently, until his eyes closed and he sagged down into wool and straw and warm light, and slept. Sel woke him, coming back. Melanthos had gone to the bakery to eat, and then had disappeared again, after promising Gentian, alone with the work, that she would

210 Patricia A. McKillip

come back soon. Soon, a stretchable word, was elongating itself across the afternoon. Sel unpacked wine and cups out of a basket, meat pies and oatcakes, bread shaped like scallop shells, cheese, and smoked fish. She ate nothing, he noticed, just sewed his surcoat back together while he ate hungrily. Soft threads of blue flowed across the mirror again, transfixing him. Sel turned to the mirror; the threads melted away.

"It's like that," Sel said. "But you'll see her clearly. Just wait."

His eyes moved from the mirror to her face. It was too heavy and coarse for ordinary beauty, its earthy coloring too strong. But there was a power, a mystery in it: she knew things, had seen things that he hadn't. That and its strange sorrow drew at him. He could still find, beneath the chips and scars of time, the younger face, with its wide cheekbones and strange, wide-set eyes, its wild hair, its full mouth smiling at the world, that would have made its own beauty out of what it was. Her head was bent now over his surcoat; her long hair spilled over her, cloaking a big, graceful body she seemed to want to keep hidden under one thing or another.

He asked, as she pulled gold thread neatly through two halves of a broken tower, "How did you find this place?"

"It's always been here, at the edge of the stone wood. I came up one day trying to get Melanthos out of here — she'd gotten spellbound by the mirror — and I stayed."

"She embroiders, she said."

"Yes. Pictures of what she sees in the mirror. She never

keeps them. She throws them out of the window and they go—elsewhere. They disappear."

"Not entirely," he said, and showed her the embroidery he had taken from the dark tower in the glade.

She looked down at the pale, troubled, lovely face, the ripples of pale thread that formed her hair, her creased brows. "That's one of hers," she said, nodding. "So you found it—"

"I found others. They seem magical, in some way. They guided me . . . Do you also make them?"

"No. Only Melanthos does."

"What did you make?"

Her eyes flickered to his face, away. She took a stitch or two, rebuilding the tower. Then she dropped her hands in her lap and stared out the window at the restless water that ran beyond the edge of the world, and pulled the sun and the moon and the stars every night down into its secret country. "I was born in—I was born so close to the sea that I fell in love with it when I was young. I knew the names of all the fish and the seals, and I understood the stories they told as they talked among themselves. Then Joed came along, and stood between me and the sea. Then my daughters came, Gentian and Melanthos, and I couldn't see beyond their sweet faces. Then Joed died." She lifted the surcoat, pulled another stitch. "He died in the sea. So, I thought, since I love Joed and I love the sea, that I would go there."

He was silent a moment, struggling with that. "So you made this—" he prompted gently.

"I made my skin. To take me."

He began a question, then answered himself. "The face on it—a seal's face—"

"A selkie skin."

"But would it work?"

Her lips moved, formed a crooked, wry smile that chilled his heart. "In one way or another." She knotted the gold thread and snapped it, then pulled out a length of dark blue and threaded the needle again. He watched her, troubled, not knowing what to say. Finished with answers, she asked him, "Now tell me a story. Tell me how you came from Gloinmere to Skye, looking for a woman in a mirror."

He told a story of a king bewitched by something monstrous and magical, who had disguised herself as the enchanting lady from Skye, and imprisoned the true lady in a tower from which there seemed no escape. Only one other in all the land knew the truth of the matter besides him: the bard who had traveled to Yves in the sorceress's company.

"I couldn't tell the king," Cyan said painfully. "I could not warn him. I had no proof until after the wedding, when she showed me what she was, and mocked my helplessness. So I did what I had to do: I rode out of Gloinmere to Skye."

Sel's hands had fallen still; she watched the mirror through Cyan's tale, as if she saw it unfolding there. "If she can't leave the tower or look at the world without dying, then how will you rescue her?"

"I have no idea. But it must be done. So far I haven't even found the tower. It keeps disguising itself as other towers."

"Maybe you'll see an answer in the mirror."

"I hope so."

Sel picked up her thread again. "What other towers have you found?"

"One with a dragon around it—"

Sel's hands fell again; she looked at him in astonishment. "Melanthos saw that one."

"And a small dark tower in a ring of trees, where the Bard of Skye talked me out of dying."

She gazed at him, her eyes unfathomable. "What kept you from it?"

"She reminded me that I love a woman in Gloinmere . . ."

"Well." She took another stitch. "I love a man in the sea."

"He's dead," he said softly, venturing, he felt, into a place with shifting ground and uncertain paths.

"So?"

"Is there nothing—no one—you love enough to stay for?"

"My daughters are grown; they can do without me. The seals swim into the harbor and call my name. It's the only love I know, now, and there's nothing to keep me from it."

"But what of the grief and confusion you will cause for those who love you?"

"They'll understand." She made a knot, reached for the scissors, and snipped the thread; he felt as if she had cut in two the breath he drew for his next argument. She handed him the surcoat, said, while he pulled it over his head, "Tell me about this woman you love in Gloinmere. What is her name?"

"Cria. Cria Greenwood."

"Pretty. Does she love you?"

"I don't know," he said starkly, heartsick at the thought. "I left her without explaining why, and at the worst time . . . Her father wants her to marry a very wealthy lord she does not love. But she might have done it by now; I wasn't there to give her any reason not to."

She stared at him. "You left her? You just rode away?"

"Yes."

"Without saying good-bye? Without even seeing her? Without—"

"Yes," he said, his face growing white, stiff with worry and fear under her incredulous eyes. "Without."

"Well, then what can you expect?"

"I don't know. You tell me. If I vanish out of the life of someone I love without a word, what can I expect?"

"She'll think you don't love her—she won't understand any longer who it was she thought she loved—" She paused, the blood pushing up like tide into her own face, as he held her eyes. "It's not like that for me," she protested. "It's different. My daughters know I love them—"

"So Cria should know I love her. Even if I never return. She shouldn't think—she shouldn't wonder if every word I ever spoke to her meant something else. She shouldn't relive every moment we had together in her mind, wondering what she had done wrong, what she did that drove me away—"

He saw the tide wash into her eyes; they glittered with underwater colors. "It wouldn't be like that with them. And I need this. I need this more than they need me."

"Yes," he said, and reached out to hold the broad, strong hands that had put his towers back together. "You need. But it can wait. Can't it? The sea will be there all your life on land. Can't you stay human awhile longer, to finish your loving on land? The sea will wait for you. Joed disappeared and left you grieving. You will pass that grief to all those who love you here, if you leave them like this."

"So you might have."

"So I might have," he whispered. "That was the only time in my life that I have been terrified of someone. I might have lost what I love most, running like that out of Gloinmere because of a woman with eyes like a snake and silver scales on her feet, who routed me with a laugh . . ."

She gazed at him, her eyes dry again, deep and mysterious as what sang ceaselessly beyond the tower. He searched for an answer in them, found neither yes nor no to his pleas, only the fathomless, color-flecked darkness. He looked deep, shifting slightly, his hands tightening on her hands, sensing the human pain they shared beneath the mystery. Then he remembered the inhuman figure she had become within the tower, something masked, powerful in its strangeness because he knew no word for it. Something that did not need to be rescued; it would free itself.

Beyond her, the mirror changed.

She felt him start, and turned. "There," she whispered, as blues and birds shaped themselves, and the rippling hair, the familiar face, bent over needlework, the needle just drawn out of the cloth and pulled taut.

Wonder caught his throat; he swallowed dryly, waiting for the needle to fall, her face to shift a little, perhaps lift a moment, so that he could see her more clearly.

Nothing happened. Her hand held the needle in the air; her lowered face, with its pale crescents of lashes, its curved, unsmiling mouth, did not move. He bent toward the mirror, puzzled by the stillness. Then he realized what he was seeing, and the breath went out of him as if he had been struck.

Sel saw it, too, then, coming up on her knees. "She's thread—she's made herself into thread!"

He cried out in despair, "Where is she? Is she dead?"

"No—she did this herself! We watched her sewing herself into cloth. She's made a picture of herself for the mirror to see, something that will sit and embroider forever and never leave."

"But where—"

"She freed herself. She left the tower."

He stared at Sel, his heart hammering. "Then she's dead."

"Is she?"

"If she leaves the tower—"

"But she hasn't left. Look. She's still there."

He closed his eyes against the tears of terror and frustration, opened them again to see the motionless image, the lady in the tower, trapped forever with no way out but death, and no word to speak except in thread.

He heard Sel move then, and the rustlings of her threads; he turned blindly, caught her wrist before he even saw the selkie face. "No—"

"She made that," the selkie said again, insistently. "She made that like I made this, to escape. She made her choice.

Maybe she is dead, but she took her chance and she didn't die trapped."

He did not answer, just tightened his grip. He heard the sea then, waves pounding against the cliff, pouring over it, into it, all around them, though he felt nothing but sunlight. Her breathing, he thought, dazed. She is turning the air she breathes into tide. He felt something slap at him then, like a wall of water trying to drag him away. The second time, it jarred him to the bone. He clung grimly to her wrist, trying to find breath. Wind smelling of brine moaned through the tower; spindrift fell like rain over them. He felt the tower tremble underfoot.

Just before it fell he heard Melanthos's voice. "Mother!" she cried in horror through wind and the wave that smashed through the tower. Cyan, swept off his feet, no longer knew what he held, human flesh and bone, or selkie sea bones and slick, silky skin. He only held fast with all his strength, and went with her into the sea.

TWENTY-THREE

T he selkie, diving in and out of the waves, felt the land drag at her, no matter how fast, how frantically she swam toward the secret kingdoms. Even in the pale, freckled seal's body plunging into the weltering, briny heart within each rising crest, she could not outswim her own name. It clung to her, tugged at her, like land, like love, not letting her go free. Voices cried at her, seal and human, dead and alive. The human voices tore at her selkie skin, caught at threads of her awareness of wind and water and scent, and unraveled them. They refused to let her be. They made their own demands, voices fighting with the wind, with gulls, with the sharp, imperative barking of the seals, trying to tell her something. Finally, fretted by these vague human disturbances, deep within the selkie skin, Sel opened an ear and listened.

She heard Melanthos's voice first, crying somewhere in the waves. Appalled, she stopped her wild surge toward open sea. Then she felt the odd pull on her body. The knight, still clinging to her with both hands now, weighted with sword and boots full of water, was racked like a fish out of water, trying to breathe. Melanthos could swim, but Sel didn't like the sound of her voice: she had never before heard Melanthos afraid. She started to dive, then arched upward again at the bubbles that fled out of the knight when they went under. His fingers loosened.

She felt a moment's panic and became herself suddenly, treading water in the middle of the sea while her skirt wrapped around her like seaweed, and her hair plastered itself over her face. The knight began to slide away from her, go without her, like Joed had, into the country beneath the waves. She caught at something as he drifted down: the silver chain around his neck. Floating on her back like an otter, she dragged him up and into her arms, turning him to face the sky.

Then she bellowed for the harbor seals.

They came at the names she called, the old, secret names that leaped out of memory straight to her tongue. They flung themselves off stones, streaked from under the docks, cutting through the water beneath the breaking waves, invisible until they came close and she saw their swift, streaming bodies beneath the green, surfacing into light. She spoke to them, remembering words now. They nudged the knight away from her, rolling him over, balancing him among their bodies. He did not move. His face, pale and still as shell, dipping and rising above the restless swells, twisted her heart. But she had no more time for him; she had to see to Melanthos.

How she got to her daughter, she was not sure. A wish brought her, it seemed, or the sheer edge of fear that cut through time and the bewildering tangle of wind and tide. She was just there, suddenly, beside Melanthos, who was at least barefoot in the water, and who had shed her clothes down to her shift. She was beating the sea with her fists, as if it were a locked door, and screaming Sel's name. Her wet hair blinded her; when Sel caught her arm, she swung a mole's face at Sel and gulped in a passing wave. While she choked, more seals caught up with them. Sel draped her over one and sent her, still coughing, toward land.

She saw then what she had done to the tower. It had broken like a rotten tooth, sending a small avalanche of stone and grass and raw earth down the cliff to scatter into the waves. Sel stared at it, still moving to the break of waves like something half-sea, half-human, a mermaid without a tail, a seal with hands and feet and a woman's face.

She dove deep into the water, swam until she could hear, beneath the rushing, soughing waves, the faint, wild singing in her blood. Memories came more quickly now, things fallen deep into her mind, that had been fastened to coral or stone, and so overgrown with moss and weed they had been unrecognizable for years. The tower falling into the sea had jarred them loose.

She could do that, destroy something that old and magical with the force of her longing. She could become seal; she could become sea, or something so like it that sailors or fishers would see her only as a glint of light beneath the

water. A realm existed within those glints, those half-caught
glimpses that humans fashioned into tales or songs. Her
father had taught her some of the songs. No doubt he
wished he hadn't, when she left him. But he had taught her
to be curious, and so she was, drifting in the dusk among
the seals, listening. And so she heard Joed, whistling as he
spread his nets on the sand to check the knots and pick the
barnacles off. She recognized the song.

A wave spun her this way and that, dragged her on her
hands and knees along the sand. She rose out of the waves,
streaming water, as unsteady on her feet as if she had yet
to learn to walk in the world. Joed was not there to greet
her with that look, startled and enchanted, as if some sea
tale had taken shape under his nose. That was many years
ago, and she had learned to walk in shoes, and cry true
tears, and to forget. As she waded ashore, seals passed her,
still carrying the knight on the raft they had made of their
backs. Lurching to dry sand, flippers struggling, they
parted company at the knot of staring humans. The knight
hit the sand hard, and came to life abruptly, retching brine.
Sel heard the long, harsh draw of his breath as she stepped
out of the tide.

They all had Joed's look in their eyes: stunned, transfixed. Gentian was there, dropping pearls out of her eyes,
clinging to the baby like a spar. Anyon looked as if he had
tumbled down the cliff after the tower, his clothes and skin
grimy and torn. He was holding Melanthos, who was weeping endlessly, soundlessly, overflowing with water, but
otherwise motionless. Someone else had come down: a
stranger, who seemed to know the knight. She stood beside

him as he learned how to breathe again, but her eyes were on Sel.

Sel faced them, twisting water out of her hair and skirt, as mute as she had been when she walked out of the water to Joed. A wave, washing around her ankles, carried a shadow in, left it lying on the sand. She picked it up: her selkie skin, sodden and torn, but whole. She shook it out, held it up to the sky, looked at the blue through its eyes.

Then she sighed. "I couldn't leave you," she said. She went to put her arms around Gentian first, because Melanthos was stronger. Gentian burst into noisy sobs; the baby wailed, startling the knight, who began coughing again.

Melanthos spoke first through the din, her voice high and unsteady. "Where exactly were you going?"

"Back home."

"Home." She took a step out of Anyon's arms, her face as white as spume. "Where?"

"In the sea. Where do you think you got your eyes?"

Melanthos swallowed. "I don't — I didn't —" She was still streaming tears, as if she were wringing herself dry. She put her hands over her mouth and whispered, "What is it like?"

"Ancient," Sel said slowly, remembering. "Strange, to human eyes, like the stone wood. Beautiful in ways you wouldn't recognize at first. Like this world." She drew a breath of its fishy, salty, mist-dank air, and was surprised how good it tasted, like Brenna's bitter ale, or Joed's skin.

"You came out of the sea?" Anyon said, struggling. "You were born there? Like a fish?" He touched Melanthos tentatively. "What about her? And Gentian?"

"Half-fish." She went to Melanthos then, took her daughter's face between her hands, and brushed at the tears with her thumbs. "Don't cry. It unnerves me. I'm back now."

"I unnerve you," Melanthos said, sniffing thickly. "I unnerve you." Her voice rose suddenly. "You turned into a seal! And look what you did to the tower! You were running away from us to die, or to live at the bottom of the sea or something—what exactly are you?"

Sel opened her mouth, closed it. They watched her, even the baby, their eyes wanting answers. The knight, quieter now, the color coming back into his face, had no suggestions; he looked as curious. "I don't know," Sel answered finally, helplessly. "I don't know what I am in this world."

The stranger's eyes drew at her suddenly, amber and full of light. She was quite tall, with long, heavy black hair, that fell straight as anchor line past her knees. Her face was brown as earth, young-old, still beautiful, but beginning to predict its future. She smiled as Sel looked at her, and Sel felt oddly as if the wind had glanced at her, or the grass. As if she had been recognized by something wild.

"My name is Sidera," the woman said before Sel could ask. She laid a long, graceful hand, ringed with a silver band, on the knight's shoulder. "I have been looking for this man. I didn't expect to find him carried out of the sea and dropped at my feet by seals."

"I never meant for him to come with me," Sel said ruefully. "But he wouldn't let go of me and I forgot about him when I changed. I nearly drowned him. Are you all right now?" she asked Cyan. "Other than soaked and shivering, like Melanthos?"

He gazed at her, still stunned. "I came to find a woman in a tower," he said, his voice worn ragged with brine. "I had no idea she would tear the tower apart and rescue both herself and me."

"I brought you to the wrong tower," Melanthos said abruptly. She had ducked into Anyon's dry hold, her wet shift clinging like skin, the goose bumps rising on her arms. She had, to Sel's relief, finally stopped crying. "I was hoping you could say something to help my mother, do something. I thought that maybe she would talk to you, if you made it past the magic. You didn't seem afraid of anything. Even dragons."

"There's still a woman in a tower," he said slowly. "In my mind if nowhere else. I must find out what happened to her. If she is alive or dead, or still trapped. There are others who also need to know."

Sel nodded. "Then you must." She pushed the wet hair back from her face, and felt the sand caught in her clothes. "But not at this moment," she added, feeling a little weary herself, suddenly. "You could use a rest, and a splash of something hot. Anyon, he left his horse next to the tower — it's probably halfway across the plain by now. Could you —"

"I'll call him," Sidera said, and frowned a moment at the sand, so still that Sel thought she had become invisible and left an image on the air. She raised her head, and all their watching faces lifted at a whinny above their heads. The gelding peered over the cliff at them. Sidera smiled.

"We've met," she explained, or thought she did.

"It's the way I called the seals!" Sel exclaimed. "You feel them in your mind. You think their thoughts."

Melanthos gazed openmouthed from Sidera to Sel and back again. "Teach me," she begged. "Can you?"

But it was Sel the woman looked at when she answered. "I will."

Sel took them all home with her, sent Anyon to Brenna's for ale, and Gentian to her own home for more blankets and some of Rawl's clothes for the knight. She went to the bakery for what was left of the loaves and tarts, disentangling herself from a crowd at the door wondering if she and Melanthos had fallen down the cliff along with the tower, and that was why no one was there to sell them bread.

"It was old," she said absently of the tower. "It just fell apart. No one was hurt."

Of the strangers glimpsed in the streets of Stony Wood, she said only, "A knight of Yves, passing through. And his friend." Beyond that she would not say, not even when someone asked why her hair and boots were damp, and why the knight left a trail of water on the cobblestones, and where Melanthos had left the rest of her clothes. But her own children were not dissuaded. Even Gentian had left Rawl's supper to his imagination and stayed with Sel. Her mermaid's eyes had lost their torment; now they looked clearly at Sel, wanting to know. Melanthos, bundled in blankets and dropping crumbs of almond tart among them, watched Sel like a hawk watching a hare. The knight, dressed in fisher's clothes and drinking ale, seemed still remote, a stranger, his own eyes haunted by his search, and by the face still visible beneath the scarred and blackened disk that hung on Rawl's old shirt. Sidera wandered among them silently, sometimes watching Cyan, sometimes Sel; she waited, too. Even Anyon, who fluttered within walls like a firefly in a jar, sat beside Melanthos patiently, his eyes on Sel. Sel stopped finally, stopped pacing, patting the baby, straightening clothes drying beside the fire, checking the tide line in cups of ale. It was like being caught in a web, she thought, that their silence, their watching eyes had made; they left her, finally, with no room to move.

She sat down on a stool beside the fire, looked at her daughters.

"Once," she said, awkward with the tale, for she had never told it before, "I lived in the country beneath the sea. I don't know what I would have been to you if you had seen me then. Maybe there are no human words for it. I have to put human words on all my memories; that changes them. I had the best of all worlds, so I thought. I could swim with the whales, pick gold off the bottom of the sea, and push my face through the roof of that world to find the wind and sun, and watch the fishers and the folk who lived in air. Even in my world, with all the things that you might call magic, my father had great, strange powers. He could sing a sailing ship to sleep in a gale, slip it safely past the wind. He could build a palace out of a single pearl. He could heal a fish torn by the hook and tossed away, with the touch of his hand. He taught me things. I don't know how much I can remember now, or if I can still do them, or what they might be worth to anyone in this world . . .

"And so I lived between sea and land, not knowing that I wanted anything at all, until one day I heard your father whistle a song my father knew. I looked at him, all brown and hard and smooth, like a piece of driftwood, his eyes like a seal's eyes, curious and kind, and I took shape out of whatever I had been at that moment, and walked out of the sea.

"I never went back until today." She lifted a hand, dropped it lightly, struggling a little to explain. "I don't know if I went back out of sorrow and loneliness. Or because all that I had forgotten drove me to find it again. I didn't know, until today, that I hadn't left that part of myself in the sea; I had brought it to land with me, and forgotten it was there . . ."

"What?" Gentian whispered. "What did you forget? What have you remembered?"

"I don't know yet," Sel answered simply. "And after what I did to the tower, I'm almost afraid of knowing."

Sidera raised her head, shook her long, gleaming hair back, a little like a seal, Sel thought, looking out from a wave. But her eyes were not seal's eyes, nor human, nor anything that Sel had ever been seen by. The moon, she thought, feeling her heartbeat under that bright, clear, unfathomable gaze. I have been seen by the moon.

"I will help you remember," she said to Sel. "We need you."

TWENTY-FOUR

Thayne Ysse rode the dragon to the North Islands.

He watched the world below him out of dragon's eyes. Gold burned in random fires through the darkness. He could smell it, a dry, metallic sweetness, a whiff of honey mixed with the lingering traces of humans. Death, they smelled like, no matter what perfumes they wore, but that itself was not unpleasant to him. The land seemed a great, dark living body, with veins of liquid silver running across it, that breathed and moved and dreamed. It was a sleeping dragon on a vast plain of water. Thayne, tracking scents of gold through the scents of trees, smoke, the thick tangled odors of animals and humans, did not smell the sea until he reached it.

He remembered his human face then. He could feel himself move, separate his bone from dragon bone. His

230 Patricia A. McKillip

thoughts detached themselves from smells, began to form
words again. He knew his name; its letters flamed within
the dragon's brain. He saw the seam of land and sea where
the waves rolled and broke in a creamy lace of foam
across the sand. Yves sank beneath the waves; Ysse rose
out of them, the crescent moon of land among scattered
stars of other islands. He felt the dragon's question in his
mind, a sudden, wordless faltering over the unfamiliar
scent, the end of land and gold.

Thayne guided it far over the empty sea, away from
farms and animals. Only a fisher in a coracle, too busy with
his nets to look up, might have seen the dragon fly toward
the northernmost horn of Ysse. There Thayne guided it
down onto a stretch of sand walled by barren, windswept
cliff. The dragon breathed a weary lick of flame at the sea,
in protest of the wet and cold. One drooping eye regarded
Thayne bleakly out of the thinnest of slits. Thayne walked
to the edge of the tide. The fishers rarely came close to this
wild, rocky shore; the nearest boat was far south. He felt a
brief, warm, ashy sigh of dragon on his back and turned.
The gold covering its vast body, heaps of coin, jumbled cups
and crowns and gold-hilted swords, bones wearing rings,
armbands, pieces of armor, clung to the dragon as if held
there by the force of its desire. Thayne swallowed something metallic, sharp, bittersweet in the back of his throat:
the taste of ash, dragon fire, gold.

He picked a coin off the dragon's back to show his
father and said, "Stay quiet. No one should disturb you. I'll
come back for you soon."

On the top of the cliff, he glanced back. The dragon

had curled tightly around itself, tucking head and claws and tail close into its body. Its visible eye had closed. Thayne began the long journey to the southern horn of Ysse.

He reached the ancient, crumbling castle at night, running a boat he had borrowed in on the tide. He pulled it to shore and stood silently a moment. He could feel the dragon sleeping, a massive, shadowy power in the dark, like a dreaming mountain full of caverns, secret underground rivers, deeper veins of molten fire rooted in the heart of the world. Then he heard soft, uneven steps, the rhythmic beat of something hard against the ground between the steps. A figure appeared in the open gate, swung the crutch for another step, and stopped dead.

Craiche whispered, "I can see your eyes in the dark."

Thayne went to him, held him tightly, wordlessly. He had journeyed so far from the man who had left Ysse with the dragon only a picture in his mind, that he thought not even Craiche would recognize him. He said, "I brought the dragon."

Craiche shook his head a little, letting the crutch fall to cling to Thayne with both hands. "You are the dragon." His voice shook. "Did it—was it hard?"

"It seemed impossible." He loosed his brother, picked up the crutch. "I had to fight the battle between Yves and the North Islands all over again."

"Did you win?"

"Yes." He dropped his arm loosely over Craiche's shoulders as he balanced himself again. "There was a knight of Gloinmere who came to Skye at the same time, looking for that tower. We fought—"

"Did you kill him?"

"Nearly." He was silent a moment, remembering the eerie, desperate battle among the bones and gold. "But he told me something only he could have known to be true. That he was the man who carried you down the hill in the dark when you were wounded."

He heard Craiche's breath catch; the crutch struck earth and stopped again. "Who was he?" All the pain of the memory that Craiche kept so well hidden behind his smile surfaced suddenly, knotted in the words.

"Cyan Dag. The man who was busy, at the same time, saving Regis Aurum's life."

"Why did he—" Craiche stopped, swallowing bitterness. "Why did he bother with me?"

"I don't know. I didn't have time to ask him that. Maybe, if he survives the war we will bring to Gloinmere, you can ask him yourself."

Craiche was silent, moving again across the courtyard. No one else was awake; even the tower their father loved was dark. As they passed it, Thayne felt something other than dragon thought flare like an ember in his mind: an emanation of power within the ancient books.

He breathed, surprised. "So he is right about that, too."

"What?"

"Our father. He never bothered with books when he could think. Now he can smell the power in them. How is he? Did he realize I was gone?"

"Well." Craiche's voice eased; Thayne felt his smile flash before he saw it, in the torchlight at the steps. "He got it through his head well enough that Thayne had gone to get the dragon. But he couldn't connect Thayne the dragon hunter with the man who led him out of the tower at night and brought him supper. He kept wondering where that man was. So yes, he missed you."

"One of me," Thayne said wryly.

"Where did you put the dragon?"

"On the north horn of the island."

"And the gold? Did you bring that, too?"

"Gold enough for us all to fill our plates with it and eat it for a year. Gold—you won't believe what you see."

"We should hide the gold. Ships out of Yves sail among the islands sometimes."

"No one," Thayne said grimly, "would touch that dragon's gold and live."

"Take me to see it."

"I will. In the morning."

When they woke in the morning, the dragon was in the yard.

Thayne was pulled out of a dream of some dark, bleak, dangerous place in which someone he could not see had just said something profound and vital that he did not quite understand. He reached for what he thought was his sword and stumbled out of bed before he opened his eyes. He bumped into his father in the hallway, barefoot and brandishing a sword.

"We are besieged," he shouted at Thayne. The scantily bearded young man who milked and herded the cows ducked nervously behind a door. Thayne heard the shouts from the yard, the impatient bawling of cows.

"There's a great thing in the yard, my lord," the cow

man said to Thayne. "I couldn't get to the barns."

"Arm the house!"

"It's your dragon," Thayne told his father. "The one you sent me to get in Skye." His father stared at him.

"Bowan? You're back home."

"I came back last night. You were sleeping."

"Your eyes are strange. Are you dead?"

Thayne rubbed them, swallowing a bitter laugh. "If I were Bowan, I'd be dead. I'm Thayne. Your son."

"Oh."

He dropped a hand on his father's shoulder, feeling the cold that had seeped beneath the dragon's scales and disturbed its sleep. "Come and see it."

"Bowan."

"Thayne."

"Why are you carrying that?"

Thayne felt it, then: the smooth grain in his hand instead of metal, the lighter weight of aged wood. Some sort of staff, he held, with a knotted bole on one end worn smooth as a skull. "Must be something of Craiche's," he guessed, bemused. "I thought I had picked up my sword."

"It looked at me," his father said, gazing mesmerized at the bole. The shouts from the yard grew in force, as the household awoke; dogs had begun to howl. Thayne heard Craiche's voice in the din, trying to quiet the dogs.

An ember flared in the dragon's brain: impatience, annoyance at the noise, the cold, the chaos of smells, the unpredictable world so unlike the stillness of the burning waste. Thayne moved quickly, still carrying the staff like a shepherd, the anxious members of the household flocking in his wake, as he went out.

The dragon had coiled itself into the yard like a sea creature in its shell, its bulky body spilling from house to barns, from wall to wall. Its head was raised; it peered curiously into the tower where Thayne's father played with magic. The gates were completely blocked by a wing. Dogs on the steps barked furiously at its other wing, then slunk back, whining at the smell of sulfur. The treasure on the dragon's back, clinging like a crust of sea life on a rock, hurt the eyes like the rising sun.

Craiche was standing among the gold, his face butter yellow in its glow. He lifted a golden helm, tried to fit it over his head, then shook the skull out of it, laughing. He dropped it into place. An etched and hammered mask of gold swung toward Thayne, its eyes dark slits in the gold, its mouth a thin, grim line.

Thayne wondered suddenly what it would take to persuade Craiche to stay home from this war. He did not broach the subject then, just said quickly, "Craiche, get down. It's a wild, dangerous thing and it could crush you if you fall."

"It's beautiful," Craiche said breathlessly from within the helm. "It will do what you tell it. Let me fly it with you. You have to move it out of the yard. And you can't expect me to march all the way to Gloinmere."

A wing shifted, perhaps harried by a dog, perhaps to unfurl for flight. Thayne gripped the staff in his hand tightly. "Craiche," he began, then did not bother. The dragon's neck sprawled over most of the stone steps in front of the doors. Thayne walked onto it easily, down its broad, flattened back. The dragon, one eye still studying the disorderly contents of the room at the top of the tower, rolled its other eye down at Thayne. It snorted very gently; the acrid smell of damp ash blew through the yard.

Thayne, standing over its heartbeat, listened to it, until the massive, measured pound and wash of blood seemed to flow through him. His thoughts seemed enclosed by a glittering patchwork of scales. He felt again the intimation of secrets, enchantments within the room, and understood what treasure had lured the dragon to this unlikely tower.

He looked up at it, filled suddenly with the dragon's longing. "Yes," he said to himself and the dragon. *Yes*, said bone and marrow, filling with the word, in wordless dragon's language. *Yes*, said the staff in his hand.

It flared suddenly; light spat out of the bole above his hand. It narrowly missed Craiche, who lost his balance anyway with surprise, and sat down abruptly on a pile of gold. Thayne heard their father shout his name. Craiche took the helm off his head and stared at Thayne.

"What is that?"

"I have no idea," Thayne said tightly, wading through coin and armor to help his brother. "I thought it was yours. Are you hurt?"

Craiche shook his head, pulled himself up with Thayne's hand. He bent to peer into the bole, making Thayne's skin constrict with horror.

"Craiche —"

He straightened. "There's something in there. A jewel or an eye."

Thayne turned the eye toward the open gates. "Our father must have brought it down from the tower." He added dryly, picking a sheathed sword out of the pile for Craiche to use as a crutch, "It took that for him to remember my name."

He moved the dragon outside the yard, where it lay along the wall, its wings jutting upward like great, shining sails, its neck looped backward along its side, its heart pushed as close as it could get to the tower.

Then he sent messengers to all the North Islands, along with a single gold coin bearing Regis Aurum's face.

By day he plotted a war, sending gold among the islanders to feed themselves, repair their houses and boats and barns for the families they would leave behind, buy arms and horses from mainland traders who asked no questions and left them alone, once they got a glimpse of the watchful dragon on Ysse. Thayne had moved the gold into the tower. At night he could wade through it and climb the stairs without a torch, it glowed so brightly; it never seemed to sleep. At night, he learned.

His father stayed with him, watched him pore over ancient books, inhaling words like air, feeling them become part of him, his bones adjusting to give them room, his heart taking a new shape. Occasionally, he struggled with the magic in the staff, trying to control its light. Sometimes it slept, deep in the dark, glittering faceted eye in the bole, no matter what Thayne did to coax it awake. Sometimes it spat its pale, dangerous fires for no apparent reason, and an ancient tome would flutter into ash, or a rock in the tower walls would crack. Once it shattered the jar his father had said was full of pearls. The smell blinded Thayne with tears, sent him stumbling with his father down the stairs. Outside, the dragon loosed a sudden snort; the stones around them trembled. For once, his father remembered his name.

"Is that the best you can do, Thayne?" he asked acridly. "Blast Regis Aurum out of Gloinmere with a stench?"

"It would work," Thayne said inarguably, sagging against a gatepost and wiping his eyes. "They must have been very old pearls."

When he slept, he was plagued with dreams.

Women came to him from all across the islands. They walked silently through the gates, sometimes one or two, sometimes endless numbers of them, crowding around him where he stood on the steps, watching them. Some were young and lovely, dressed in worn wool and linen, their hands and bare feet already grown broad and callused with work. Others had lined, weary faces, and children clinging to their knees. Others could barely walk; they looked at him out of eyes like cloud. No one ever spoke. They simply stood in the yard, gazing at him, until he jerked himself awake, and stared thoughtlessly into the dark. Awake, he understood their sorrow. But he could not let it touch him; even in his dreams, he refused to speak.

Finally, in his dreams, one woman spoke.

She sat in the tower with him, among the gold, holding the staff he had found. Her hair was white as bone, her eyes as black as emptiness. She turned the eye on the bole at him. He felt its light pour into him, trying to change the shape of his heart, which, he knew in the dream, was a helm made of gold, with two dark slits for eyes and a thin slash for a mouth. As relentlessly as the light melted the gold mask, he reshaped it with his own powers, showed her the expressionless, merciless face of war.

She said, "Then I will take Craiche."

"No," he shouted, and woke himself. It was barely light. A servant on his way to the kitchen opened the door to look at Thayne questioningly. Thayne shook his head, rubbing his face. He dropped his hands, felt the fear boring into him.

"Craiche," he whispered. "I need you to stay here with our father. Craiche, I am tying you to this chair for a good reason; when they untie you, don't try to follow us, the dragon will be gone. Craiche —"

Craiche eased the door open with his crutch then, startling Thayne. "I heard you shout."

"Craiche, you are not going with us to Gloinmere. You will stay here with our father —"

"Don't be absurd." He backed out again, yawning, closing the door as he went. "You're dreaming. I'm riding the dragon with you."

"Who are you?" Thayne demanded helplessly, of the harper from Skye. "Who are you?"

But though she haunted his dreams, she did not answer.

TWENTY-FIVE

Cyan Dag, having gone through fire and water for the lady in the tower, found himself at a loss. No embroideries fluttered across the village cobblestones to point his way. No crones with eyes as black as a raven's shadow appeared unexpectedly to tell him where to go to find the tower with or without the lady in it. As each day passed in Stony Wood, he felt himself regain strength, but with it came a gnawing worry, a restlessness that impelled him to move without knowing where to go. The image of the dragon laden with gold, burning like the sun through the rain-lashed sky, haunted him. It would find its way to Gloinmere, he had no doubt; he had to return to warn Regis Aurum. But he could not leave Skye without knowing if the woman the king thought he had married was alive or dead. He had seen the dead turn into thread before; that he had been too distracted by dragons and selkies to rescue Gwynne of Skye from such a fate filled him with horror. He held her delicate, troubled face in his hands, still visible behind the clouds and jagged lightning bolts that warped the disk. He gazed at her intently, thoughtlessly, as if she might become aware of him, turn her eyes to him, and tell him what to do. Others had answers for him; she remained silent.

Find her, the bard had told him. *Free her.*

You cannot free her, the king's snake-eyed wife had told him. *You will only kill her.*

She freed herself, Sel had said.

She was alive or dead, free or thread, his harrowed thoughts told him; he had to find her to know which.

Or would he find her only to cause her death?

He wanted to question Sidera, but like her sister, she seemed to vanish when he tried to find her. She was with Sel in the stone wood, Gentian told him, or with Sel among the tors, or here, just a moment ago; she would be back soon. Even Melanthos had disappeared, seduced by the magic leafing and branching out of Sel. It seemed a private matter between Sel and Sidera, and not, Cyan remembered warily, without danger. But, desperate, he found his way into it one morning, walking along the cliff to the broken tower, where he discovered Melanthos and Anyon sitting on the ring of stones, watching Sel make trees.

Sidera was with her, standing between tower and wood, as still and dark as if she had been rooted with the stone trees. But her eyes flicked at Cyan and she smiled, turning human again for a moment. Melanthos, leaning against

Anyon and looking oblivious of him, patted the tower stones beside her for the knight to sit.

"She's making a riddle in the wood," Melanthos said softly to him as Sel wandered through the stone wood, pulling new stones, or old trees, out of the earth, so like the real wood that Cyan could not see the difference.

"They even cast a shadow," he murmured, astonished. Melanthos nodded, her eyes sparking with the muted fires within the stones.

"I can see through them," she said. "I can tell the difference between stone and air. But I don't know how she makes something out of nothing."

Having broadened the small wood, spilled it beyond its familiar boundaries, Sel followed Sidera's instructions, and pulled a cloud out of the sky. It fell like sea mist over the wood; sky and sea and village vanished behind it. So it seemed to Cyan. Melanthos, pushing closer to Anyon in the sudden chill, saw it from a different perspective.

"She's hiding something from the villagers."

"What is it?" Anyon asked.

"I don't know yet. Watch."

Cyan, watching, saw Sel turn herself into stone, her eyes flat, dark, reflecting nothing. She spoke. The word split the air with fire as abrupt and pure as lightning. The mist grew bright, pearly around them. Cyan, gripping the tower stones, felt for an instant that he was back in the dragon's tower, with Thayne Ysse pulling fire out of gold. Anyon had disappeared. Cyan, blinking away the brilliant aftermath from his eyes, saw him pulling himself out of the tower ring, where he had fallen in surprise. Almost before he got himself settled again, Sel spoke another word. This one kindled the cloud around them gold, and toppled a stone out of the ring. Cyan felt the force of it in his bones. He stared, amazed, at the woman who had, scant days before, stood mute before him in the tower, cloaked and masked by threads, trying to find a way out of her life. Now she was a stranger with wild crackling hair, speaking trees and stone and fire into existence. Even Melanthos was speechless, one hand gripping Anyon's shoulder as she watched the stranger, her face turning the luminous hues of the clouds.

Finally Sidera spoke, and the storm ended. The stranger turned into Sel again, weaving her hair back into its braid, and mildly expressing a misgiving.

"It's more magic than I'd ever need for Stony Wood. Or all of Skye, for that matter."

Sidera only gave Sel a fox's unfathomable glance, and said, "You never know what you might need to know."

"For instance," Anyon said, with unexpected enthusiasm, "if the boats are lost at sea. You could light their way."

"More likely set them on fire," Sel suggested wryly, bending to pick her hair tie out of the grass, and startling Cyan with her smile. It might have been a mermaid's smile, something that barely surfaced on her face, yet shone everywhere out of her, as if her bones were alight. Around them, the strange mist was dispersing, revealing, beyond the mystifying wood, a cluster of astonished villagers trying to see through Sel's illusions.

She looked a question at Sidera, who said calmly, "You know them. Do what's best."

The maze of stony stumps around the true wood vanished. The villagers, mothers with children, tavernkeepers, old fishers with hands lumpy and crippled with age, moved cautiously toward Sel. A tall, massive, fair-haired woman, clutching a child to her thigh, her eyes as round as kelp bladders, said uncertainly, "Sel?"

It was, Cyan thought, a fair question.

"It's me, Brenna," Sel said. The smile still hovered within the bones of her face, just beyond sight. "I'm learning some magic."

They were dumbfounded again. One of the old fishers shifted, planting his feet as if the ground rocked like a boat beneath him. He asked, "What for?"

"Because it's there. Because it might come in handy. You never know."

"You never do," Brenna echoed faintly. "But your own private lightning storm?"

"Well. Not all of it is practical. But suppose the ovens go cold around my bread? Suppose one of your children falls sick, and you need more warmth than your fire can give? Or your animals in the barn need a less dangerous fire? Besides, it's not all fire. I can knot up a torn net in a breath, untangle a tide under a full moon, tease a wind out of a tantrum. I could always do those things. I just forgot."

"That high tide some years back," a man with a leather needle stuck in his shirtsleeve said suddenly. "Raging under the full moon so that the boats were trapped after dark beyond the harbor. The waves began to quiet for no good reason, each one sliding in slower than the last, and breaking with no more force than wash water tossed out the door so that the boats could come home — was that you?"

Sel nodded, a splinter of light flickering gold in one eye, as at a memory. "I wasn't married very long then," she said softly. "I wanted Joed safely into harbor, out of his boat and into my arms. It was after that, with Melanthos and Gentian growing up, I began to forget things. Now I'm remembering them again."

They gazed at her, their eyes no longer apprehensive, Cyan saw, but full of wonder, and calculating their good fortune at having a sea witch wash ashore into their lives.

"I've missed your visits to the tavern," Brenna said. "I wondered what you were doing instead."

"I was trying to remember. Ale helps, for that, but it doesn't go deep enough."

"But what about the bakery?"

"What about it?" Sel answered, surprised. "I'm not going anywhere. Except maybe to your tavern. I could use a splash of ale."

Melanthos slid off the tower stones, went to Sel's side; Anyon followed. Sel put an arm around her daughter's shoulders, threw a look like a plumb line into her daughter's eyes. Melanthos smiled. Cyan looked beyond them then, for Sidera. But only a dark, glittering stump stood where she had been, asking its constant questions: Stone or tree? Once alive or never? He sighed noiselessly, and followed the villagers back to Stony Wood.

The next morning, after he had dressed himself again in his towers, packed the loaves and the salted fish that Gentian had given him, slung pack and sword onto the gelding's saddle, and prepared to mount, he found Sidera beside him.

"Where are you going?" she asked.

He pulled himself into the saddle, looked down at her. "I have no idea. Somewhere in Skye."

She only nodded, as enigmatic, he thought, as one of the stumps in the stone wood. She smiled up at him, stroking the gelding's head. "I will see you in Gloinmere," she said.

"I thought you disliked courts."

"I will see you there," she repeated, as if she was giving him the answer to some riddle he hadn't thought to ask. She stepped back, her eyes as lucent and unreadable as polished shell. "Be careful," she added as he turned the gelding. "This is the most difficult tower."

He twisted in the saddle to stare at her. "More difficult than what?" he demanded. "Than dying?"

"It's the most difficult to see. Look at it with your heart, Cyan Dag, and you will survive it."

"What about the lady?" he asked desperately. "Will she survive?"

But the gelding was already moving, leaving Sidera behind, looking, with her face and hands hidden within her hair, like a peculiar smudge of shadow in the morning light.

He rode south along the coast, away from the three hills, the stone wood, all the towers he had found. When the road he followed wandered inland, around a steep, impassable mountain looming over the sea, he went with it. The road met a river, meandered along it through orchards whose trees had lost the young fiery green of spring; hard

buds of apple and pear clustered among the summer leaves.
The water curved westward again at a leisurely pace. The
valley broadened around it; fields of barley and rye and
shallots scented the tranquil air. People passed him on the
road: farmers with their harrows and carts, merchants,
young, laughing riders with hawks on their fists or bows
and arrows trailing ribbons from their shafts. In the distance, where the river flowed toward the ocean, he saw
what seemed the walls and houses and sea-misted towers
of a small city. Perhaps the folk within it could help him,
he thought: suggest a direction, remember an odd rumor.
The river had grown broad and slow; trees shadowed him,
lining both sides of the road. He smelled a sweet, unexpected scent blown across the water and glanced toward it.
On a small island in the middle of the river, white lilies
massed along a stone wall half-hidden by trees and vine and
the warm, dusty cloak of shadow and summer light. It
seemed a small fortress. Separating shadow and leaf and
light as he rode beside it, he discovered the dark, worn
crenellation of four towers joining four walls. Sunlight
glancing off the slow river trembled on the stones, blurring
them slightly, as if he were seeing it underwater. Most of
the windows had been blinded by a green web of ivy. Those
he could still see were opaque; nothing stirred within them.

Still he studied it idly, wondering who had built it and
abandoned it, and why. As the gelding's steady, even pace
took him past the foremost tower, he saw something flicker
in a high window. A shard of light splintering from something very bright caught in his eyes. He blinked away the

blur of fire-white light, and saw a face within the silver disk on the window ledge.

He reined sharply. The sounds of murmuring water, the distant voices from the fields, the rooks he had disturbed in the trees behind him, all spun to a fine clarity in that moment. He felt his heart pound. He looked up again, swallowing dryly. For a moment he saw only the ornate mirror on the window ledge, the tower's eye gazing at what passed down the road.

And then the mirror fell, shattering against a cornerstone into a rain of glittering fragments at a careless sweep of sleeve, as a woman leaned over the ledge to look down at Cyan.

He felt his heart crack like the mirror before he shouted, "No!"

He wrenched at the reins, sent the startled gelding splashing into the river, where it had to swim a pace or two through a tangle of water lilies. Cyan, drenched and trailing lilies, waded onto the island beside the gelding. He searched frantically for a door, tearing great swaths of ivy from the walls, sending a cloud of small gold birds fleeing across the water. He uncovered a rotting portcullis closed across an archway near the tower. Ivy trailed across the far arch, hiding the inner yard. He slammed into it. The old wood groaned under him, rattled like bones. Something flying over his head startled him before he tore through the portcullis. It changed shape as it descended, elongating, wrinkling, growing new wings. It hit the water and floated. The slow current tugged it straight. Cyan, staring, saw circle after circle of embroidery on an endless length of linen: the changing images of the woman's silent, changeless days.

He hit the cracked wood hard and fell through it onto a damp tangle of grass and weed within the archway. He paused then, drew his sword, and spilled the river water out of its sheath. He sheared impatiently through the cascading ivy that hid the courtyard. The yard was choked with weed and wildflower, brambles and climbing roses. The stone fountain in the center of it was dry and filled with dead leaves; the figure in the fountain's basin poured ivy from its urn instead of water. He waded through weed as through water, feeling it drag at him as he made his way toward the door in the inner wall of the tower. The only other way out for her was through the window. He could only hesitate a breath before he guessed, door or window, and he dared not change his mind.

The arched wooden door was warped and blackened with moss; it did not give at his first pull. At the second, the iron ring he gripped came out of the door into his hands. He stared at it incredulously, then flung it away, and began to pry between wood and stone with his sword. The door made a sound like a tree split in two, and fell suddenly, ponderously, out of the stones on top of him.

He remembered, after a moment or two, why he was lying underneath a door. He pushed himself out from under it, and stood up shakily, wiping blood from a cut on his forehead. The tower steps made a neat, marble-white fan unfolding around their central core. They might have been freshly laid, never walked on until he came up them, leaving the first faint stains of grass and earth on them, wearing down the first shadow-thin layer of stone. He heard nothing as he moved but his own steps, his own breathing. The tower was as still as death. She had turned into thread, he thought numbly. Or she had gone out the window while he came through the door. She had flung herself into the river, wound herself in her embroidery and let it drag her down among the water weeds and lilies.

He reached the door at the top of the tower and opened it.

She stood at the window, her back to the world, her hands clenched, hidden in her skirt, watching him enter. He saw the face in the silver disk, lovely and white as marble, her pale hair rippling down her back, her eyes as blue as the summer sky behind her. She was trembling, he saw. She could not seem to speak. She let a tear fall instead. He watched it slide down the curve of her cheek, pass her mouth, and trace the long, graceful line of her throat before he remembered to move.

He said nothing, either, simply knelt and bowed his head to the true Queen of Yves and the North Islands and Skye.

She whispered, "You looked at me."

He raised his head, not making sense of the words then, or much of anything at that moment, except that he had found her and she was alive

He said, "My name is Cyan Dag, my lady. I was sent from Gloinmere by the Bard of Skye to find you."

She shifted slightly; her voice found its timbre. "Idra."

"She said—she said you would die if you looked at the world. If you leave the tower—"

"You looked at me," she repeated. He was silent, still

looking at her, perplexed. Color flowed beneath her skin; her eyes grew bright again, heavy. She moved then, crossed the room quickly and knelt in front of him to take his hands. He shook his head a little, feeling her wonder, and a sense of sorrow past endurance. Tears stung his own eyes; her face blurred.

"I don't understand."

"They knew I was here. Farmers passing to their fields saw my mirror every day. Knights pointed to my window, told one another about me; I could see them talking. Sometimes I even heard them. Fishers moored their boats among the water lilies and wondered aloud what I was doing here. I was cursed, they guessed; I would die if I looked past the mirror, at the world out of my own eyes. They were half-right. I was some magical, fey being, fit to tell stories about to pass the time of day, to wonder about and pity, and try to imagine what might be so compelling to me that I might fling my life away to look at it." She was trembling again, he felt as she gripped his hands; her voice was dry and hollow, still not yet freed. He wanted, only a little less than his own life, to put his arms around her, hold her and her fear and grief, until she no longer felt the tower around her. "They passed me every day, the fine knights, the poets, the folk of the city and the fields. I was part of their lives, like the rooks, the tower, winter, sun. They knew me. But you are the only one who ever looked beyond the mirror at me. You are the only one who ever saw that I was real, and came to help me."

"I still don't—"

"If I looked at the world I would die. If the world

looked at me, saw me with courage and compassion, and reached out to help me — how could I not live? How could that not make me free?"

He tried to answer, could not. She brushed at the tear furrowing down his own face, then touched the disk that had fallen out of his shirt.

"My face," she said wonderingly. He raised her face with his fingers, felt her poised in his hands like a bird, to stay or fly. She stayed. He kissed her very gently, feeling Regis Aurum's eyes on him across two lands.

He stood up, suddenly as drained as if he had fought a battle and lived. "You're not afraid of leaving?"

She gave him the beginnings of a smile. "It's the world," she answered. "I should be a little afraid. Will you take me to Gloinmere?"

"Shall I take you to your father, first?"

"No. I want to see Regis." She turned, for one last glance out the window. "I have lived in Skye all my life, yet I have no idea where we are. You will have to guide me."

He followed her down the steps, keeping his sword unsheathed. He was still wary of the woman far away in Gloinmere, who wore the mask of the queen's face, and drank out of her cup, and who would turn a black venomous eye their direction when she found her tower empty. But he found nothing to disturb him until he reached the bottom step. He paused there, his taut face easing into a smile as the Lady from Skye, moving eagerly out of the tower into light, reached up with both hands toward the sun.

Her shadow swept back across the weeds and fallen leaves to Cyan's feet. On the white marble of the threshold he saw her hands.

Six fingers, his stunned eyes told him, on each shadow hand opened to the light. He made some sound. He saw her look back at him before the sun seemed to rise behind his eyes in an explosion of light that blinded him. *I have ridden across Yves and across Skye*, he thought bewilderedly, *to free the evil that threatens the king*. He felt his body move, though he knew he must be still frozen with horror and confusion on the threshold of the tower. The dazzling light faded a little; he saw her through a pounding wash of red, watching him as he crossed the tangled yard. He could not see her face, only the blurred shape of it within her hair. She did not speak; she raised one hand. He did not falter; he moved in fury and desperation to meet whatever deadly magic she conjured out of the air against him.

It was a small thing compared with the sorceries he had met in Skye: a splinter of silver that caught briefly in his eyes. But it brought him to a halt.

He stood staring at her, his sword poised to strike, his body trembling with the effort that stopped the blow. She did nothing else: her upraised hand, long-boned and slender, with the plain band of silver on the longest finger, was the only magic he recognized. He saw her clearly then, the face that had terrified him, that he had worn like a talisman over his heart, that he had hated, that for an instant and forever he had loved.

He could not move.

When, or how, she disappeared, he did not know; she

had already blurred behind his tears before she left him. Still he did not move for a long time after that, feeling the pain of his failure, his helplessness, like a weight over his thoughts and body, as if he had been cast in iron and left like a statue in the abandoned courtyard. Finally, wearily, he sheathed his sword, remembering the long road between Skye and Yves, and the dangers still converging on Gloinmere. He swallowed the rust and charred, cold ash of bitterness, and walked out of the dark archway through the tower walls to find his horse.

Three Sisters rose around him, flooded with light from the setting sun. He stared at them, at the meadow grass under his feet, at the little stream where the gelding was drinking, at the squat black tower he had just left. The confusion welled through him again; he wanted to beat answers out of the tower with his fists, but it would not answer, he knew; it never did.

"How do I find my way out of you?" he shouted at the blank, dreaming faces of the hills. "When will you let me go?"

They did not answer, either. He called the gelding, and mounted slowly, wondering if all the paths to come in his life would loop forever back to those three hills, that tower. He turned the gelding away from the sun, toward what he hoped with all his heart was Yves.

Someone cried, "Wait!"

He reined, recognizing Melanthos's voice. She rode up beside him, barefoot and tangle-haired, her horse whuffing nervously at the stolid gelding. Cyan did not look at her; she had to wheel her mount close to his to see his face.

She whispered after a moment, "What is it? Was she dead?"

His head rose abruptly; he found her eyes. "What do you—how do you—"

"I found this," she said, her voice small, shaken. "In the tower in the stone wood. It's not one of mine. I came looking for you. I wanted to know."

He gazed wordlessly at the embroidery she opened. The dark-haired knight with the three gold towers on his surcoat walked out of the dark tower onto a swath of light from the setting sun. He was alone, except for the face in the silver disk over his heart, barely visible, a stitch or two of blue and gold beneath the jagged lines of power worked across the silver.

Cyan raised a hand to the disk, pulled it out of his shirt. She was still with him, harrowing his life. His hand closed over it, to snap the chain, fling the disk into the grass. But he kept it; it had saved him, he remembered starkly, from water, from fire, from Thayne Ysse's blade, from the dragon.

Melanthos was still watching him, her strange eyes questioning, disturbed. He said painfully, "She is free. But I think—there is a reason that she was trapped in the tower, and I might have set someone very dangerous to Yves loose in the world. I must get back to Gloinmere to warn the king. Also—" He sighed, shook his head, one hand splayed over his eyes. "There is the matter of Thayne Ysse and the dragon. He took it, to help him war with Yves. While I stayed here to free—" He stopped again. Melanthos's hand closed around his wrist.

"My mother," she finished. He dropped his hand, oddly surprised. "I'm sorry. We kept you here. No one—no one would have guessed that the tale would end like this. We never thought the woman in the tower might be dangerous."

He was silent, gazing at Melanthos, remembering how her face had changed, when he had last seen it, beneath the changing colors of her mother's power. He whispered, words transforming an image in his mind, "The woman in the tower."

"Which?" Melanthos asked, perplexed. "My mother? Or the woman in your disk?"

"Your mother. She has grown very powerful. I saw Thayne Ysse take the same fires from the dragon that your mother drew out of herself."

"Because of you."

He shook his head quickly, remembering the strange, masked face of the selkie. "No. She sewed my towers back together, and then she freed herself. I did nothing."

"You went with her into the sea. You wouldn't let her go alone. She had to return to the human world to rescue you."

"I didn't dare let go of her." He smiled a little, brushed her tangled, smoky hair with his fingers. "It was you who called her back. Thank you for finding me again."

"I had to, when I saw this. You, walking out of the dark tower alone—she must have embroidered it."

"She saw me coming," he said bitterly.

"Then she was here in this tower all the time?"

"She must have been. Sidera said that this tower is best

at seeming." He gathered his reins, an eye to the setting sun. "I must go. I want to find my way out of these hills before nightfall."

"Come back to Stony Wood," she begged. "Tell my mother about the woman, about Thayne Ysse's dragon and the danger to Gloinmere. I don't know anything about war, or the world outside of Skye. But if Gloinmere is in danger because of sorcery from Skye, then how long can Skye itself stay peaceful?"

"I don't know. But at least you have Sel to fight for you. I can't stay any longer in Skye; I have been away far too long." He urged the gelding again toward Yves, and raised a hand in farewell to the selkie's strange-eyed daughter, whose eyes, as they watched him, seemed to have lost their glinting lights and become as dark and secret as the stones behind her. He took her fey smile with him out of the hills.

TWENTY-SIX

Thayne Ysse sat in the dragon tower arguing with Craiche. Behind them, their father searched his books for a spell that would, he said, turn the dragon invisible over Yves, so that no one would see the path it took toward Gloinmere, only the mysterious devastation that charred the earth as the army from the North Islands marched through Yves.

"You can't go alone to Gloinmere," Craiche insisted. "If you get killed, the dragon will escape, or be taken by someone in Gloinmere. Then who will protect the North Islanders? We'll be slaughtered. By the same king, in one lifetime—"

"There's not enough magic in Yves to string a bow with, let alone capture a dragon," Thayne said tersely. "And noth-

ing will happen to me. You stay here with our father. Someone has to."

"I'm going with you."

"So am I, of course," their father said, glancing up from
a book. "I'll take the dragon if you fall, Bowan. Leave Regis
Aurum to me. I have a score to settle."

"Of course," Thayne said, reining in his temper. He
dropped his head in one hand, drew his fingers back
through his hair, and straightened again. Craiche watched
him with an obdurate, maddening calm. "If I die in Gloinmere, so will you. And then who will rule the North Islands?"

"It won't matter," Craiche said softly. "You know that.
If you fail in Gloinmere, Regis Aurum will send his army
here and the only thing left alive when they finish with the
North Islands will be the sand crabs."

Thayne was silent, knowing that Craiche was probably
right. He said harshly, "Then what? Should I stop this
war?"

"It will be inevitable, when Regis Aurum finds out
about the gold. And the dragon. And you."

Thayne shifted restively, stilled himself. Craiche had
changed in the past weeks. Thayne himself had changed his
brother from a clear-eyed, reckless boy who laughed at fate
to a young man driven, more deeply even than Thayne, to
extract justice out of Yves, and the ancient powers of Ysse
out of Thayne. Craiche had sat through every war council
Thayne had called; he had an answer for every argument
Thayne could raise. Even his smile had changed; it flashed
out then, deceptively sweet, edged with danger.

"Besides, I want to see Regis Aurum's face when he finds a dragon in his yard."

Thayne rubbed his eyes. He slept badly, those days, still disturbed by dreams. "I can force you to stay," he heard himself say. "I could seal the walls around this house so that you could not find the gates, or see out any window, or find your way to the top of any wall."

"I know that spell," their father said.

Craiche only looked at Thayne patiently. "But you won't, or you wouldn't have told me that."

"Craiche. Please."

"Please what? You don't have to ask. You just told me so." He paused, no longer smiling, his eyes quizzical, curious. A thread of uncertainty worked itself across his brow, as if he had seen too far into Thayne. He reached out impulsively, let his hand drop between them on the table. "What are you afraid of?"

A woman in a dream, Thayne thought. *A feeling in my bones.*

"Something," he admitted finally to Craiche. "Something feels wrong. I'm not seeing something I should see. I'm doing everything we planned, but I'm missing what's standing under my nose and shouting—"

"I found it!" Their father spun across the floor behind Thayne, dropped a tome, weighty with gold leaf and pearls, in front of Thayne. "Here. Do what this says, Bowan, and the dragon will become invisible even in the noonday sky."

Thayne slumped wearily over the book. Despite himself, the words, in a precise and graceful script, charmed their way into his thoughts.

He looked at Craiche, who said, "It's not a bad idea. If you keep the dragon quiet, no one will know we're coming until we're already there, disrupting the king's dinner in Gloinmere. He won't have a chance to prepare for us."

"Cyan Dag will prepare him."

"Only if he gets there before we do."

"There must be rumors of dragons in Yves by now. Anyone dropping a hook off a boat on the north side of the channel would see it."

"Maybe," Craiche said. "But who would believe it?" He bent down, looking under the table for his crutch, neatly avoiding Thayne's eyes. "We should leave soon. The men are armed, the horses are shod, the dragon lord of Ysse has nothing left to learn—"

"That," Thayne said soberly, "is what I'm afraid of: what I will not learn until we face the king in Gloinmere."

He spent his dreams, as always during those nights, in the company of the harper from Skye. Sometimes she played her harp, a single deep note over and over again, measured to his heartbeat. Sometimes she spoke in a language he did not know, the words urgent, compelling, so that he twisted his thoughts into knots trying to understand. And then she would speak the one word that would wake him like a cold slap of water from a bucket.

Craiche.

He interrupted her that night, in the midst of her dire, incomprehensible chattering. "All right!" he shouted at her. "Then tell me what to do. You tell me. Tell me. You sent me to find the dragon! What did you expect me to do with it?"

She was silent, so silent he wondered if he had died in the middle of his dream. Then she smiled, and he knew he must be dead, because he was more afraid than he had ever been in his life.

She told him.

A morning later, before the sun rose, he cast a spell over the dragon, a web of words and air that wound around it strand by strand, and hid all its glittering scales, its massive claws, the slitted, golden pools of its eyes. He finished finally at sunrise, and found the dragon's shadow still underfoot, with the bulky shadows of packs and arms, and Craiche's crutch dangling from behind one wing. Thayne opened the eye in the bole of the staff Craiche tossed him, and let the shadow flow into it. He found his father beside him, gazing at the empty sand where the dragon had lain outside the tower. It had melted, here and there, into hard, shimmering pools of glass.

"You are Ferle's heir, Thayne," his father said with wonder. "You were born with all the magic of Ysse. But what have you done with Craiche?"

"I can still see him," Thayne said. He embraced his father tightly, moved as always by the briefest recognition. "Stay well and safe."

"My greetings to Regis Aurum." His father gave the absent king his tight, wolfish smile. "I would bring them myself, but someone must guard the secrets in this tower."

"No one could do it but you."

"Bring his crown back with you, Bowan."

"I will."

The dragon lowered its neck. To his father's eyes, and

the eyes of men watching over the wall, Thayne knew he must be mounting air. But his father only raised a fist in salute and farewell, before Thayne turned himself invisible.

"I can't see you," Craiche breathed as Thayne coaxed the dragon above the sea. "Or the dragon. I can't see anything but air beneath me."

Thayne put a hand over Craiche's eyes. "See out of mine, then," he said. He lifted his hand, aware of Craiche in his mind, a thread of quicksilver thought, restless, unpredictable. He added, as Craiche blinked at him, "For a change."

Craiche turned to look back at Ysse, a quarter moon of land hanging above the mainland in a sea of silver fire. "Where are the boats?" he asked after a moment. "They should be starting across the channel by now. We'll have to wait for them."

"They're not coming."

He felt the quicksilver flash of astonishment behind his eyes before Craiche swung around to stare at him. "What do you mean they're not coming?"

"I—"

"You bought half the horses in north Yves, and arms from every trader beyond Yves—"

"So we're armed," Thayne said evenly. "I gave orders last night for the army to stay on the islands unless I send for them."

"You mean until—"

"No." He felt the dragon fire in his eyes then, a wash of gold that blurred the sea and stopped Craiche's breath.

"It's you and me and this dragon against the king in Gloin-mere."

"Why?" Craiche whispered.

"It's a promise I made to someone."

"What promise?"

Thayne didn't answer that. He smiled thinly, and dropped a hand on Craiche's shoulder. "The dragon alone could destroy Gloinmere. So could I. There's no one in all of Yves who could fight me."

"But they wanted war—they wanted another chance at Regis Aurum and his knights! With you and the dragon protecting them, they could have taken Gloinmere, and crowned you King of Yves with Regis Aurum's crown!"

"I know."

"Then why?"

Thayne looked at him silently, feeling himself, with all his power, balanced on the thin edge of a blade, halfway between all he wanted and what he most feared. He said, "Don't fight me over this. You're with me now because you are the measure of what I win or lose in Gloinmere."

"I don't understand."

"I don't want you to understand." His fingers dug fiercely into Craiche's shoulder. "I never want you to understand. All I want you to do is stay alive."

He saw himself suddenly out of Craiche's eyes, in an odd merging of their sight: a honed, powerful figure, the dragon fire flaring and ebbing in his eyes, and all the ancient forces of Ysse in his mind, the first Lord of Ysse in a thousand years who could take all he wanted from the world, but for something even more powerful that restrained him.

"Who," Craiche whispered, "made you promise?"

They had left the sea behind by then; land, green with summer, flowed in its own frozen waves and hollows beneath them. Thayne's hand loosened, hovered for an instant near Craiche's face, which was turning hourly, it seemed, into the feral, graceful, impetuous ghost of their father's. He shook his head, again without answering. "Just stop warring with me. I am the Lord of Ysse and you are my crippled younger brother who would be walking on two legs instead of three now if you had listened instead of fighting seven years ago. Let me do what I will."

They reached Gloinmere near dusk, a day later. Thayne stripped the cocoon of invisibility from the dragon as it settled in the yard. The whole of the castle on Ysse could have fit in the yard at Gloinmere, but not even the high walls and towers could dwarf the dragon, who peered into window and turret at whim. It snorted at the astonished guards running along the walls; they tumbled back into one another, arrows and crossbows flying like straw in a storm. Thayne heard an uproar from within as the dragon laid its smoldering eye against a window in the hall. The doors flew open; guards and knights, brandishing sword and pike and bow, started down the steps. Thayne raised the staff in his hand, sent a tidal wave of cold fire that swept into them, battered them off their feet, and sent them sliding helplessly back into the hall. The fire died; Thayne waited. A few unarmed men came out, quickly pulled those fallen and washed against the walls back into the hall. The doors slammed shut again. The dragon, raising its long neck higher than the highest tower, opened its jaws and loosed a butterfly of flame that turned the pennants flying there into cinders.

The guards at the gates had vanished into their turrets. Along the walls, a helmed head appeared briefly here and there, then ducked back down again. Someone, not thinking too clearly, shot a burning arrow over the wall. The dragon, moving so quickly it startled even Thayne, picked the arrow out of the air like a frog snatching a fly, and swallowed it. A little flame drifted out of its teeth. It dropped its head over the high wall, and what was left of the guard fled into the towers.

Thayne raised his voice. "Regis Aurum!" The bells in the high tower hummed. Craiche, his face puckered, dropped to his knees and put his hands over his ears. From within the hall came an answering volley of exploding crockery. "The North Islands have come to Gloinmere with their tribute to the King of Yves."

The doors swung open again. The King of Yves strode out furiously, alone, his broadsword in one hand. He stopped abruptly, the expression on his face changing as he raised his head and kept raising it, until he finally found the dragon's eyes, each one as broad as an open door, staring down at him. Thayne saw him swallow. He looked at Thayne then, seeing him instead of the vague, pinched, impoverished face that every man from the North Islands wore in his eyes.

He drew breath. "Thayne Ysse. I've heard tales of

power in the North Islands, but I thought that's all they were. What do you want?"

"Justice."

The king's face hardened. "Then leave that monster outside my walls and come to me with courtesy. What will you do? Burn Gloinmere and call that justice?"

"It would be." Thayne heard his own voice shake.

Still on his knees, Craiche whispered, "Don't tell him — show him."

"You in Gloinmere have eaten the North Islands to the bone for centuries. You pick at the carcass and demand more. If we had nothing but stones to eat, you would demand stones. You drive us to our knees, and slaughter us when we refuse to yield our lives to you. You want our oaths of fealty and tribute, but what of mercy or good faith or justice have you ever shown us? What have you ever given the North Islands but the back of your hand and the sole of your boot? Ysse, not Yves, ruled the North Islands once. Ysse, not Yves, will rule the North Islands now. You can give me the courtesy due from one ruler to another, and if you and your knights set one foot in the sea between us, to fight us for our freedom, I will shake the stones of Gloinmere down around your ears."

The king took a step, his face streaked with rage. "Then do it now, because I will hunt you down as a traitor to Yves when you leave Gloinmere —"

Thayne heard metal slide from a sheath. Craiche pulled himself up, stood beside him, sword in one hand and gripping a wingbone with the other for balance. "Then I will kill you," he said, his stripped, level voice sounding so much like their father's that Thayne's skin pricked.

He shifted, sending an undulation down the dragon's back that made Craiche lose his balance. He vanished behind the wing again. Regis, his voice cracking, shouted, "Who was that?"

"The next ruler of Ysse," Thayne said, and lost his temper. He raised the staff, the eye in the bole glittering at Regis Aurum, holding him motionless, transfixed, while Thayne poured what thoughts he had left into the bole until he could see Regis through all its power and its eye. "Enough," he said very softly. "Come to me. Come."

The gate opened behind him.

He turned abruptly, startled, the power in the staff flaring out of it at whoever had entered. He caught a horrifying glimpse of a woman standing helplessly in its luminous path. Then the light surged back at him, streaming into the staff with such force that he thought the gate had flown off its hinges and smacked into him. All his own power exploded from the staff into his mind.

He struggled out of that dazzling star, felt Craiche's hands holding him, helping him up. He blinked his vision clear as he rose, and saw the king again, staring over the coiled neck of the dragon at the woman in the gate. Thayne could not find words; Regis Aurum managed.

"Who are you?"

"I'm the baker," she said, "from Stony Wood."

TWENTY-SEVEN

The dragon drew her eyes then, its luminous scales glowing in the fading light as with inner fires, its head reared on the immense stalk of its neck, staring down at Sel out of cauldrons of molten gold. It was absolutely still. So was she, stunned still, for she had never seen anything so beautiful or so menacing in her life. Its jaws opened slightly, revealing teeth like wedges of crystal, as if, she thought incredulously, it smiled.

It was more than dragon. That she recognized, though she could not have said where its boundaries of dragon ended, and the unknown force that knew her name began. Somewhere in its fiery, nebulous thoughts a familiar eye had opened, looked at her. The smoldering confusion of emotion from the humans in the yard pulled at her attention before she could pursue the question. She studied the men, remembering what Melanthos had told her.

The brown, burly man with the sword in his hand and the hectic blood in his face, standing alone on the steps defending his house, must be the King of Yves, the North Islands, and Skye. The gold-haired man whose powers had rebounded back at him would certainly be Thayne Ysse, who had brought the dragon to war with the king. The young man beside him, as dark as Thayne was fair, Melanthos hadn't mentioned. He wore the same fearless, intractable expression as Thayne, and stood so close, his hand gripping Thayne's arm, that Sel guessed he must be family.

She saw the sudden glint in the bole of the staff Thayne carried, a flash of wicked, warning fire. He held it loosely, without intent, but she didn't like the look of it. She sent a jolt of thought into the skull-smooth bole, avoiding the power in the eye. The staff jumped out of Thayne's hand. He staggered, loosing a cry that was part curse, and hunched over his hand. She looked past him to the man on the steps.

"Regis Aurum?"

The king nodded, searching for a word. He brought it out finally. "Baker?"

The dragon swiveled its head suddenly, its jaws opening wide, and hissed at a parapet wall. The archer hiding there, crouched and aiming at Thayne, shouted and dropped his bow into the yard.

"My daughter persuaded me to come here," Sel told the king. "She said that Cyan Dag was afraid that he wouldn't get here to warn you about Thayne Ysse and the dragon.

I came as fast as I could. Faster sometimes than others. I'm still learning things."

"Cyan Dag?" The king took a step, remembered the dragon. "Have you seen him?"

"Yes. He passed through Stony Wood." She paused, remembering the knight who had found her in the tower and followed her into the sea. "He helped me when I was in need. When Melanthos told me he was in distress, I thought I'd return the favor." She sensed a turmoil of conflicting thought on the dragon's back, and added curiously, "You'd think that if Thayne Ysse were truly going to burn down Gloinmere, he would have done it before the dragon landed in the yard. What's he waiting for? The dragon could do it easily."

The king stepped back warily. Thayne Ysse only threw her a grim, harassed glance. *Something,* she thought. *Something not as it seems.*

Behind the king, the doors began to open. Thayne Ysse whirled abruptly, slamming them shut with a gesture. Fists battered furiously at them; they refused to budge. Sel raised her voice.

"Shall I go up and talk to him?"

"Talk!" Regis Aurum answered furiously. "He talks too much. I should have dragged him to Gloinmere seven years ago, put an end to that flea-ridden, gadfly family. But I mistook his pledges for truth —"

The dragon's head fell so quickly toward him that the king barely had time to upend his blade with both hands, aim it at the lowering throat. It stopped as suddenly, just out of reach. The king quelled a visible impulse to throw his sword at it.

"I never pledged you anything," Thayne retorted passionately. "Kneeling to you in the rain was hard enough; a word would have choked me."

"Your father pledged fealty."

"He was wounded; he barely knew—"

"He knew," Regis Aurum said levelly, "that the North Islands have belonged to Yves for centuries. The only thing that you can claim there is your name. You asked for war when you refused to offer fealty to me in Gloinmere when I was crowned. I gave you what you wanted."

"You nearly destroyed us." Thayne's back was to Sel, but she saw the power gathering in him again, as clearly as she could see the shining bones of transparent fish deep in the sea. The air shimmered around him, roiling, pulsing.

Regis, oblivious, snapped, "I will."

Sel moved then, the way she had crossed vast distances through Yves. She focused her attention on a gleaming scallop of the dragon's folded wing, and took a step toward it. She was there, suddenly, on the dragon's back, feeling the blaze of Thayne's fury like an open oven in the bakery.

He loosed it at her instead of Regis when he found her unexpectedly beside him. She hid herself within the lightning shock and flare of air, moving with it like a selkie within a wave, safe from any storm. She reappeared. He stared at her, the air fading around him to the color of twilight.

"What are you?"

"Thayne," the young man murmured edgily, leaning on

a sword for balance. "Use the dragon before she stops you. You're not fighting, you're just talking, and they'll find a way to kill you."

"He has a point," Sel said. "What are you doing here if you didn't come to destroy Gloinmere?"

He answered tautly, "I thought the dragon might persuade the king to listen to me."

"Listen!" the young man repeated in horror. "I thought we came to fight!"

Thayne's fists clenched. "I promised—"

"What? What did you promise?" He reached out to grip Thayne with both hands. The sword slid away from him; he clung to Thayne for balance. "Who made you promise? Thayne, she could kill you, if you don't fight!"

Thayne shook his head wordlessly. Sel saw the young man's withered leg, dragging next to the one muscled with labor. She picked up the staff, pushed the bole under his arm.

"Who are you?" she asked.

He didn't answer, didn't look at her; all his bewildered attention was on Thayne, who breathed, "She'll kill you if I do."

"Who?" Sel demanded abruptly. "Who will?"

Their faces swung toward her, one confused, the other desperate. The young man loosed Thayne slowly, swallowing. He echoed Sel's question.

"Who?"

"Just be quiet and let me think. This is my brother Craiche," he added to Sel. "He was wounded in the battle the North Islands fought against Yves seven years ago."

Sel grunted. "You lost more than the battle, then. Your father and your brother wounded. Is your father still alive?"

Thayne started to answer, then raised his head, listening. Sel heard the faint, ragged thrum of many running feet spiraling up the stone steps within the towers. "He recovered," Thayne said tersely. "But his mind wanders. He can't remember my name, but he knew enough to send me to Skye to find the dragon. Are you really a baker?"

Sel nodded. "I'm used to it. I'm not used to this." As she spoke, Thayne's eyes changed. She felt the dragon stir, one eye turned down to meet his gaze. It drew its wings together over their heads. Arrows shot from archers' windows in the towers pattered like rain against the dragon's scales. "It seems your brother is right," she added. "You can burn down Gloinmere or leave with the dragon. You should do one or the other before they kill you."

He looked at her, his eyes like the dragon's, fuming with light. "I thought you were fighting for Regis Aurum."

"I don't know either one of you. You're not afraid of the king. You could feed him to the dragon if that's what you want—"

"I don't! What good would that king's heart do to anything alive? He'd go to his death with the same arrogance in his eyes, the same oblivion worse than contempt with which he views us even while he demands our hope, our loyalty, our lives. I don't want war. The cost will be too great. I want freedom for the North Islands from Yves."

Sel was silent, weighing certain things in her mind: Craiche's leg, the look in the king's eyes, Thayne's mysterious restraint, her own unlikely power. She drew breath, barked like the selkie she might have been, "Regis Aurum!"

The dragon's wing dropped down between them; its other curved more closely over them. The king gripped his sword more tightly and stared at her. "What?"

"Come here."

He balked; she pulled him when he did not move fast enough, hauling him in like a fish in a net. Thayne, breathing something inaudible, moved to stand in front of Craiche. But he left the sword in the king's hand, for it was worth nothing, there on the dragon's back, except to help Regis Aurum think.

"You've brought this on yourself," Sel said to him. "You've driven Thayne Ysse to this. Look at his brother. You made war on boys not old enough to grow beards —"

"I didn't war on children!" Regis snapped. "And I nearly died myself in that battle."

"You've fought a war without weapons since then," Thayne said bitterly, "against even our children."

"You started the war!"

"You drained everything but the breath out of the North Islands to punish us for it!"

"I'll concede the air you breathe to you. But the ground you walk on is mine."

"What of Skye?" Sel asked.

"Skye is also mine. By heritage, by marriage —"

"Even the magic in it? This dragon came out of the heart of Skye. If we ever offend you, and you bring your knights to fight us, beware what you might face."

Regis Aurum stared at her. So did Thayne Ysse and the dragon. Sel would have stared at herself if she had an extra eye, for the words had come out of nowhere, solid as stone piled on stone, making an unshakable argument for peace.

The king asked incredulously, "Are you threatening me?"

Sel thought about it and nodded. "I am. If you go to war with Thayne Ysse and the North Islands over this, then Skye will go to war with you. And you'd better learn some magic, Regis Aurum, because your weapons will be useless there."

The king opened his mouth; for a moment nothing came out. The blood raged into his face and faded. "The Lord of Skye would never war against his own daughter—you can't speak for Skye—"

"It's not the Lord of Skye you would face," Sel said grimly. "It's all the folk whose faces you have never seen. Like the folk in the North Islands, they have names, and lives they think important. Unlike the North Islands, Skye has not forgotten its magic."

The king blinked. He glanced up at the dragon, whose head had curved back above them, as if it were listening. One eye loomed over them like a bright, swollen moon. He said heavily to Sel, "I thought you came here as a favor to one of my knights, to defend Gloinmere."

"That knight," Thayne Ysse said tautly, "of all your knights, had some pity for the islanders. He left your side while you were wounded, to save my brother's life."

"How do you know that?" Regis Aurum asked sharply. "He never told me that."

"I know because I nearly killed him myself, battling

over this dragon in Skye. But he knew my brother's name. So I let him live."

The king's eyes narrowed; in the torchlight, his face lost color. "You are a very dangerous man, Thayne Ysse. That knight, of all my knights, I value most."

"So do I," Thayne said simply. "We will tear three lands apart if we war with one another. And war it will be, nothing less than that, unless you yield the North Islands to me."

The king was silent, motionless, his eyes on Thayne, seeing him, Sel guessed, for the first time. He swallowed something, said softly, "Now I know what you tasted in the back of your throat when you knelt in defeat to me in north Yves."

Thayne shook his head. "You don't know even now. You haven't lost anything you loved."

Regis lowered his sword finally. "I can't fight dragons. Or my wife's land. Not over a handful of islands with nothing on them but sheep. I claimed the North Islands when I was crowned, with no more thought than my father gave the matter, or his father before him. I spared them a thought once a year at most. Still, I would go to war with you over barnacles and sand, if you gave me any choice." He looked at Sel dourly. "I don't see that I have a choice. I have never lost a battle on the back of a dragon before."

Thayne drew breath soundlessly, loosed it. He shifted, brought Craiche forward, one arm tight around his shoulders. His eyes turned briefly as gold as coins. "As you said, it's only sand."

The king sheathed his sword slowly, studying them

both. "You look like your father," he said abruptly to Craiche. "I saw him once or twice, when my father was alive. Come into the hall, before someone plots another attack. I need to make this very clear to my knights: that the North Islands belong to Ysse, and that you owe nothing more to me." He added, seeing the reluctance in Thayne's eyes, "Arm yourself if you want, but come in peace. Which you have already done, very effectively. You could have taken Gloinmere from me. Perhaps Yves itself. You have no reason to trust me, but perhaps I have some reason to trust you."

Sel found herself silently consulted by the Lord of Ysse. She said, "Cyan Dag seems to love him. That must mean something."

The dragon flattened a wing like a bridge to the steps. The king offered his arm to the baker in a gesture that melted her heart. "It's time he came home," Regis murmured as they made their way across a carpet of bone and glittering scale. "My wife sent him on some errand, two days after we were married. I haven't seen him since."

"I thought he came to Skye looking for the dragon," Thayne said after a moment. "Why else would he have entered the dragon's tower?"

"He told us in Stony Wood that he was looking for a woman . . ."

The king pulled futilely at the doors, then stood aside to let Thayne unseal them. The doors flew open as if the entire household were pushing at them. Men stumbled out. Swords flashed, seeking hither and yon, but the Lord of Ysse and his brother were suddenly nowhere to be found.

The king raised his voice for calm. A woman followed in the wake of the chaos, stood at the doorway looking at the dragon. The shouting and turmoil dwindled in Sel's head into something heard within the chambers of a shell.

It was the woman in the mirror: her lovely face with its grace and luminous eyes, her hair, though in this world she wore it so smoothly coiled and braided, it might have been carved of ivory. She felt Sel's stare and smiled at her, a private smile, as if they shared a secret. The king, restoring order finally and coaxing Thayne Ysse back from nowhere, led him to the woman in the doorway.

"This is the Lord of the North Islands, Thayne Ysse, and his brother, Craiche," he said. "And this is Sel, who came from Skye to tell us all what to do. Make them welcome in my house."

"From Skye!" the Queen of Yves said, taking Sel's hands, as the astonished and vociferous knights and guards followed the king into the hall. "Tell me where you live; perhaps I know it."

"Stony Wood," Sel answered, her voice grown small with wonder.

"Yes," the Lady from Skye said with delight. "I rode down the coast once from my father's house, to see the strange stone wood." She put her hand on Thayne's arm as he waited behind the crowd so that Craiche would not get unbalanced in it. Some impulse from the dragon made him turn as the last guard drifted after the king. Sel felt it, too, as she lingered in the queen's gentle grasp: the glance of a dark eye out of the dragon's mind. The four of them stood alone outside the noisy hall, watching the dragon change.

A tall old woman with hair as white as bone and eyes as black as the eye in the bole stood in the yard where the dragon had been. Sel heard Thayne loose a sharp, incoherent word. I *know you,* she thought with wonder. *You watched me in the mirror . . .*

She smiled at Sel as if she heard her thinking, her heartbeat, the next thought still finding words in her head.

"You won't need this now," she said to Thayne, and picked her staff out of the clutter fallen off the dragon's back.

He whispered as the old woman turned her back to them and faded into fire and night on her way to the gate, "I should have known."

TWENTY-EIGHT

Cyan Dag returned to Gloinmere at twilight, weeks or years after he had left; he was not certain which. It was still summer, the fields and orchards told him, patterning the rolling land around the city like a rumpled quilt. But which summer, they did not say. He had ridden hard from Skye, driven all the way by the vision of charred, broken towers, the city emptied, its occupants killed or fled, the knights of Gloinmere scattered, the king nowhere to be found, and the Leviathan of the North Islands flying over the ruins.

But the walls and towers of Gloinmere were as yet intact. No dragon shadow flowed across the rising moon. It would be easier to face the dragon and Thayne Ysse together, Cyan felt, than the king's bewildering and dangerous wife. He still wore the battered disk over his heart, a reminder of his unfinished quest. He would show it to the king, who by now might have glimpsed something in his smiling wife that had begun to disturb his dreams, something amiss in her shadow, something chilling that happened to her eyes when she danced.

So Cyan hoped, or he would be forced to lay the stark bones of the tale out before the king and try to convince him that they truly shaped some marvelous and deadly beast that in Yves existed only on a tapestry.

He rode through the gate into the yard, barely noticing the startled expressions he caused as the guards opened the gates and the stabler ran to take the gelding. He walked wearily up the steps into the hall, where the king sat at supper with his court. Tables lining the long carpet to the dais grew oddly quiet as he passed, in his dusty, patched surcoat, his hair loose and untidy down his shoulders, the warped, tarnished disk hanging on his breast. He kept his eyes on Regis, wondering how to begin. The king, staring at him, seemed as mute. He gestured sharply at the musicians for silence and rose. As he passed behind the gold-haired man sitting beside him, Cyan's steps faltered; he felt, for a moment, as if he were trying to walk through tide.

The queen drew his eyes, then, the woman who had forced him out of Gloinmere, haunted his journey across Skye, and met him at his journey's end. She watched him thoughtfully, lifting one hand that flashed gold in the candlelight from every finger as she touched the arm of the woman beside her.

Cyan stopped. Regis reached him then; Cyan started to kneel, but the king embraced him, pounding dust out of his tunic as Cyan stared in disbelief over his shoulder. The baker from Stony Wood, his eyes were trying to tell him, was sitting next to the queen.

"How—" he began blankly, but the king was already talking.

"I know," he said. "I know. Gwynne told me where you had gone and why—"

"What?"

"That she had asked you to go very quickly and quietly to Skye, to rescue a kinswoman of hers trapped in a tower. She told me that of all my knights you were the only one who could see his way clearly in Skye."

"I didn't—I couldn't—is that Thayne Ysse? Eating supper in your hall?"

Regis nodded, his mouth tightening briefly, as he contemplated the sight. "I had to yield the North Islands to him when he came with his dragon. That woman from Stony Wood threatened to raise all the magic in Skye against me if I didn't."

"Sel did?"

"Thayne Ysse said you faced that dragon in Skye. I've never seen such a monster in my life."

"It spoke to me," Cyan said dazedly, "instead of killing me."

"It didn't speak to me. It didn't have to."

"Where is it?"

"Thayne said it must have gone back to Skye." He paused, eyeing the disk. He lifted it, looked more closely at the face in the cloudy silver while Cyan held his breath. "That's Gwynne."

"It's the woman I was sent to find."

The king dropped the disk. "She looks just like Gwynne." He gripped Cyan's shoulder tightly, studying him. "You look like you've been on a battlefield. Who slashed your towers?"

"The dragon."

The king's face changed, as if he had caught a sudden glimpse of the strange and dangerous path Cyan had followed out of Gloinmere. "Get the dust out of your hair," Regis said tersely. "Then sit with us. I want to hear what happened to you in Skye."

Cyan bowed his head, grateful for a few moments away from the queen's eyes, to gather his straying wits and piece them back together. She gave him just time enough to wash and change. He stood weighing the disk in his hand, wondering how much to tell Regis then, and how much in private later, when she entered.

She walked through the door without opening it. The face she revealed stunned him, with its flat, dark, lidless eyes, the bones pushing out beneath them, widening her lipless mouth, her white skin livid and shining, like something born in shadow and water that evaded light. His fingers locked protectively over the disk. Beyond that he could not move. He could only watch her helplessly, as he had when her silver ring had flashed in his eyes beyond the tower walls, and he had let her live.

This time, her ringed hand moved toward the disk. He shook his head a little, wordlessly, his hand tightening. He felt as though she reached through him for his heart. But not even habit could move him to raise his sword between them. His heart had glimpsed some mystery that his mind, warring against terror and rage and bewilderment, could not yet grasp. Her fingers freed the disk from his grip. He felt the touch of the sixth, the touch of magic, and closed his eyes.

She said, "You won't need this now."

The chain links parted suddenly. He realized only then, as it slid into her hands, how heavy it had been.

He looked at her again, and pleaded without hope, "Where is Gwynne of Skye?"

"In the hall, eating supper beside the king."

He had to grope for air before he could speak again. "Then who— Then what— Who are you?"

The disk had vanished. She answered as the dragon had, her terrible, inhuman eyes holding his. "You could have killed me, Cyan Dag. You let me live. You tell me who I am."

He began to tremble then, on the verge of an answer as he looked back at the long journey he had taken and saw everything change. Suddenly there was not one thing that he had done or not done that he could explain with any certainty. He knew nothing then, it seemed, except her. He bowed his head, gazed at the silver ring she wore, that they all wore: the bard, the witch, and the woman before him.

He touched her hand tentatively at first, and then less fearfully, drawing all six fingers into his hold and lifting her hand until the silver spark of magic that his heart had recognized caught light again between them.

He said, "You are the third sister."

She smiled. It was an unlovely sight by human standards, but he felt all his fear of her drop away like another chain, ponderous and invisible, that he had worn since he left Gloinmere.

He whispered, "Why?"

"We needed you." She raised her other hand to hold his in both of hers, as if she were coaxing him to follow her across air. "We needed you to help Sel, and Thayne Ysse and the North Islands. We wanted all your courage and your gentleness, your determination, your loyalty and your gift for seeing and for doing, as when you heard the young boy crying in the rain, what must be done."

"I don't understand."

"Regis Aurum married Gwynne of Skye, that day in Gloinmere. I came with my sisters to the wedding, since the Lady from Skye is something of a cousin of ours. I wore her face here with her permission, twice: when I danced with you, and again when I frightened you and sent you on your way to Skye. And I wore her face in Skye. I was the woman in the mirror whose story Sel told to herself. I was the woman in the silver disk. I was the woman in the tower."

He was still trembling, still trying to see where it was he had gone, what he had done while he thought he was doing something else entirely. "You sent me to rescue you—"

"You rode out of Gloinmere to rescue the woman in the tower. What you truly did, while you searched for me, was to rescue Thayne Ysse and the North Islands from seven years of bitterness and hardship. You rescued Sel from her dark tower. I told her the tale she was living, and you helped her end it. Because of you, Thayne Ysse opened the door in himself for magic to return to the North Islands. Because of you, Sel remembered her great powers and brought her magic into Yves, so that there is peace now between Thayne Ysse and Regis Aurum. Because of you."

She held him upright, he felt; if she let go of his hand he would have fallen. "Who are you?" he asked again, the question his heart was asking by now with every beat. "Who are you in the world?"

"Three sisters," she answered simply. "Idra weaves. She wove your life into a perilous and complex path, and you changed everyone your life touched. We needed help, and Idra chose you. She was right, and we are very grateful."

He was silent, swallowing the mystery she gave him, since she gave him no answer to his question that he could understand. He felt the stones beneath his feet again; the dry, silken grip on his hand loosened a little. He said bewilderedly, with only a touch of bitterness, "She could have asked me. You could have trusted me instead of terrifying me."

"If I had asked you to outface a dragon, catch a selkie in the sea, persuade Thayne Ysse to trust a knight of Gloinmere, face death by water, sword and sorcery, and survive to bring magic into Yves, what would you have said?"

He blinked, and felt the blood ease into his face. "No one," he told her, "could do all that."

"You did," she said gently, and loosed his hand. "You won't see this face again. You won't recognize me after this. But we three will watch over you, and return to you, as long as you let us, the peace and magic you have brought back into the world. I have many faces, and I might be any woman you meet, anywhere."

She stepped away from him; he felt as if she had taken the disk away from him again. *But wait,* he wanted to plead. *Stay here. Ask me something else. Send me anywhere.* He watched her strange face and body blur and waver and merge into smoke and shadows. Just before she faded, he saw her eyes again, full of color and light now, and reflecting, it seemed to him, all the worlds he had glimpsed in the dark tower. He heard himself say abruptly, words coming out of no-where, "Show me your true face."

Stunned again, he stood for a long time after her shadow faded on the flagstones, watching that face flame again and again in his heart until, emberlike, the memory burned itself down, hid itself, and only flared, now and then, at unexpected times.

He returned finally to the hall.

He saw the face in the disk again, framed now by can-dle and torchfire, and stopped, his heart still raw. Gwynne of Skye, her eyes smiling, watchful, said softly, "I am glad for Regis's sake that you returned safely from Skye, my lord. Sel told me that you met one of my kinswomen while you were there. My elusive cousin, Sidera. And of course you met her sister at my wedding, the Bard of Skye."

"Yes, my lady." He took her hand, raised it to his lips, grateful to her for bringing such mysteries into the light of day. "I met a third sister. I never knew her name."

"Her name is Una."

"Thank you."

Thayne had risen to greet him. So had the young man beside him, who moved a little awkwardly out of his chair. His lean, dark-eyed face and sweet, fearless smile were unfamiliar. Then he put his hand on the back of his chair for balance, and Cyan remembered the boy's slight weight in his arms, the face he never saw on the rainy night in north Yves.

"Craiche?"

"My brother," Thayne Ysse said, touching Craiche's shoulder. "This is the faceless knight of Gloinmere who saved your life."

"I never thought I would meet you," Craiche said, his smile suddenly gone. "I don't think I believed that you were real. You came out of nowhere, like a knight in a tale, and carried me to safety, and went on your way. I never—I always wondered why you took the trouble."

Cyan gazed at him wordlessly. *Idra weaves*, her sisters had said. Out of that single frail thread, an incident during a battle he had long forgotten, she had woven Cyan's life and Thayne's hope. "You were hurt," he answered finally. "How could I not help? You saved my life in the dragon's tower," he added, and Thayne flushed.

"Sit down," Regis said, gesturing to servants for a chair and food and wine. Cyan sat, flanked by Ysse and Yves. He raised his cup to Thayne.

"To the Lord of the North Islands."

"And to the baker from Stony Wood, who saved the towers of Gloinmere," Regis offered. "I'm hoping she'll stay awhile, teach me some magic."

Cyan met the selkie's eyes, with their deep, underwater smile. "Are you going to?"

"Give up the secrets of Skye to Yves?"

"You must stay, Sel," the queen urged. "My cousins taught me a few things; together you and I could bring the magic back to Yves. It was here once. I can feel it, in stone and moonlight, in earth under my feet." Her smiling eyes, alight with magic, moved from Sel to Cyan. "In certain, ancient towers."

A voice, deep and sweet, wandered away from flute and viol, singing, as they followed, of some impossible love. Cyan felt his heart melt and crack like ice in a fire. "Cyan," the king said, as the flute picked up the singer's note and sang with her. "We have waited long enough. Tell us what happened to you when Gwynne sent you to Skye. What of the woman in the tower? Did you find her? And how did you meet Thayne Ysse and Sel along the way? What improbable events brought them both to supper with me here in Gloinmere?"

Cyan found the singer much later. The king had left the hall; the servants were taking up the cloths; the musicians were putting their instruments to rest in velvet pouches and rosewood boxes. She wore her green tabard; her hair spilled in a soft dark cloud out of the gold clip at her neck. He watched the way she laughed at something the flute player said, and touched his arm lightly. Then she turned, and saw the knight, and her eyes grew as dark and still as the tower among the hills in Skye.

He went to her as uncertainly as he had moved toward

any magic. She smiled a little, tightly, an unfamiliar expression.

"My lord Dag."

"You're still here." He studied her silently, noting the shadows beneath her eyes, the slightest cobweb line beside her mouth. He said softly, "I left you without a word."

"Yes."

"I had no time to say good-bye, to tell you why I was leaving. I thought— I thought—"

"That I would be dressed in fine clothes and holding the arm of some wealthy lord of Yves by now? Because you left me?"

"Yes. No." He drew breath. "I thought you would be given no choice."

"So did I." She paused; he saw the memories bloom, painful and distressing, in her eyes. "So it happened. My father wanted me to marry, you had vanished, and I was desperate. So I went to the queen for help. You go for help to those who possess what you desperately want. She told me to stay here and sing. She persuaded the king to talk to my father, to tell him that I loved the greatest knight in Gloinmere, and that the king would help you in any way he could, and deny you nothing. So my father, in high dudgeon, told me not to bother coming home, and left me here to fend for myself."

"And do you still?" he asked steadily.

She looked at him without answering. Then her face answered, pulled suddenly between laughter and tears. "Oh, Cyan. When I saw you walking through the hall in your patched surcoat, your hair falling down around your face and covered with dust, wearing nothing of arms or armor but that strange tarnished silver on a chain, looking as little like the greatest knight in Gloinmere as a page in a doorway, what could I do but fall in love with you all over again. I sang to you. Did you hear?"

"I heard."

He touched her face, then drew her into his arms, felt the silk of her hair against his cheek, and then against his eyes. When he could see again, blinking dark, feathery strands out of his eyes, the hall was silent, empty around them, but for the echo of music, and a strange shadow cast in a crosshatch of torchlight on the floor: three women growing out of one, their ringed hands raised in greeting or farewell.